Ble
LANDING

DATE DUE

Also by Terrie Todd

The Silver Suitcase

Maggie's War

Bleak LANDING

211678

TERRIE TODD

Waterfall
PRESS

Scripture quotations marked (NIV) are taken from the Holy Bible, New International Version®, NIV®. Copyright © 1973, 1978, 1984, 2011 by Biblica, Inc.™ Used by permission of Zondervan. All rights reserved worldwide. www.zondervan. com The "NIV" and "New International Version" are trademarks registered in the United States Patent and Trademark Office by Biblica, Inc.™

All other scripture quotations are from The Authorized (King James) Version. Rights in the Authorized Version in the United Kingdom are vested in the Crown. Reproduced by permission of the Crown's patentee, Cambridge University Press

The following hymns are referenced and in the public domain:

"A Child of the King," Harriet E. Buell (1877)

"It Came Upon the Midnight Clear," Edmund Hamilton Sears (1849)

"I Heard the Bells on Christmas Day," Henry W. Longfellow (1863)

Published by Waterfall Press, Grand Haven, MI

www.brilliancepublishing.com

Amazon, the Amazon logo, and Waterfall Press are trademarks of Amazon.com, Inc., or its affiliates.

ISBN-13: 9781542046336
ISBN-10: 1542046335

Cover design by Laura Klynstra

Printed in the United States of America

I can think of several real-life reasons why my fictional heroes tend to be pastors. I dedicate this book, with much love and appreciation, to

Don & Donna Lee

Glen & Linda Letellier

Ken & Melanie Driedger

Jerry & Karen Orthner

Jake & Erica Enns

Chris & Kim Elford

Greg & Linda Langman

Ray & Gloria Willms

Peter & Mandy Ralph

Nathan & Tamara Weselake

Soldiers, all.

You will be a crown of splendor in the Lord's hand, a royal diadem in the hand of your God.

No longer will they call you Deserted, or name your land Desolate.

—*Isaiah 62:3–4 NIV*

Chapter 1

Bleak Landing, Manitoba, Canada. June 1934

The day Victor Harrison locked me in the school outhouse, I swore two things. First, that I would leave Bleak Landing forever at my earliest opportunity. And second, that if Victor ever came near me again I'd cut off his ugly head and feed it to the magpies.

I knew better than to say the words out loud. Pa said I was probably going to hell as it was, being as how we didn't have a good Catholic priest to hear our confessions. Far as I knew, the nearest was a hundred miles away, in Winnipeg. Might as well have been a million miles for all the good it did me, stuck here in Bleak Landing.

Pa said that's why he used the willow switch on me. When he was sober, Patrick O'Sullivan called me his darling girl. "Bridget, me darlin' girl, you've got the devil in you, sure. With no priest to grant absolution, the only way is to dole out your penance meself. I'm doin' you a favor, lass. You'll thank me for it in the end."

When he wasn't sober, he didn't speak with as much eloquence or aim the switch with as much precision, but the bruises he left were still as black. Once, when I was ten, I worked up the nerve to ask him who was doling out *his* penance. It did not go well for me. Now that I was twelve, I knew better. I'd learned every trick I could to stay out of my father's way and protect my own sorry hide. And maybe Pa was right; maybe I *should* have thanked him. If I hadn't learned to take care of myself, I might not have escaped the outhouse that day.

From my seat in the two-holer, I heard Victor's smelly sidekick, Bruce Nilsen, daring him to lock the door.

"If you're so tough, you do it," Victor argued.

"Chicken! Victor's a chicken, *Victor's a chicken*." I could hear Bruce's sissy singsong as I scrambled to finish my business.

"Am not."

A third voice chimed in, but I didn't recognize it. "He's in love with her, that's what. Victor won't lock Bridget in because he's sweet on her."

"Am not. Can't stand the sorry sight of that redheaded woodpecker."

"Are, too. I seen you watching her when you thought no one was looking."

I was sure that would be all it took for the cowardly Victor to step up and prove his undying hatred for me—or his undying loyalty to Bruce. Before I could pull up my knickers, I heard the block of wood on the outside of the door turn into place. I unlatched the inside hook and pushed gently on the door to confirm it, not wanting to rattle the door or sound desperate in any way. It was locked, all right. I kept my evil head-chopping plan to myself and made no audible threats.

The June heat was making the stink in the little building unbearable. The smell brought back memories of our awful voyage from Ireland when I was seven, with the stench of overflowing chamber pots radiating from the steerage compartment. Flies buzzed around me now as if I was some kind of corpse, but I refused to give Victor the satisfaction of hearing me holler or cry. Surely, before recess ended one of the little kids would need the outhouse, and I could make my escape with my dignity intact.

That's when I heard Miss Johansen ring the bell, calling everyone back inside.

The playground grew quiet as the children returned to the one-room schoolhouse that doubled as a church on Sundays. Pa said we'd burn in hell for sure if we worshipped with the Protestants, but one Sunday morning when I was eight and Pa was sleeping off a bender, I slipped out and sat under the oak tree just behind the school, out of sight from any window. I could hear the people singing about amazing grace and wondered what was so amazing about it. I hadn't seen anything amazing from any of them. Didn't they know they were doing the devil's work? Now that I was twelve, I wondered how it could be possible that my pa was the only one in all of Bleak Landing who was right about God.

When the singing ended that day, I heard someone dismiss the children ten and under for their Sunday-school lesson. They filed outside and gathered in the shade of the apple tree flanking the playground. I scooted behind my oak and peeked around it. The teacher was Victor Harrison's mother. I recognized her from the times Pa sent me to their farm to buy eggs. I always hoped Victor wouldn't be around when I arrived, and usually he wasn't. The one time he was, he mostly ignored me. That was also the time I wasn't watching where I stepped. I got all the way back to the road with my dozen eggs and tripped over a big old tree root sticking out of the ground. The eggs went flying from their basket, and my dress tore when I tried to catch myself. I could feel blood seeping through the stocking that covered my left knee, but it wasn't the knee I worried about. Every last one of them eggs was broken, and I knew Pa was going to beat the clumsy out of me.

I sat there wondering how I could manage to dodge hell if I stole two or three eggs from each farm I passed on the way home.

Mrs. Harrison came running. "Are you all right?" she asked.

"Yes, ma'am. But I've broken the eggs." I bit my lip to keep the tears from showing and refused to look at her.

"Let's have a look at that leg."

I lifted my skirt and lowered my stocking. A cut as long as my little finger crossed my knee, and bits of wool stuck to the blood congealing there.

"Don't fuss about the eggs. You come with me."

I looked up at her. What was she going to do? "I'm fine, ma'am." I pulled the stocking back over my knee and stood to leave.

"Bridget, please. Let me clean that knee up and get you some more eggs."

"I haven't any more money."

"Don't you worry about that. I can find more eggs. Truth is, the hens are laying more than I can keep up with right now. You'd be doing me a favor. And I sure don't want to lose your pa's business, now, do I?"

I looked around to see if Victor was within sight, but saw no sign of him. I picked up my egg basket and followed Mrs. Harrison to her house.

"Victor!" she called out. The boy's face appeared from around the corner of the house. I looked away. "Please sweep up those broken eggs and run them over to Mr. Berg's pigs before they attract some varmint." I thought for sure Victor would argue, the way he always did with the teacher, but he obeyed his mother without protest.

Mrs. Harrison led me inside and directed me to sit on one of eight matching kitchen chairs. I'd never seen such a thing before. In fact, I got so caught up in the surroundings, I hardly noticed her cleaning up my knee, even when she applied something that stung.

The Harrisons' farmhouse was neat and tidy, furnished with pretty curtains and rugs. From my seat in the kitchen, I could see part of the living room in which stood a sofa and matching chair, both decorated with finely embroidered pillows and crocheted doilies. I could almost hear Pa telling me to put my eyes back in my head before they popped clear out. Mrs. Harrison wrapped a strip of clean white cloth around my knee and tied it in a knot.

When Victor's sister Peggy came in, Mrs. Harrison instructed her to fill a glass with water for me. I watched in wonder as she used a small pump right there by the kitchen sink and then handed me the glass. I drank it all.

Mrs. Harrison sent Peggy to the henhouse with my basket. "Make sure you find a full dozen," she told her. "While we're waiting, I'll mend your stocking, Bridget."

Before I could protest, the woman grabbed her sewing basket and began to darn the hole in my stocking. I hadn't even noticed her pulling it all the way off my leg. "You'll want to soak this in cold water when you get home," she said. "Gets the blood out."

I'd never seen anyone stitch so quickly or neatly. By the time Peggy returned with the eggs, my stocking was back where it belonged. Mrs. Harrison handed me the basket and smiled. "There you go. Right as rain."

I knew I should have thanked her, but my voice refused to cooperate. It did that sometimes. So I simply took the basket and walked carefully home. That night I lay on our couch, which doubled as my bed, wishing Mrs. Harrison were my mother and wondering how it might feel to have her touch my cheek or brush my hair. But that would make me a sister to Victor. What could be worse than living under the same roof as the boy who once called me "Carrots" and loved to mock my father's Irish accent?

If my mother had lived, would our home be filled with pretty things, too? The one article I had of my mother's was her locket. Though I could no longer picture Ma's face, I often went to bed with the locket in my hands and fell asleep remembering the sound of her voice as she sang "Too-Ra-Loo-Ra-Loo-Ral" to me. The beautiful necklace was an heirloom from *her* mother, who was born to more affluent parents during more prosperous days. The front featured a silver Celtic knot wrapped around a shamrock shaped from emeralds. Inside the locket nestled the worn likeness of my great-grandmother. Pa assured me it was valuable and would be mine forever. But the year I turned eleven, my mother's locket went missing from its little box on the mantel. I had a hunch about it. Pa hadn't found work in a while, and I knew he was growing desperate for money and more desperate still for a bottle. So when he went to use the outhouse, I searched his coat pockets. Sure enough, I found my locket, wrapped in Pa's handkerchief. I immediately put it around my neck. When Pa returned to the house, he looked directly at the locket. Our eyes met. We stared at each other in silence while I mustered up all the defiance I could.

"She wanted me to have it, Pa."

The stare-down lasted a full ten seconds. Finally, Pa looked away and grabbed his coat. "Would have saved me a heap of trouble if she had lived instead of you." Without a backward glance, he left.

I've kept the locket around my neck ever since.

All that was why, when I'd tried to imagine our home with matching furniture and dainty doilies, I couldn't see past the rickety kitchen table with two mismatched chairs or the lone couch-bed, its stuffing trying desperately to escape forever.

I understood the impulse. Escape from my present and smelly predicament was exactly what I needed. A gap too narrow for my finger let in a streak of sunlight between the outhouse door and its frame. I studied the walls of my prison carefully until I spotted a place where the wood had splintered, and I carefully peeled back a long, narrow strip. When it broke off in my hand, I ignored the sliver that poked through my skin and pushed the stick through the gap in the door. I nudged at the latch, gently so as not to break my stick. Little by little, the latch lifted until finally it stood completely vertical, and I pushed the door open.

I squinted in the bright sun and took a gulp of fresh air. The first thing to meet my eye was Victor Harrison's ugly face.

"Miss Johansen sent me out here to—"

But he didn't finish his sentence. My fist, seemingly of its own volition, had struck his nose. Hard.

"Oww!" Victor's hands flew to his face, but I marched past him into the schoolhouse and took my seat. The room grew quiet.

"Where is Victor?" Miss Johansen demanded. But before I could answer, Victor entered, wiping blood from his nose with his sleeve. The other students immediately started twittering. Victor took a drink from the water dipper and sat on the boys' side of the room, back row.

"Bridget and Victor, you will both please remain after school today. I'd like to talk to you. Now, everyone, please direct your attention back to the lesson at hand." Miss Johansen turned to her chalkboard and carried on teaching, but I didn't hear much for the rest of the afternoon. The smell of that outhouse lingered in my nostrils and probably on my clothes. Rebecca Olsen, who shared my bench and desk, scooted away from me as soon as I sat. But then, she always did.

~

An hour later, Miss Johansen dismissed school for the day. I stayed in my seat while all the other students except Victor filed out. After the last of them left, Miss Johansen said, "Bridget. Victor. Please come sit in the front."

The seats at the front were smaller, but I lowered myself into one and watched out the corner of my eye while Victor sat, leaving a desk between us and looking completely ridiculous with his lanky knees nearly touching his swollen nose.

"Which one of you wants to tell me what happened out there this afternoon?" Miss Johansen waited. I stared at the tips of my braids, somewhere near my midsection. I didn't hear anything coming from Victor's direction, and I'd be darned if I would be the first to talk. But then Miss Johansen asked me a direct question.

"Bridget, why didn't you come in after recess with the rest of the children?"

I paused. "I was using the outhouse, ma'am."

"You were in there for an awfully long time. Were you ill?"

"No, ma'am. The door was locked from the outside."

"I see. And do you happen to know who might have done such a thing?"

I looked up at her, and she was looking at Victor. The coward sat there, staring at the floor.

"Can't say for sure, ma'am," I said. "Since I couldn't see."

"I did it." Victor kept looking with intent interest at the floor and added lip chewing to his repertoire. His long legs were now stretched out ahead of him, crossed at the ankles, and his arms lay folded across his chest. He surely was the goofiest-looking creature the good Lord ever made, if indeed the good Lord actually made him. Pa figured some folks were devil-born, and I wondered if that was the case with Victor. Maybe his sweet mother found him abandoned in her henhouse one day and took pity. The thought almost made me smile.

"I see," Miss Johansen said. "Can you tell me what would possess you to do such a mean thing?"

"No."

"Then can you tell me how it is that after I sent you out to find Miss O'Sullivan, you returned with a bloody nose?"

Silence.

I tried to suppress the grin I felt forming on my face. What boy would admit he'd been whomped by a girl?

"I did that," I said. I wanted to add "and I'm proud of it" but held my tongue.

"Surprise, surprise," Miss Johansen said. "All right. Here's what is going to happen. Victor, since you feel the outhouse is such a pleasant place for a young lady to spend an afternoon, you'll be cleaning it inside and out before you return home today. Bridget, for your inappropriate retaliation, you will clean the chalkboard and brushes and sweep the floor. I will be speaking to both your parents as well. Now get busy and make sure this behavior never repeats itself. You two ought to be setting an example for the younger children, not continuing this stupid feud you've been fighting since your first day."

The fact that Miss Johansen remembered this detail about my first day spoke volumes about her interest in her students, and this made me admire her all the more.

Chapter 2

*W*hile I served my detention, I thought about my first day of school. Seven years old, and all I'd wanted was to go home to Ireland, go back in time to before Ma and Pa ever got on that boat with my little brother and me. Sure, we were hungry then—but hunger felt normal. The boat did not. Cramped in steerage with hundreds of others, my poor pregnant mother felt ill from the moment we boarded. The disease took my little brother, Tommy, and then Ma, while we were still on the boat. I was too little to understand that, in the end, it was Ma's broken heart just as much as it was the tuberculosis that ripped her from us. She mustered the strength to brush my hair just before she passed into unconsciousness. Two days later, my hair was still neatly braided from her work as I stood beside Pa, watching them lower Ma's body into the cold water far below.

So Pa and me were the only two from my family who got off the boat on this side. I remembered little about the long train trip from Canada's east coast to Manitoba and understood even less. How Pa ended up in Bleak Landing while the other surviving Irishmen stayed in Newfoundland was a mystery to me until the day I overheard him saying he'd won his plot of ground in a card game during our sea journey.

So here we were, in a ramshackle hut that was worse than the one we'd left behind and cold as the grave. I didn't know it was possible for winter to be so severe. Pa said we lived in the promised land now and I'd be going to school to learn to read.

I felt almost excited, that first day. Pa had made it sound good, and the stove in the middle of the classroom provided more heat than the pitiful fireplace at home. But then Miss Johansen called me up to the front and said, "Class, we have a new student." She looked at me. "Can you please tell us your name and a little about yourself?"

The teacher talked funny. I looked around the room. Not one student had red hair like mine. Most of them were fair-skinned with blond or light brown hair and blue eyes. I'd learn later that their names all ended in *s-e-n* or *s-o-n*, though I hadn't learned even a single letter at that point.

The teacher prompted me again. "Can you tell us your name?"

"Bridget O'Sullivan," I said. I heard snickers. What else did the teacher want me to say? I looked at the floor, and thankfully, she didn't press me further. But then she said something that made me want to crawl into a hole and never come out.

"Bridget and her father have come all the way from Ireland. How many of you remember studying about the Irish potato famine in our history lessons last year?" A few hands went up. "Well, that's the country where Bridget was born. Sadly, her mother and brother did not survive the voyage. I will expect you all to treat her with kindness and welcome her warmly to our school."

She might as well have just hit me over the head with the water dipper.

"Rebecca Olsen, please raise your hand," the teacher said. A girl with tightly woven braids identified herself. "Bridget, you may take a seat next to Rebecca."

Relieved, I moved toward the girl who'd lifted her hand. As I passed a blond boy with pronounced ears and buck teeth, I heard him whisper,

"Woodpecker!" This brought another round of snickers. I slid in beside Rebecca. As I did, she scooted as far from me as she could without falling off the bench, and I heard more giggles. I stared at the surface of my desk, studying the various scratches former occupants had carved into its wood and wishing I could read what they said.

But all that was five years ago. By the end of that first day, I'd learned the boy who called me "Woodpecker" was Bruce Nilsen, and with one swift poke to his left eye at recess, I'd killed the nickname on its third use. Bruce's pal Victor Harrison wasn't as easy to persuade. Victor's name of choice for me was "Carrots," and I got riled every time he used it, no matter how much I tried to hide it. The odd thing was, any time anyone else tried to call me "Carrots," Victor put a stop to it quick as anything. I never could figure out why everybody did whatever that boy said. By the time we got to Grade Six, he was some kind of hero with the little kids. He'd reached the physical height of any man in Bleak Landing, except he was as skinny as a stick. The Grades One and Two boys would line up at recess and take turns riding around on Victor's shoulders, where they'd pretend to be king of the world.

The girls figured Victor was pretty swell, too. But then, he acted nice to *them*. I thought Rebecca Olsen's eyelashes would bat themselves right off her face whenever Victor got within ten feet of her, and Margaret Mikkelsen made a fool of herself trying to act coy. Made me feel embarrassed to be a girl. Maybe that's why I stuck to myself most of the time.

Though I never succeeded in making friends, I learned to read better than anyone in the school, even the oldest of them. Before my first year ended, Miss Johansen was calling on me to help the other students—most of whom were older and had been in school longer. This did not endear me to them any more than if I'd suddenly sprouted horns. But in time some of them—the girls, at least—appreciated me as a good tutor and welcomed my help. Usually.

More importantly, I learned I didn't need friends. While the other girls played their made-up games or braided each other's hair, chatting endlessly about dresses and boys, I sat under the big oak tree with books Miss Johansen loaned me. She had no fewer than three of Jane Austen's books on her personal shelves, and I figured she must be the wealthiest and most generous person alive. I'd read them all several times over, and my favorite so far was called *Sense and Sensibility*. And though she wouldn't allow me to take it outdoors, I spent many a recess poring over the school's copy of Mr. Webster's dictionary.

After I'd finished my detention following the outhouse incident, I walked to the front of the classroom where the heavy dictionary sat on its special stand and flipped it open. One of my favorite things to do was choose a new word and mull it over on my walk home from school. I'd spell it in my head, repeat the meaning, and put it into sentences. Once I even tried a sentence out on Pa, but he told me to quit talking fancy or he'd smack me upside the head and remind me of my place.

This time the word *gregarious* jumped off the page at me. The dictionary said the word described someone with a "liking for companionship."

I pushed the school door open just enough to look around the yard. Victor was nowhere in sight, and I guessed he had finished his work. I stepped out into the bright sun, thankful it was Friday, and started my walk home. It was only a mile, but that was far enough for me to work on *gregarious* until it was in my head for life.

"Bridget O'Sullivan is *not* a gregarious girl." I kicked a stone and followed it down the dusty road.

"If Bridget O'Sullivan was more *gregarious*, perhaps one of the other girls would have unlocked the outhouse door." I kicked the stone with my other foot.

"Victor Harrison is far too *gregarious* for his own good." I gave the stone a sideways kick as hard as I could, sending it off the path and out of my life forever.

At the thought of Victor, my fists automatically tightened. His latest actions were the last straw. I would be hearing the story of my outhouse imprisonment for months, even without popular Victor saying a word. The other boys would praise his courage for showing the dirty little Irish girl her place. The girls would twitter and giggle behind their hands. If they were half as clever as I was, they'd come up with catchy rhymes, like calling me "Bridget the fidget" when I avoided the outhouse, even when I needed it desperately.

Good thing they weren't.

And good thing I didn't care. The fact was, that day's experience only made me more determined to leave Bleak Landing at the first opportunity. I told myself that one day in the not-too-distant future, I would wash the dust of this hateful community right off my feet and catch a train for Winnipeg, where no one knew me. There, I'd become a completely new person. Why, I might even become gregarious.

And I would never, ever, *ever* return.

Chapter 3

Our house sat on the north edge of Bleak Landing—the last building on Fattigdom Road. The word is Norwegian for "poverty," and I couldn't help wondering what the founding fathers went through to make them give such depressing names to everything. Pa wasn't home when I got there. With any luck, that meant he was working today. Pa never kept a steady job, but he managed to find work most days helping farmers or carpenters. They couldn't always pay him in cash, but he often brought home food and firewood. He was known to be a good worker when sober and a harmless jester when drunk.

Harmless, that is, to everyone but me.

Already behind because of my detention, I changed into my overalls as fast as I could and headed for the garden—Pa's pride and joy. I never did figure out how Pa could be so meticulous about his vegetable garden but not give two hoots about the condition of our house. I guess that made us a good team. I kept the house as clean as I could and nagged Pa when he dragged mud inside. Pa insisted on planting the garden himself so the rows would be perfect and harassed me if I didn't keep up with the weeding and watering.

I'd been working for about half an hour when I saw Miss Johansen approaching. I stood up straight but didn't move or let go of my hoe.

"Hello, Bridget," she called out. "Is your father home?"

"No, ma'am."

"I was hoping to speak with him. I've just come from Victor's house, where I spoke with his mother about what happened at school today."

I wasn't sure what she wanted me to say. I never knew what time Pa would get home or what frame of mind he'd be in when he did. The only thing I felt sure of was that I'd be in far deeper trouble when he found out I'd gotten into hot water at school than I would already be in for not having my chores done. Maybe I could get rid of my teacher before Pa got home, and he'd never need to know.

"Victor's mother is a very kind lady," Miss Johansen continued.

"Yes, ma'am, she is."

"She suggested that Victor probably deserved what you gave him and hoped your father would go easy on you." She looked around at the garden for a moment. "I wonder why she'd say that about your father."

When I made no reply, she put her hand on my elbow until I raised my eyes to her. "Can you think of any reason Mrs. Harrison might say such a thing, Bridget?"

I looked briefly into her blue eyes and then turned my attention back to my hoeing. "I've learned it's best to get these things over with sooner rather than later, ma'am." And it was. The anticipation could be worse than the punishment. So I felt almost relieved when Pa came around the corner, toolbox in hand. I could tell by his walk that he was sober. "Here comes Pa now."

Pa walked straight toward us. "What's this, then? Teacher come a-callin'?"

"Good afternoon, Mr. O'Sullivan."

Pa looked from Miss Johansen to me and back again. "My girl in some kind of trouble, then?"

My teacher paused. "Not at all, sir. Your daughter is my top student. I was passing by and stopped to drop off this book for her." She reached into her bag and pulled out a copy of *A Vindication of the Rights of Woman* by Mary Wollstonecraft. She held the book out to me and nodded for me to take it. She knew I'd read the book more than once already, and I could see her own bookmark sticking out of it. It seemed I was being granted an impromptu reprieve. I was glad, though, that Pa couldn't read the title. Pa couldn't read much besides his own name. He surely wouldn't approve of Miss Wollstonecraft's axioms.

"Glad to hear it," Pa said. "But you'd best keep the book. Bridget's got no time for story reading. Not with the corn six inches high and the weeds nearly eight."

"I see." Miss Johansen returned the book to her bag. "Well, it's a lovely day for garden work. Perhaps you wouldn't mind if I stayed and helped awhile?"

"Ain't got but the one hoe. And you still in your school frock." Pa's tone alone dismissed Miss Johansen.

"Very well, then. I'll see you at school on Monday, Bridget." She turned and continued walking into town, where she stayed at Sigurdsons' boardinghouse.

Pa watched her leave and then turned to me. "What did she come here for?"

I resumed my hoeing. "To loan me a book."

"Why didn't she do it at school?"

"She was passing by, like she said." I bent to pull an extrastubborn stringy vine and tossed it to the side.

"Don't treat me like I'm daft, girl. If you're in trouble at school, I'll find out, sure. You best be mindin' your ways or you'll be stayin' home and gettin' something useful done. No point in education if you throw it away misbehavin'."

"No, sir. There isn't." Whatever else Pa might say, I could agree with him on that point. I kept working and he went inside the house.

Later, as we sat at the table eating potatoes and more of the Harrisons' eggs, we heard a knock at the door. Pa looked at me and raised his brows. No one ever came to our house, and now we'd had two visitors in one day. I'm sure my own brows reached for the sky, too, when I opened the door and saw Victor Harrison standing there.

"Hello-Bridget-I-came-to-apologize." He stared at his feet and spoke so fast, I wasn't certain what he'd said. But his swollen nose sure made his face look funny.

I managed not to laugh. "Excuse me?"

"You heard me. I came to apologize."

"Your mother make you do this?" I asked, hoping Pa hadn't heard.

"Yes."

"May your cat eat your liver and the devil eat your cat, Victor Harrison." It was the worst insult I knew. His eyes went from my face to just behind me, and I knew my father stood there.

"Young Harrison, isn't it?" Pa said.

"Yes, sir."

"You came all this way to apologize to Bridget? What for, lad?"

Victor glanced at me, then down at the ground. "I'm sorry I locked you in the outhouse."

Pa laughed. "Is that all? Your ma made you come all the way here to say you're sorry just for that?"

"And because teacher kept us after school." Victor Harrison was making my life worse by the minute.

Pa stopped laughing. "What do you mean? The both of you?" He looked at me, and I nodded as slightly as I dared. "I knew that teacher had more to say than she let on." He turned back to Victor and took a closer look at his face. "Where'd you get the puffy nose? Did Bridget do that to you?"

Victor's face turned as red as my hair.

But Pa wouldn't let it go. "Not much of a man, are you, lad?"

Victor looked down at his shoes. "No, sir. That's what my pa said, too. I'd best be getting home. Just came to say I'm sorry and it won't happen again."

Pa watched Victor leave, then slowly closed the door and turned around.

"You lied to me."

I hadn't. Not really. I may not have disclosed the whole truth, but I hadn't outright lied. I knew, though, that it was better to keep my mouth shut and not argue with Pa.

"If there's one thing I cannot tolerate, it's lyin'."

It seemed to me there were a whole lot of things Pa couldn't tolerate, especially when it came to me. But I kept quiet.

"It's one thing to get in trouble at school, but you will not lie to me. Turn around."

He grabbed the willow switch from its corner of the room and began to strike before I could find anything to lean on. I stumbled forward, bracing my fall with my arms so that my left wrist hurt worse than my backside. Pa wasn't done. I didn't try to count the number of times the switch came down on my back and buttocks. What was the point? The only thing I knew for sure was that Victor Harrison could apologize until his tongue turned purple, but I would never forgive him.

His anger spent, Pa threw the switch into the corner. "Don't you ever lie to me again. And if you get into another fight at school, I'll give you twice that. Your poor mother would be disgusted with you, her own daughter fightin' with boys and lyin' to her pa. She'd want you to be a lady. Best start actin' like one."

Finally he left the house, and I didn't see him again until morning. While I wrapped my aching left wrist in strips of fabric for support, I thought about the lady Ma would have wanted me to be. The best example I could picture was Victor Harrison's mother.

Chapter 4

July 1935

The grown-ups were calling it the hottest, dirtiest summer on record. I figured most of our topsoil was somewhere in Ontario by now, having been replaced entirely by Saskatchewan's. Until the wind changed direction, that is. Then it would all fly back again in an eternal swirl of dust. I spent my days outside, pumping pails of water and carrying them to the pathetic mounds of potato plants and cornstalks Pa and I were trying to grow in our garden patch. The dust and grasshoppers made the effort a losing battle. Each night I filled a basin with water and washed myself from top to bottom, but I never could get all the dust out of my hair. Though I was tempted to chop it off, I could never quite bring myself to do it.

"You have beautiful hair," Miss Johansen had said to me more than once. "I'd love to brush it out and style it for you sometime."

"I do my own hair," I told her, clenching my teeth so she'd know I meant it. I suppose it sounded a little rude, but nobody was touching my hair.

The one consolation was that everybody else was covered in dust, too. At least our well still produced. Not everyone was so fortunate. Several of the homes and farms surrounding Bleak Landing sat abandoned, the last pig or chicken already eaten or dead of starvation. Somehow, Pa managed to keep bringing home flour and enough cash to send me to the Harrisons' for eggs most weeks. When we didn't have money for eggs, Mrs. Harrison took my Irish soda bread in trade. Pa taught me how to make it, and some days that's all we had to eat. I tried making dandelion-leaf sandwiches after someone said they were good for eating. That's when I decided there were two kinds of "good for eating"—that which tasted good, and that which provided the body some nourishment. The dandelions definitely fell into the second category, but we ate them without complaint.

I looked forward to my trips to the Harrison farm despite the possibility of seeing Victor there. The oldest in his family of five children, he was nearly always working with his father on something. His sister Peggy was ten; Nancy, seven; Anna, six; and his brother, Bobby, was four. They had a dog named Bingo who greeted me with a friendly tail wag no matter how dreary the day. Just like everyone else, the Harrisons struggled to keep everybody clothed and fed, but for some reason Victor's mother didn't carry that weary, hopeless look all the other adults did. She always greeted me with a sunny smile and spoke kindly to everyone, even her own children. While none of them wore new clothes, they managed to stay clean, which was more than I could say for most of us in Bleak Landing.

Maybe it was because the Harrisons' house was built better than most; I'm not sure. Maybe it had something to do with the plaque hanging on the wall above the table. It said: *As for me and my house, we will serve the Lord. Joshua 24:15.* Did a person's house magically stay clean if they hung scripture on its walls? I doubted it. Maybe if they followed its principles, though. I didn't know. But I knew that when I stood inside that kitchen where I was always offered a drink of water, I longed to make a little bed in the corner behind the stove and call that place home.

This was, of course, ridiculous. But having something to daydream about on my walk home with the eggs made it easier to ignore the dust kicking up around my feet and the hoppers whirring across my path. Nasty things. Sometimes they landed on my arms and legs and hung on as if they'd been glued there.

So I imagined myself trading places with Victor Harrison. He could go live with my father. He certainly stood tall enough now to hold his own with Pa. Besides, they kind of deserved each other. And I could be a big sister to Peggy, Nancy, and Anna. Oh, sure, we'd have to share a bedroom, but at least it would be an actual bedroom. I could call Mrs. Harrison "Ma," and she'd teach me how to be a lady and how to do my little sisters' hair and remind them to sit up straight. Little Billy could take the place of my brother, Tommy, who had died. Instead of spending Sunday mornings in my overalls hauling water in summer and stoking the fire in winter, I could put on a pretty dress and sit in church singing about amazing grace with my family, right there beside my ma and my sisters.

I supposed, though, that whatever that amazing grace was about, it wasn't for the likes of me.

I had managed to finish Grade Six without getting into more trouble at school, mostly by avoiding the other students. Victor Harrison and Bruce Nilsen, however, served enough detention time to keep the floors and the outhouse clean as a whistle. If those two weren't climbing on the schoolhouse roof, they were tying the ribbons of Francine Lundarson's dress to the back of her chair or dipping Margaret Mikkelsen's braids into an inkwell. At least they left me alone most of the time—except with their words, which I knew could never hurt me. Certainly not unimaginative, childish words like "carrots" or "leprechaun." Bruce got my dander up whenever he tried to mimic an Irish brogue, though. For one thing, he was no good at it. For another, I did *not* speak that way! I knew my father did, and my father was the last person I wanted to sound like.

Pa had been leaving me alone lately. I didn't know if he was just running out of energy or if I'd grown wiser about how to avoid his angry outbursts. Whatever the reason, he was more prone to simply leave the premises when he got mad. I figured my biggest troubles were behind me and I could look forward to better days.

Then one hot night I overheard a conversation that piled a whole new layer of dread on me. Pa was outside in his undershirt, sitting on the porch step trying to keep cool. I was tossing on my couch bed. I had left the windows open in hopes of a breeze, having long since given up on trying to keep the dust out of the house.

Just when I thought I might be close to dozing off, I heard someone talking to my father.

"Good evening, O'Sullivan."

"Evenin', Roper. What brings you 'round?"

"Wonderin' when I can collect on my winnings. Thought tonight might be just as good a night as any."

Pa hesitated. "You're drunk, Roper. Go home and sleep it off."

"Not so drunk I can't remember your offer, even if you was too drunk to remember making it."

I crept off the couch and over to the window to peer out. I couldn't see the man talking to Pa, but I could hear him more clearly.

"That's because I didn't make you no offer. Now get on home before I sic my dog on you." Pa was always threatening to sic his dog on people, and sometimes the threat worked. Not tonight.

"You ain't got no dog, O'Sullivan. And if you ever did have a dog, you probably gambled it away in a card game. Just like you did your daughter."

I saw Pa's head jerk up. "I did no such thing."

"Did, too. So sure your hand would win that last round, you promised me first chance at your girl. But I won fair and square, and now I've come to collect."

"She's a child, Roper."

"Thirteen. You said so yourself. Old man Larssen started peddlin' his girls around at twelve. I figure I'm doin' you a favor by coming here and saving you the effort of bringing her to me. Now how about it? You gonna make good on your deal, or you gonna make me tell everybody you're a fella who goes back on his word?"

I heard the familiar warning sound of Pa's fist smacking against his palm. "I suggest you get off my property this minute, Roper. What kind of man do you take me for?"

"Oh, I think we've already established that, O'Sullivan. Just don't bother askin' to join any more card games around here once word gets out. And it will, I'll see to that."

Pa stood there, sturdy as a rock, fist in hand. For the first time in my life, I understood the glorious security of feeling protected. The man I feared had become my champion. Whatever Pa may have promised in one drunken moment, he was my hero in this one. I'd never felt more proud of him.

But just as quickly as it had arrived, my joy drained away with Pa's next words.

"I'll make good on my promise when my girl is ready." He turned his face away from Mr. Roper's. "Come back when she's fifteen."

Chapter 5

April 1936

*V*ictor Harrison liked his school assignment, for a change. Each class was supposed to prepare a current-events report as a group project, using the newspapers Miss Johansen brought to school. Since he, Bridget, and Bruce Nilsen were the only Grade Seven students, the three of them had to work together. Bridget bossed them both around like she was some kind of drill sergeant. Victor found it funny, but he could tell it rankled Bruce.

"Crazy woodpecker thinks she's so smart," Bruce complained on their walk home from school. "Her pa don't even own a radio."

Victor knew that Bruce's family had only acquired *its* first radio in the past year, but he didn't mention it.

Bruce wanted to do the report on the Canadian athletes who would be competing at the 1936 Olympic Games, in Berlin. Bridget thought Canada should boycott the Olympics to protest the way the Nazis were treating people. She wanted to focus the presentation on propriety and justice, exposing the German leaders who, she said, "ought to be skinned alive." In her opinion, Canada and the United States should be opening their arms to immigrants, providing a safe haven for folks who had to flee their homelands.

Bruce defended Germany. "Pa says the Nazis have the right idea: do away with the weaker races and you'll have a better world. Why should we let them come here and drag our country down?"

Bruce was always saying stuff like that, and sometimes Victor wondered why he still hung around with the guy. But he couldn't remember a time when he and Bruce were not pals. One of his earliest memories was going to the Nilsen house with his mother when Bruce's baby sister was born. Both boys were just four at the time.

"Can I show him my sister, Mama?" Bruce had asked.

"Yes, but be quiet and don't touch her," his mother said.

Bruce had led Victor to a back bedroom where a tiny baby lay sleeping in a basket. Victor already had a little sister, but he couldn't remember her ever being this little. He watched, wide-eyed, as Bruce picked her up. Suddenly, the infant slipped from her brother's arms and landed on the hardwood floor. She began bawling, and Bruce quickly grabbed her and lay her back in the basket. He skedaddled out of the room as quick as a bunny, with Victor on his heels.

In the years after the incident, rumors about the Nilsen girl abounded among the people of Bleak Landing. "She ain't right" was the usual summary. Some said she was born that way; others suggested something had happened to her later. The only thing Victor knew for certain was that the girl was seldom seen, and when she was, she sat silently with a vacant stare in her eyes. One day she simply wasn't around anymore. When Victor asked Bruce about it, he said that his sister was at a special school in Winnipeg and that Victor shouldn't ask about it again. Victor never did. No other children were added to the Nilsen family, and the two boys seemed to have some unspoken agreement that they would both remain silent about the day Bruce had dropped the baby.

While Bruce and Bridget argued about the Olympics, Victor dug through the papers and found an amazing story about a jockey in California named Ralph Neves who was declared dead after a horse rolled over him. The very next day, though, he was out riding again and went on to get enough second-place wins that he took home five hundred dollars and a gold watch presented by Bing Crosby. Victor convinced Bruce and Bridget that they should present Neves's story instead. Which was just as well, since the Olympic boycott plans eventually fizzled and the games went on in August as planned.

When it came time for them to give their presentation, Bridget played the role of a news reporter interviewing Ralph Neves, played by Bruce. She stood on a stool to emphasize Neves's short stature, and threw herself into her portrayal as though her life depended on capturing the attention of millions of radio listeners. Victor had never seen her so animated nor heard her so articulate, and she commanded the attention of the entire room. After the class applauded, Miss Johansen gave a brief evaluation. "I think you two might have been born for the stage. Well done, Bridget and Bruce. And Victor, you make a very convincing racehorse."

For a few brief moments, Bridget's face was so radiant that Victor couldn't stop looking at her. But by dismissal time, she'd returned to her serious self and couldn't be bothered to give the time of day to either boy.

A week later, a completely different assignment seemed to reveal a completely different girl.

Victor chewed on his pencil and stared at the blank sheet of paper in front of him. He really hated Miss Johansen for this new assignment. *Show me one real man who writes poetry,* he thought. Although Edgar Allan Poe had probably been a pretty swell fellow. At least he knew how to scare the girls with stories like "The Tell-Tale Heart" and his poem "The Raven." Maybe, Victor thought, he could write something like that. He gazed out the classroom window for inspiration. He'd seen a raven a time or two. Crows and magpies. Robins, sparrows, blue jays. Even seagulls had been known to dot the prairie landscape before things got so dry. Nothing poem-worthy, though. The birds he saw most were his mother's laying hens.

"Victor Harrison, keep your eyes on your work, please," Miss Johansen singsonged from the front of the room. "And for those of you who have chosen to write a limerick, remember the rules. Five lines long. Lines one, two, and five must rhyme. And lines three and four must rhyme. Don't forget to keep your rhythm consistent."

Victor leaned forward over his page and wrote "The Chicken" for a title. His eyes roamed again. Just ahead and to his right sat Bridget O'Sullivan, in that dilapidated brown dress she always wore. Her red hair hung loose today, but short bits near the front made him wonder if she'd taken a butcher knife to it. The choppy-looking pieces reminded him of Chester, the Rhode Island Red rooster that strutted around the Harrisons' farmyard, his comb sticking straight toward heaven and his feathers always ruffled. Victor suppressed a chuckle and, with a wicked grin, started his poem.

Five minutes later, he scrawled his name across the bottom and raised the sheet of paper high in the air. "I'm all done, Miss Johansen. Can I be excused?"

Miss Johansen frowned over the top of her glasses. "*May* I be excused."

"Sure you can!" Victor grinned. "Can I be, too?"

The class broke up laughing, and Victor looked around the room to bask in the appreciation. The only one not laughing—in fact, not even looking—was Bridget O'Sullivan. She still seemed intent on her poetry.

"All right, settle down!" Miss Johansen warned. "Victor, this wasn't supposed to be a race. And no, you may not be excused. In fact, for disrupting the class—again—you'll be staying after school to clean the chalkboards and brushes. Again. Now, are you pleased with your poem?"

"Yes, ma'am."

"Please stand and read it for the class."

Clearing his throat, Victor rose from his seat and stood in the aisle. He held the paper up so the light from the windows fell squarely on his page. He read in a strong, clear voice:

There once was a naughty red chicken
Who deserved a really good lickin'
With her feathers a mess
And her ugly brown dress
She stunk up the place like the dickens.

The classroom erupted. Victor took his seat and was thumped on his back by Bruce, who sat behind him. Even the little kids thought the poem was funny, though they clearly had no idea who had served as the poet's muse.

"How inspiring," Miss Johansen said in a flat tone.

"Thanks," he said, knowing full well she was being sarcastic. He wasn't about to let her make him feel bad. He surveyed his captive audience again, enjoying the admiration and the knowing grins of his peers, the elbow pokes he saw exchanged, and the nods in Bridget's direction. She appeared, as usual, to be the only one who wasn't amused by his antics. She stayed focused on the page in front of her, her pencil scratching against it. Only one thing had changed: Bridget's face was now the same shade of red as her hair.

Victor looked at the surface of his desk, feeling an immediate flood of regret. In an instant, he could hear his mother's prayers, how she included Bridget O'Sullivan nearly every night along with the petitions she offered for her own children. How she asked God to make Victor a man of conviction and integrity, a man who would do good in the world and have compassion for those less fortunate. A man who'd be a leader of men and stand against injustice. He glanced again at Bridget's sorrowful face and hung his head. He was anything but those things. He was just a boy who cared more about getting a laugh than he did about people.

In that moment, Victor loathed himself.

"Is anyone else ready to share their work?" the teacher asked.

One by one, students stood to read their poems. Some were well constructed; some sadly lacking. Most were funny, but none received a reaction anywhere close to what Victor's had. After each, Miss Johansen called on the class to identify whether or not the poem was a limerick and to discuss its rhythm and rhyme.

The last to finish was Bridget O'Sullivan. "Are you ready to read your poem, Bridget?" the teacher asked. "It's nearly dismissal time, but I'll give you half a minute."

Victor braced himself, expecting Bridget to seize the opportunity and pour out a limerick that would pay him back a thousand times over. It would almost be a relief. He could take his medicine, endure the ribbing of his classmates, and feel they were even. But the girl said nothing.

"Have you completed it, Bridget?" Miss Johansen asked.

"Yes, ma'am."

"Well then?"

"I'd prefer not to read it, Miss Johansen." Bridget rose from her desk and walked to the front of the room, where she handed her paper to the teacher.

Miss Johansen scanned the page and stared at it for several long seconds. She swallowed so hard, Victor could see the bump in her throat move up and down. Finally, she sniffed and cleared her throat before speaking in a near whisper.

"This is lovely, Bridget. Well done."

As he waited for the teacher to read Bridget's words, Victor felt his curiosity rise. But to his disappointment, Miss Johansen merely added the paper to the stack already on her desk. In a louder voice, she said,

"Class, you're dismissed. Enjoy your weekend and please don't forget your seed collections for Monday."

The room cleared quickly, but Victor fiddled with his books and papers as an excuse to remain at his desk. As students passed him, some of the boys patted his shoulder or extolled his brilliance. Even the girls were all smiles, and Rebecca Olsen stopped to talk. "I loved your poem, Victor. Want to walk me home?"

"Can't," he muttered. "Gotta clean the boards."

"I could help you," she offered.

"No, thanks. I don't think that would sit too well with Miss Johansen. You better go on home."

Rebecca shrugged and kept moving. "Your loss." Behind her came Bridget, her gaze focused on the door.

"Bridget." Victor stopped her with a hand to her arm. "I'm sorry."

When she looked him in the face, Victor thought he'd never seen so much anger and sadness wrapped up together in one pair of eyes. She looked down at his hand on her arm until he removed it. Then she looked him in the eye again.

"Whatever for?" she said. "Because you wrote an imbecilic poem about some stupid chicken? Why apologize to me for your ineptitude? I couldn't care less. Leave me alone."

He watched her leave the building. *I'm sorry, God,* he prayed. *I'm really, really sorry.*

With his heart still heavy, he walked to the front of the room and cleaned the boards. But not before he stopped in front of Webster's dictionary, opened it up, and read the definition of *imbecilic*.

Chapter 6

April 1937

On my fifteenth birthday, I woke to the sound of Mr. McNally's rooster and the smell of his chicken coop wafting through our open window. Spring had come early to Bleak Landing, but the drought and economic depression raged on. The Great Depression, they called it, thanks to former US President Hoover, who'd thought "depression" sounded better than "panic." To Pa, what Canadians called a depression still seemed like a step up from what he had known back in Ireland. For me, it was simply life.

Pa had declared that once I reached fifteen, I would no longer need school. I begged him to let me continue until the end of June and finish Grade Eight.

"Whatever for? You already know more than the teacher."

That much was almost true. Miss Johansen had confided to me that she'd completed Grade Nine and then passed an exam that earned her a one-year teaching permit, back in 1928. Every year since, the school board had simply renewed her permit. She was doing a good job, and no one felt inclined to seek out a more qualified teacher. Of course, it hadn't hurt that Miss Johansen kept agreeing to smaller and smaller salaries as everyone tried to survive the troubled times. Pa told me more than once how grateful I should be for getting to go to school at all, and I knew that much was true. I knew Miss Johansen read widely to stay one step ahead of me, and she passed on every book she studied for me to devour as time allowed.

I'd been the oldest student in the school all year. Next oldest was Bruce Nilsen. He claimed he was going to become a lawyer one day, and I believed it. Somehow, though no one seemed to understand why, his parents defied the economy and continued to live prosperously. That's why Bruce was still in school. Victor Harrison had left after Grade Seven to help out full time on his father's farm. Rebecca Olsen had been working at her father's general store since the end of Grade Six, and Susan Andersen had found a job as a telephone operator around the same time. Rumor had it both girls were on the hunt for husbands.

A husband was the last thing I needed. By fourteen, I'd determined I would make my own way in the world. Trouble was, I hadn't a cent to my name, and though I'd looked for work, nobody could pay. But today was my fifteenth birthday, the day I would leave Bleak Landing forever. I'd already made arrangements with Mr. Nilsen, Bruce's pa. The man drove to Winnipeg regularly, returning to Bleak Landing only once a month or so. He'd agreed to give me a ride to the city and introduce me to his friend Mr. Thompson, who managed a textile factory. Mr. Thompson and the owner, Mr. Weinberger, liked to hire country girls because they had a good work ethic and worked for less pay. In exchange, I would pay Mr. Nilsen one half of my first paycheck. The other half would cover my keep in the dormitory on the factory's top floor.

Mr. Nilsen had no use for my father. I didn't know what his grudge was, although I suspected it had something to do with a card game. The situation worked in my favor, though. Mr. Nilsen was happy to make arrangements with me secretly, just to spite Pa. He told me to meet him at the Shell, Bleak Landing's only gas station. The station was closed now, since no one in town besides Mr. Nilsen seemed to have the means to buy fuel. I guess he made sure when he was in Winnipeg that he had enough gas to get himself to Bleak Landing and back again.

I arrived at the Shell before he did and took a seat on the concrete curb in front of the abandoned pump.

The setting seemed appropriate for my last moments in this forlorn little place. It was a warm day for April, and already dusty first thing in the morning. Truth was, we hadn't seen the sun clearly for weeks thanks to that haze. It did make for pretty sunsets and sunrises, I'll give it that.

The brown skirt and white blouse I wore may not have been the best choice for the day, but it's not as though I had a lot of options. The canvas duffel bag I carried held my entire wardrobe: two dresses, a work shirt and pair of overalls, a nightgown and some underthings, and the good winter coat that had mysteriously appeared on our doorstep the December before last. I'd tried to put my hair up to look older, but it was hopeless. In the end, I'd simply tied it at the back of my head with the hair ribbon Miss Johansen had given me for winning a spelling bee two years before. At least it was a step up from the two braids I'd learned to do myself at the age of seven and worn all my life since.

I looked around at the dusty gravel road and the tumbledown buildings across the street. The grass was dead except where weeds sprouted through the broken concrete. So many people had left Bleak Landing, seeking work in bigger cities. It felt like a ghost town, especially early in the morning. I'd managed to leave the house without disturbing Pa, and all I could think about was ridding myself of this place forever. From today on, the word *bleak* would no longer be part of my vocabulary. I wasn't naive enough to think life was going to be easy, but it would certainly be different. It had to be.

Mr. Nilsen pulled up in his gray-and-black car. He rolled down his window. "Hop in. You can throw your bag in the backseat."

I did as I was told and climbed in beside him. "Thanks, Mr. Nilsen, I really appreciate this." I smoothed my skirt and brushed some of the dust from my sleeves, mostly for something to do. My heart pounded at the knowledge that I was actually making my escape.

"About that." Mr. Nilsen paused to light a cigarette. "I know we agreed on your first paycheck—"

"*Half* my first paycheck."

"Right. Half. Here's the thing. I'm going to need a little collateral."

I looked at him in disbelief.

He blew smoke out his window. "*Collateral* means—"

"I *know* what collateral means." Did the man think I was born yesterday? That I'd never read a book? "That was not part of our deal."

"Well, it is now. How do I know for sure Thompson will hire you for the garment factory? He might take one look at your sorry hide and say you're too skinny or something. And if he does hire you, how do I know you won't take your money and run?"

"Where would I run? Please, Mr. Nilsen."

"And how do I know that shylock will even pay you?"

Now I was really confused. What did any of this have to do with a Shakespeare character? "Shylock?"

"I mean the owner, Mr. Weinberger. He's a shylock."

I stared at him, not comprehending.

"You know, a Yid? An Abe? They're even worse than the greaseballs and the micks, like you and your pa."

I sighed. No wonder his son was so narrow-minded.

"Mr. Nilsen, I don't have anything for collateral. I'll earn the money and pay you back, I promise."

"Oh, but you do have something." His eyes went to the locket at my throat. "You think there's anybody in Bleak Landing who doesn't notice that necklace you wear all the time? Anybody who doesn't know it's worth a good price, even in these lean times? I'm surprised you've managed to hang on to it, knowing that daddy of yours."

I covered the locket with my hand, wishing I'd packed it in my bag. "It was my mother's. It's all I have."

"And you'll get it back, no problem. All I'm asking is that you let me hold on to it for you, just for a while. As soon as you make good on the money, you can have mommy's little trinket back. Shoot, it'll be safer with me than if you keep wearing it."

I studied the man's face. His light blond hair and fair complexion contrasted with the darkness of his expression and the cold glint in his eyes. "Please don't do this, Mr. Nilsen."

"It's your choice, girl. You can hop out and go home to daddy right now if you prefer to hang on to your bauble. But I can't wait much longer, so make up your mind. There's a job for you in the city, and a roof to go over your head, too, but they won't wait long. Girls are flocking to Winnipeg looking for work, and not all of them are ignorant little immigrants like you."

I looked out the side window, my eyes beginning to sting. If I returned home now, Pa would discover what I had planned and make me pay. And just as soon as I healed from whatever bruises he inflicted, I'd be expected to earn my keep in a manner I was not prepared to accept. Surely Ma would understand. And I'd get her locket back as soon as possible—in a month, at most.

"Well? Come on, girl. Wait any longer and somebody's going to see you leaving town with me."

Slowly, I removed my mother's locket and held it out to him without a word.

"Good choice." Mr. Nilsen slid the locket into an inside pocket of his coat. "You won't regret it, you'll see." He started the car, and we rolled down the road.

I had not left Bleak Landing since our arrival eight years before, but I did not turn around now for a last look.

Chapter 7

I knew my eyes were probably bugging right out of my head, but I couldn't help it. I'd come through Winnipeg when I was seven years old, but now I wondered if I'd been asleep on the train the entire time. I sure couldn't recall having seen so many buildings or people in one place before. I started feeling really nervous, and my heart pounded as though it was driving fence posts or something.

Mr. Nilsen's chuckle grew into a full-blown laugh as he saw me turning my head from side to side to gawk at the new world around me. Did it never end? How would I ever find my way around?

"How many people live here?" I asked.

"Plenty. Around two hundred and twenty thousand, with more coming every year."

A low whistle escaped my lips as I surrendered any attempt to appear nonchalant. I don't know what I expected, but it wasn't this.

Mr. Nilsen pointed out something on our left.

"See that? It's a hockey rink, come winter. That's where the Monarchs play. Proud gold medal winners at the World Hockey Championship two years ago. And they won the Memorial Cup this year."

I didn't care much about hockey or any sport, and marveled that anyone in the world still found the means to attend games when so many people went without food or work. It seemed like a good sign, though. I was gladder than ever to be somewhere besides Bleak Landing, where even the curling rink had sat abandoned the past winter.

Mr. Nilsen turned down Broadway Avenue. At school, I'd seen pictures of the Manitoba Legislative Building with the shiny Golden Boy on top, but seeing him now was a whole different thing. The bright sun glinted off his bare bottom as he stood balanced on the ball of one foot, his right arm holding a torch high, the other grasping a sheaf of wheat. I knew he was seventeen feet tall, but he looked tiny from where I sat gawking in the car. I craned my neck as we drove by, trying to get a look at some of the other statues on the grounds.

"This here's the famous Fort Garry," Mr. Nilsen said. "Better get a good look at the outside, because you're not likely to ever see the *in*side."

I faced forward in my seat and saw what he was talking about. The grand hotel stood like a fortress, its stone walls decorated with fancy carvings. Next came the railroad station, nearly as grand but not as tall. Would I ever see the inside of *that*? I wondered. Where would I go by train? Not back to Bleak Landing, that's for sure. Still, I tried to get my bearings and memorize where it was so I'd know, should the need arise.

Mr. Nilsen turned north on Main Street, and I marveled at the cars and trolleys and pedestrians. On some streets, we shared space with streetcars running along little train tracks. On others, trolley buses scooted along, powered by overhead wires that sent sparks shooting out when they turned a corner. Were they safe? Would I ever figure out how to get around on these buses?

As we turned right and left, I lost track of street names I'd been trying to keep straight in my head. I knew I'd never find my way anywhere without guidance. Buildings looked more industrial now, and when I realized Mr. Nilsen was stopping in front of one, I read the sign sweeping across its front: **WEINBERGER TEXTILES**.

"This is it." Mr. Nilsen turned off the engine and lit a cigarette. "Might want to stretch your legs a little before we go inside."

I climbed out of the car and stood beside it, looking up at the big building. It represented my new world, and my heart fluttered like the last leaf clinging to an oak tree on Halloween night.

Mr. Nilsen got out, threw his cigarette butt to the pavement, and ground it out with his foot. "Might as well bring your bag," he said. "Let's find Bob Thompson."

I grabbed my belongings from the backseat and followed Mr. Nilsen up the steps of the factory. Inside, a middle-aged woman sat at a large reception desk, talking on a telephone. I could hear the muted whir of machinery. When someone opened a door off to my left, the sound got much louder, and I caught a glimpse of what lay beyond it: rows and rows of sewing machines.

The woman ended her call, glanced my way, and turned her attention to Mr. Nilsen. "May I help you?"

"Lars Nilsen to see Bob Thompson, please. He's expecting us."

The woman led us down a hallway to the right, where she rapped on a door marked ROBERT THOMPSON, PERSONNEL MANAGER. She opened the door without waiting for an answer and ushered us into an office. "Have a seat," she said. "I'll find him and tell him you're here."

"Thank you." Mr. Nilsen watched her leave and took one of two wooden chairs facing Mr. Thompson's desk. "Might as well sit down, Bridget."

No sooner had I set my bag on the floor than a short man with a bald head rushed in. "You made good time, Nilsen." The men shook hands over the desk, and Mr. Thompson looked at me. "I take it this is the young lady you told me about?"

"Bob, this is Bridget O'Sullivan. Bleak Landing's finest."

"How do you do, Mr. Thompson?" My voice trembled and my cheeks felt warm.

"Pleased to meet you, Bridget." The man nodded and sat in the chair behind his desk. "I'm glad you're here. We just lost one of our seamstresses this morning, and I need to replace her as soon as possible. Ever operate a sewing machine?"

"N-no, sir." I hesitated for only a moment. "But I'm a fast learner."

"Well, you'll have to be. I've got time for a quick tour, and then we want to get you started—provided you don't change your mind." He chuckled and handed me a form. "I'll need you to fill this out and hand it in to Miss Brenner before the end of the day."

I took the paper. I'd never filled out a form in my life. I didn't even own a pen!

"I'm sure Miss Brenner will be happy to assist you with it at her desk," he added. "Now follow me. You coming, Lars?"

"Not this time, Bob. My job here is done."

"Know any other girls looking for work?"

"No. Just the one."

The men shook hands again, and Mr. Nilsen moved toward the door.

"Mr. Nilsen!" I cleared my throat. "How will I get ahold of you?"

"You'll see me around." He placed his hat on his head and opened the door.

"But—"

"Unless I see you first." He laughed and walked out the door and down the hallway, my mother's locket still in his coat pocket.

I had no time to fret about that, though. "Follow me," Mr. Thompson said. He took off so fast I had to grab my bag and half run to catch up. He opened an office door down the hall from his and poked his head through it. "Miss Brenner? This is Bridget O'Sullivan. Can you take her upstairs, please?"

A short, stocky woman in a gray skirt and white blouse looked up. "Certainly." She marched around to the front of her desk while I peered over Mr. Thompson's shoulder at her.

"I'll leave you in Miss Brenner's capable hands." Mr. Thompson turned and headed back to his office. I felt like the bucket in a bucket brigade.

Miss Brenner looked at me without smiling. "Come with me." She led me through a door to a stairwell. "Might as well start at the top so you can leave your bag." As we climbed two flights, she kept talking. "We've got dorm space for forty-eight young ladies, divided into four rooms of twelve beds each. Each room is assigned a resident assistant, usually the oldest but not always. She earns a penny more per hour than the others and sees to it that rules are followed. She'll make sure you get a uniform with your name embroidered on it." She looked down at my worn shoes. "And proper footwear. Of course, the cost of the clothing will come out of your pay, but we take it out in installments, over several months, to make it manageable. We expect uniforms to be kept clean and pressed. You'll find a washtub, clothesline, and ironing board in the washroom. You can start your training today dressed as you are."

We stopped on the third floor. I saw a set of double doors on each side of a hallway, all of them wide open, and another door on the opposite end.

"Shared bathrooms are on the end," Miss Brenner said, pointing. "You'll be in here." She led me through the first set of double doors and I knew instantly why they stood open. The stifling air descended on us like a heavy cloak. Two narrow windows remained open on the far wall, their thin curtains pulled aside—someone's vain attempt to freshen the rooms. I saw twelve narrow cots lined up, six on each side. Beside each bed stood a small chest with two drawers. Most were cluttered with handheld mirrors, hairbrushes, and books. All the beds were carefully made, except for one near the middle with a bare mattress. On the stand next to it sat some neatly folded bedding, a towel, and washcloth. Miss Brenner led me to that bed.

"This will be yours. You can place your bag under the bed for now and settle in this evening. The workday ends at six p.m. and the evening is yours, but you'll find the five a.m. wake-up alarm will have you heading for bed early. Any questions so far?"

Aware that I was grinning like a fool, I shook my head. "No, ma'am. I can't think of any."

"You seem to find this amusing, Bridget."

"Not amusing, exactly. Just glad to be here, ma'am."

How could I admit how excited I was to know that, for the first time in all my fifteen years, I would be sleeping in a real bed?

Chapter 8

$\mathcal{B}$ack in Miss Brenner's office, I completed the employment form, fudging just a little. For starters, my new name was Bridget Sullivan. I figured that maybe by dropping the *O*, I could lose the nicknames and the ridicule once and for all. A new name for a new life. Where it asked for name and contact information for my next of kin, I wasn't sure what to write. As far as I knew, Pa was my only kin on the entire planet, and I was determined to break all links to my old life. That included Bleak Landing. So, in honor of Miss Johansen, whose first name was Elizabeth, I wrote "Elizabeth Sullivan" on the line. I added number 71 for a street address because that was the number of books that lined the shelves at the Bleak Landing school. I added "Kennedy Street" because it was the name of a street I remembered seeing near the legislative building as we drove by. For all I knew, I was giving the address of the lieutenant governor, but I was pretty sure no one would notice what I wrote or ever even refer to my form. My goal was to make enough money here to pay back Mr. Nilsen, redeem my necklace, and move on to something better.

"I could have sworn Mr. Thompson said your name was O'Sullivan," Miss Brenner said when I handed the paper back to her.

"He did. But he heard it wrong," I said. "It's just Sullivan."

"I see. Well, you're a fortunate young woman. Jobs are scarce these days, and positions here at Weinberger Textiles are highly coveted. I hope you can appreciate that."

"I do."

"It's a ten-hour day and you'll start at six dollars a week, with the opportunity to work your way up to eleven dollars. Out of that, we take a dollar a week for your room and board. You'll need to catch on quickly, work hard, put in long hours, and keep your opinions to yourself."

"I can do that."

She placed the form inside a folder on which she'd already written my name. "Glad to hear it. Let's get you started, then." She led me to the huge, noisy room with rows and rows of sewing machines. My heart pounded.

"Mrs. Huddlestone?" Miss Brenner handed me off to an older woman in a gray dress with **D. HUDDLESTONE, HEAD SEAMSTRESS** on her name tag. "This is Bridget Sullivan, our newest girl. I'll leave her with you."

Mrs. Huddlestone looked me up and down. "How old are you?"

"Nearly sixteen, ma'am." Well, I would be. A year from today.

"Ever run a sewing machine?"

"No, ma'am. But I can hand stitch."

Mrs. Huddlestone sighed and rolled her eyes. "That'll come in handy when it's time to sew on buttons. We're working on industrial aprons at the moment. No buttons required, but a good garment to learn on." As she spoke, she led me to what appeared to be the only vacant chair in the room.

"The most important thing you need to know is how to care for your machine."

I spent the next half hour learning how to thread, clean, and oil a sewing machine, and the next six hours after that sewing the same four seams over and over again before passing each apron to the girl on my right for the next step. Whenever I thought I was starting to get caught up, another pile of fabric would be delivered to my station. By the time the bell rang at six o'clock, I figured I could sew those seams with my eyes closed. My back ached and my stomach rumbled. My bladder was near bursting, and my fingertips felt as dry as dust. But I'd survived my first day.

"I'm Maxine," the round-faced girl to my right said as we covered our machines. Her blond hair was pulled into a thick bun, but I could still tell it was curly. She nodded to the girl on my left. "That's Rosa. She doesn't speak much English."

Rosa's nearly black hair and dark skin contrasted with Maxine's light complexion. She nodded and said hello in what I guessed was an Italian accent.

"I'm Bridget Sullivan." The new name felt good.

"You need a bathroom as desperately as I do?" Maxine asked.

I nodded.

The girls laughed and walked with me to the ladies' room. Maxine kept up a running dialogue, and as we continued on to the second-floor cafeteria, I learned that she slept in dorm room number one, same as me. "Rosa's in room two with the Italian and Ukrainian girls. They stick to their own groups, except for Rosa here. She prefers our company so she can learn English."

Rosa smiled at me again, and I wondered when she found any opportunity to speak English—or any language—around Maxine. She certainly heard plenty of it, though.

Maxine led us through the double doors of the factory cafeteria. "You'll hate the food." She grabbed a metal tray and showed me how to get my fork and knife and line up for whatever was being served. "No options. Breakfast is always oatmeal. Lunch is always soup, even in the summer. And since this is Thursday, supper will be mashed potatoes and baked beans."

When had I ever had options? I gladly received the potatoes and beans plopped onto the divided sections of my tray. This meal was topped off with a thick slice of bread, an apple, and a glass of milk. We found seats together at a long table already occupied by four girls. I was about to dig in when I saw Maxine folding her hands and closing her eyes. I put my fork down and watched her.

"Lord," she said, "for this uninspiring food I am about to receive, you have made me hungry enough to be truly grateful. Amen!" She opened her eyes and smiled brightly at me. Rosa crossed herself and dug into her potatoes.

I tried to grin back. I figured Maxine would decide soon enough that I was not friend material, so I might as well start into the food. Once I did, I had to admit there was not much taste to it. But it filled a need, and I had no difficulty feeling grateful as well. Even Maxine stopped talking long enough to eat most of her meal. Between bites, she introduced me to Betty, Helen, Frances, and Dorie.

"Pleased to meet you," I said in as chipper a tone as I could muster, determined that Bridget Sullivan would be much more gregarious than Bridget O'Sullivan had been.

"Pleased t'meet ya, too!" Helen said, and for one delightful second I thought someone here was more Irish than I. She giggled.

"Top o' the mornin' to ya," Betty chimed in. "Oh, but it be evenin', then!" Now all four girls laughed.

Dorie got into the act. "Catch any leprechauns lately?" More laughter.

"I think your accent is swell, Bridget. How long've you been in Canada?" Frances may have meant to defend me, but her suggesting that I spoke with an accent only made me want to crawl into a hole. After I slugged her, of course.

Gregarious, I thought. *Just answer the question.* "Eight years." I forced out a smile.

"Not long enough, apparently." This was followed by another round of laughter. I wondered why all the girls seemed to hang on every word Helen said.

"Well, I think it's adorable," Frances said. "Take me home with you some weekend so I can hear the whole leprechaun family. Where do you live?"

The thought was horrifying. "Oh, I won't be going home weekends. It's . . ." How could I explain my home or my father or Bleak Landing? I didn't even want to say the name. ". . . too far."

"Obviously out in the country somewhere." Helen again. "She still has manure on her shoes." More giggles.

Dorie waved her hand in front of her face. "I wondered what that odor was."

"I thought it was Irish stew," Betty said.

I resisted the impulse to look down at my shoes, knowing it wasn't true. But it was getting harder to resist the urge to stand up and punch each of them in the nose, as I'd done to Victor Harrison. I'd start with Helen. I could feel the blood rising to my face. My hands were clenched, and I pondered whether a silent but painful punch would fall into Miss Brenner's definition of keeping my opinions to myself. Probably not.

"It's funny, I didn't hear any accent at all. Still don't," Maxine said with a shrug.

I glared at her. I knew she was fibbing; though I willed her words to be true, I knew they weren't. I waited for her to twist them into an insult. Surely she wouldn't risk the ridicule of the others by coming to my defense.

But she went on. "I think it's marvelous. So exotic, sailing here from a far-off land. Your horizons are so much broader than ours."

"Her horizons are the only 'broad' thing about her." Helen laughed. "I've seen more curves on a broomstick."

"I'm serious," Maxine said. "And look at all this glorious red hair. I can't wait to see what it looks like when we brush it out!"

"Maxine imagines herself a hairdresser." Betty turned to me. "Better watch out, you might wake up one morning with it chopped into a pageboy bob!"

"Ooooh, that's what I want." Frances fluffed her brown tresses. "Can you do mine, Maxine?"

"Just get me a good pair of scissors." Maxine leaned in my direction. "I'm saving up for beauty school."

"I'll be your guinea pig, Maxine," Helen said. "Not until *after* you've done all these heads for practice, though."

"Nobody touches my hair," I said. I took a deep breath and let out a slow sigh, my fists gradually uncurling. It seemed the attention was finally off me and my Irish-ness and my country-bumpkin-ness. I was about to bite into my apple when I noticed Helen slicing hers and eating it in dainty bites. I followed suit.

When the meal ended, we headed for the dorm. It was now seven, and girls were already taking turns at the showers and washtubs.

"Lights out at nine. I'll help you make up your bed," Maxine volunteered. She helped me place the white sheets and gray blanket on my cot. "It's too hot in here for this blanket right now, but it'll cool off tonight. It's only April. Wait until July!" She tucked the pillow into its pillowcase and fluffed it with care. "There you go." She looked at my hands. "You'll want to get some cream for those fingers. The fabric sucks the moisture right outta them. I'll share mine for now."

I unpacked the contents of my bag into the two drawers allotted to me and tucked the bag back under the bed. I wanted to crawl right in, but I took the time to rinse out my clothes and hang them to dry. Afterward, I took a quick shower and pulled my nightgown over my head. That's when I remembered my mother's locket was no longer around my neck. But I refused to dwell on it. With the dust from the long day washed away and Maxine's hand cream soothing my weary fingers, I climbed between the sheets and lay back with a satisfied sigh. I'd done it! I'd left Bleak Landing behind. I had a full belly, a bed to sleep in, and a roof over my head. It even seemed that, in spite of myself, I might have made a friend.

I was so exhausted, the chatter in the room didn't even bother me, and I didn't hear the call for lights out. It had been both the longest and the best day of my life. It was only as I was fading into delicious sleep that I remembered it was my birthday. I was fifteen years old.

And I'd gotten away.

Chapter 9

Bleak Landing

*D*arkness was approaching, which meant the dishwater might benefit the potato plants before it evaporated. Victor Harrison carried two five-gallon pails from his mother's kitchen to the garden. His sisters Nancy and Anna dipped some onto each spot where they'd buried a piece of potato a few hours before. It was early in the season to plant, but the threat of another drought was greater than the threat of late frost. The sooner the potato chunks were placed in the ground, the sooner they'd produce something to eat.

With careful use, the Harrisons had so far kept their well from running dry. The rule was, except for the water they drank, every drop pumped had to be used twice. Before it was used to water plants, it was used for dishes or bathing. Sometimes both, in that order, if it didn't get too greasy. And there was little to make dishwater greasy these days. The family lived on oatmeal without milk, boiled potatoes without butter, and beans without bacon. His mother was still keeping six chickens alive, and they earned their keep by eating grasshoppers and laying eggs. Ma allowed one egg per family member per week and sold the rest, though Victor strongly suspected she was giving away more than she sold—calling it "on credit," to save her customers' pride. Or trading for other goods, like that tasteless Irish bread Bridget O'Sullivan frequently brought by. He'd far rather have the eggs and knew his pa would, too. But his mother's heart was made of gold and had a soft spot in it for Bridget. He'd overheard his mother praying for the girl at night when his parents knelt together in their bedroom. For her protection, mostly. Victor felt sure from the bruises he'd seen on Bridget's shins that his mother's prayers went unanswered.

Thoughts of that redhead were never far away, no matter how hard Victor tried to banish them. Now that he was done with school, he didn't see her much. Each time he did, it seemed she'd grown taller. And less ugly. Not that he'd taken particular notice, he told himself. He noticed lots of girls.

His thoughts were interrupted by the sound of Bingo barking from the edge of their property.

"Here comes Mr. O'Sullivan," Nancy said.

Victor thought he'd misheard his sister at first. Had she somehow read his mind? But both she and Anna stood looking toward the road, and when Victor's eyes followed, he was surprised to see Bridget's father walking toward them. *What on earth?* To his knowledge, the man had never set foot on their place. He always sent Bridget for eggs. Was he looking for work, hoping Pa might hire him?

"Bingo! C'mere, boy." Victor patted his thigh and the dog came, tail wagging.

"Good evenin'," Mr. O'Sullivan said in his Irish brogue. He looked around at the beginnings of the garden. "Got your praties in, then?"

"Yes, sir. Just planted them today. You think it's too soon?" Victor thought the man looked more worn and weary than usual, if that was possible.

"Notta t'all, not this year." Mr. O'Sullivan glanced at Victor's sisters, then back at him. "Might I have a word with you, lad?"

"With me?"

Mr. O'Sullivan nodded, and Victor wondered what on earth he'd done to offend Bridget so much she'd sent her father after him. He hadn't even seen her in a week or more, since the day he and Pa drove past the school on their way to the grain elevator and everybody was out for recess. Bridget was sitting on a swing, her nose in a book, and never looked up.

After Victor's sisters took the hint and went into the house, Mr. O'Sullivan pulled a piece of paper from his pocket. "I was wonderin' if perhaps you could read this for me," he said. "Me eyesight's not so good." He unfolded the sheet and handed it to Victor, who wondered why on earth Bridget couldn't read it to him. But he said nothing, and took the paper.

Daylight was beginning to fade, but he recognized Bridget's handwriting immediately. She was the only student he'd ever seen who wrote as neatly as the teacher. He read aloud.

> *Dear Pa,*
>
> *I know you won't be able to read this, but if I tell you what I'm doing you might try to stop me, and I don't trust anyone to keep quiet until I'm gone. I am fifteen today and I've decided it's time to make my own way in the world. I'm sure you will be relieved to not have to keep me fed anymore.*
> *Please don't look for me.*
> *Bridget*

Shocked, Victor looked up at Bridget's father. "She's gone?"

The man stared at the horizon and nodded. "Bloody girl. Just when she's old enough to start earnin' her keep, she up and abandons her ol' da." He sighed. "She'll be back." With a loud sniff, he turned and headed in the direction from which he'd come.

"Wait! Mr. O'Sullivan!" Victor trotted to keep up, holding out the paper, Bingo nearly tripping him. "Do you want your note?"

"No use to me."

"But, sir." Victor had so many questions. "When did she leave? Did she have train fare? Do you have any idea where she might have gone?"

"Don't know." He kept walking, and Victor stood watching him.

"Mr. O'Sullivan!" he called out, but the man didn't stop. "Why did you come to *me*?"

No answer. Victor watched until the descending darkness swallowed up Bridget's father. He looked down at the note in his hands, folded it, and shoved it into his pocket. Bingo looked up at Victor, and Victor crouched to lay one arm across the dog's back.

"Why did he bring this to me, boy?" Victor looked to the sky and thought of his mother's prayers. *Is this your answer, God? Are you protecting Bridget by removing her from her father's house? Did he come to me because he thought I might know something? Or that I might be with her?*

Bingo licked his face. "Well, between you and me, boy . . . I wish I were." At least then he'd know whether or not Bridget was safe.

He turned and slowly walked back to the house, where he knew his family was preparing for bed. He wasn't ready to tell his parents why Mr. O'Sullivan had come. He needed time to think it through. He sat on the front porch, scratching Bingo's ears, until all was quiet and dark. The dog lay beside him, enjoying the attention. Finally, without a word, Victor went inside, took his turn with the wash water, and lay on his bed.

But sleep refused to come.

Chapter 10

I'd been at the job two months, and my sewing machine was beginning to feel like a natural extension of my hands. In truth, I was part of a much larger machine, humans and instruments working in tandem, each doing one small part to produce something of value. Together we turned out aprons, gloves, coveralls, and winter coats, though I could not have sewn a single garment from start to finish to save my life. When buttons needed to be sewn on, Mrs. Huddlestone pulled me and a few other girls away from our machines to the buttoning table where we stitched by hand. Afterward, I returned to my machine, where a huge pile of garments had accumulated, waiting for me to run through my seams. The work was monotonous, but it felt good to be part of a team. I was so glad to be away from Bleak Landing, I could have kissed Mr. Nilsen.

If only I could find him.

I had carefully set aside half of my first pay envelope so I could redeem my locket at the first opportunity. When the other half wasn't enough to cover my uniforms, however, I needed to dip into my locket money to cover the two plain blue dresses with my name embroidered on the front. By the second payday, I had enough money set aside for Mr. Nilsen, plus extra to repay Maxine for the soap and hand cream she loaned me. With my third pay, I bought soap and hand cream of my own and splurged on a motion picture on a Saturday night. Rosa, Maxine, and I saw *The Good Earth*, starring Paul Muni and Luise Rainer, at the Bijou Theater on Main Street. I tried not to let on that it was my first time at the movies, but the other girls saw right through me. I guess I was gawking, but I couldn't help it. The theater was decorated with plaster relief figures and trimmed with gold! We bought popcorn, too, and I loved it. I had read Pearl Buck's book in Grade Seven, and to be honest, the book was better than the movie. It's a mostly sad tale, but it was still glorious fun.

It felt strange to have these girls being friendly to me, especially since they were eighteen. I remained vague about my own age, but I think they suspected I was a lot younger than I let on. Maxine treated me like a little sister who needed to be shown the ropes. We spent our free time exploring the neighborhood, and I was adapting to city life. Though I didn't care for the noise, it was less dusty than Bleak Landing and a whole heap more interesting. The sight of lines at the soup kitchen and tramps begging for food bothered me at first. But Maxine kept saying things like "I'm so thankful I'm not in that line," and "God's been so good to me." She talked about God as if she knew him, even though she wasn't a Catholic. Reminded me of Victor Harrison's mother, and I wondered if Maxine had a mother like Victor's. I didn't ask, though, because I didn't want to be asked back.

Maxine kept begging to do things with my hair, and I kept telling her no, thanks.

"C'mon, just let me brush it," she'd say.

"I'm fine," I'd tell her. I could usually count on one of the other girls begging for Maxine to do theirs, distracting her from mine.

My hair stayed in some kind of braid or bun all the time, and it hung to my waist when I let it down for washing, another chore Maxine kept offering to do no matter how often I refused. She kept up a running monologue while she watched me wash it, though, and I didn't mind. Saved me from having to talk, and I liked hearing her stories. She talked about her two big brothers, for whom she held boundless affection in spite of the tall tales they told her. When she was a little kid, they had her believing bears lived in haystacks. Later she figured out that had been their way of keeping her away from the haystack they hid behind to smoke cigarettes.

Maxine went home for the weekend about once a month and kept insisting I should go with her. I told her I couldn't go until after I got my locket back, in case Mr. Nilsen came around the factory looking for me while I was gone. It was the truth, but the bigger truth was that I had no desire to get closer to Maxine Ross. The last thing I needed was her pestering me about visiting *my* home.

I saw Mr. Thompson, the personnel manager, breezing through the production room a few times but I hadn't spoken with him since our meeting in his office on my first day. Once I had enough money to redeem my locket, I went straight to his office every day when the lunch bell rang. He was never there. Finally, after five tries, I caught him just outside his door. He was heading away from me.

"Mr. Thompson!"

When he turned around, I could tell by the look on his face that he didn't remember me. But then, why should he? With all the girls coming and going here, we probably all looked alike to him. "Yes?"

"I'm Bridget. Bridget Sullivan?"

He looked down the hall beyond where I stood. "Yes?"

I put on my sweetest voice. "Mr. Thompson, I need to find Lars Nilsen. The man who brought me here? I was hoping you could tell me how to get in touch with him."

"Lars Nilsen? I'd like to get in touch with that shyster myself. He owes me fifty bucks." He turned and headed down the hallway.

"Oh. Wait! Mr. Thompson?"

The man turned with an impatient sigh.

"Don't you at least have a telephone number? An address here in the city?"

"Had one. He was staying at a boardinghouse, but last time I tried to call, the landlady told me he'd moved out and she'd didn't know where he'd gone."

"Well, is he still in Winnipeg?"

"Don't know. Listen, kid, I have a meeting to get to. Come back at the end of the day. I'll see if I can track him down."

But when I returned after the finishing bell, Mr. Thompson was not in his office. I returned at lunchtime every day for the next week, and finally caught him at his desk. This time he recognized me.

"You the kid that's looking for Nilsen?"

"Yes, sir."

"What for?"

"He's got something of mine. A necklace."

He studied me a moment. "He steal it?"

"No, sir. He's holding it until I can pay him for the ride to Winnipeg. I can do that now. I'd like to get my necklace back."

"I see. Must be valuable."

"Only to me." I'd been standing the whole time, trying to keep my feet planted firmly in one place. There was a copy of *Cosmopolitan* floating around the dormitory, and I'd read an article about how to appear confident in order to get what you want. I worked hard to keep my eyes on Mr. Thompson's face. "The locket's been in my family for generations."

Mr. Thompson lit a cigarette and studied me. "Well, I hate to be the one to tell you this, but you can kiss that necklace goodbye." He scribbled an address and phone number on a scrap of paper and handed it to me. "Nilsen was staying at this boardinghouse, but like I said, the landlady told me he moved out a couple of weeks ago. Maybe he went back to wherever he came from."

I looked down to see an address on Hawthorne Avenue. "What's the landlady's name?"

"I forget. Something like *Chester*. Or *Crest*. Starts with a *C*. If you find Nilsen, you let me know."

That night I took a chance and wrote a short letter:

Mr. Nilsen,

Please contact me. I can pay you for the ride, and I wish to redeem my mother's locket. I am still at the place where you left me.
Bridget

I mailed the letter to the landlady's address with hopes that she'd forward it if she knew where he'd gone. I left off a return address, though, in case that somewhere was the place I'd fled. Bleak Landing was much too small and its postmaster much too nosy.

Chapter 11

December 1937

*F*ace it, Bridget." Maxine looked at me, the twinkle from her eyes gone. "That man is not going to come looking for you just to return your necklace—especially if he owes Mr. Thompson money. You must come home with me for Christmas. I insist. You can't stay here; they're closing everything up."

It was true. The factory would shut down for five whole days. We'd been informed that the dorms must be vacated and the cafeteria would be closed. With nowhere else to go, I had to admit Maxine was right. I'd be foolish to hang around Winnipeg, hoping against all odds that Mr. Nilsen might look for me. There'd been no reply to my letter. The locket was probably hanging around someone else's neck by now, my great-grandmother's picture replaced with a photograph of some stranger's sweetheart. I wondered how much Mr. Nilsen had gotten for it and what he'd done with the money. I felt sick. How could I have been so foolish?

"Your mother will understand," Maxine said. "She *does* understand."

That was the oddest thing about Maxine. She knew my mother was dead, but she talked as though death was just a doorway into another life. When Maxine was thirteen, she lost an older sister to some kind of heart disease. She told me the story one day while she brushed her hair.

"I just can't see her right now, but I will one day. You'll see your mother, too."

"How can you be so sure?" I asked.

She paused for a long time. "I suppose I can't. I just believe it. I just *know* it."

Now we sat across from each other on the Thursday morning train, heading for Maxine's home in Pinehaven. The heat in the train car was minimal, and I was glad for my warm coat—my mystery coat, left on our doorstep as if by mistake but clearly intended for me. I chose to believe that, anyway. Every clickety-clack of the train was carrying me in the opposite direction from Bleak Landing. There'd been times when I felt a pang of guilt for leaving my father the way I had, but I swept those feelings aside and tried to live in the moment.

"You'll love Pinehaven," Maxine said. "We'll get to go skating and watch some curling, and I'll introduce you to Clara and Fern and Mildred and Grace. Oh, and Joyce. Too bad the school Christmas concert will probably be over already. That's always fun. And my family always makes homemade Christmas presents . . ."

I ignored Maxine and watched the Manitoba countryside go by. The sunshine sparkled on virgin snow, nearly blinding me. Yet I couldn't take my eyes off the wonderland outside my window. Acres of poplar trees, devoid of their leaves, glistened with hoarfrost, looking like some kind of magical kingdom. The world was cleaner and brighter than I'd ever seen it, and it was easy to believe there was no such thing as drought or depression and that loved ones who'd passed on truly still lived even if we couldn't see them.

I was surprised when we reached Pinehaven well before noon. Maxine's mother met us on the platform, though it was only a short walk to their home. She greeted me with a warm smile and then turned her attention to her daughter, and the pair of them didn't stop talking for the rest of the week. Their home was filled with the warm scents of cinnamon and ginger. I heard "Away in a Manger" playing on a radio and masculine laughter coming from the next room.

Maxine's brothers, Billy and Arnie, turned out to be tall, blond, and large boned like their sister. They lived at home and worked at a lumber mill along with helping their father on the farm. In anticipation of our visit, they'd cleared snow from their pond for ice skating. After a lunch of chicken noodle soup and bread fresh from the oven, the four of us bundled up and ventured down to the ice.

I'd never owned a pair of skates. But I sat on a straw bale watching Maxine skim around the pond, and it looked like a cinch. At the movies, we'd seen newsreels of Olympic skater Sonja Henie, and I was eager to give it a try. Maxine's skates were a little big for me, but with extra wool socks and determination, I was sure I'd soon be flying across the ice on one foot. Maxine helped me lace up her skates on my feet, but I quickly discovered it was all I could do just to stand up on the snowy ground! How did Sonja Henie make skating look so easy and graceful? With Maxine on one side and Arnie on the other, I eventually made a wobbly circle around the pond. When they let go, I promptly landed right on my behind. Disappointing though my first skating experience was, I couldn't stop smiling. Billy pulled me to my feet again and I spent a while longer just trying to stay upright on the ice before giving Maxine another turn.

The sun was going down by the time we went back to the house, where Mrs. Ross had hot chocolate waiting.

"Sorry it's a little thin," she said. "But I think there's just enough for you all to have a cup."

I don't know why she apologized. It was the most delicious drink I'd ever tasted.

After the evening barn chores were done and supper had been eaten, the family gathered in the living room. A Christmas tree glimmered in one corner, and a half-finished jigsaw puzzle sat waiting on a wooden table. Maxine's mother showed me the basics of crocheting, while her siblings and father played Parcheesi on the coffee table. I felt as if I'd walked into some kind of dream where everything was filled with warmth and love and goodness. I wondered what the catch was.

"We'll be attending the Christmas Eve service at church tomorrow evening, Bridget," Mrs. Ross said. "You're welcome to join us."

Church. There it was. My father's words returned in full force. *You'll burn in hell, sure, if you set foot in with the Protestants.* I had no desire to offend the Ross family when they were being so kind and hospitable to me. But what if my father's words were true?

"I'm Catholic, ma'am," I said. I didn't bother telling her that the last time I'd actually been inside a Catholic church—or any church—was when I was six years old and still in Ireland.

"I see. Well, there *is* a Catholic church in town." Mrs. Ross picked up her knitting needles and worked on something bright red while I continued practicing a basic crochet chain stitch. "If you like, I can find out what time they hold Mass. Everyone around town likes Father Michael."

Mr. Ross piped up. "They always hold a midnight Mass on Christmas Eve. Maybe we could all go. Our service will be over by nine."

I wasn't sure who was more shocked, me or Mrs. Ross. She looked up from her red wool and smiled. "Well, wouldn't that be a fine idea! Something different. Do they allow non-Catholics to attend?"

"We wouldn't know what was going on," Arnie said, as he rolled the dice. "I think it's all in Latin."

Billy cuffed him on the shoulder. "How would you know?"

"He went there once, when he was chasing Miranda Hotchkins." Maxine said the name in a teasing singsong. "Wasn't *that* a wild goose chase?"

"Oh, pipe down." Arnie moved his playing piece around the board. "I could tell of a lot worse things you did chasing Henry Newton."

"Pipe down, both of you." Mr. Ross placed his final piece in the center square of the game board and rose from his armchair. "If they allow the likes of Arnie in, they're sure to welcome us all. Bridget, how about you come to church with us at seven, and we'll all go to midnight Mass together. What do you say?"

I had no idea what to say, but I figured I was in no position to argue. "All right."

Five faces smiled back at me, as if I'd just capped their heads with royal crowns. I had not felt this much a part of something since Miss Johansen picked me to read stories to the little kids back at Bleak Landing School. I didn't say anything more for the rest of the evening, but I didn't need to. The Ross family did enough talking for three families. All I had to do was sit back and soak it up.

And hope I wouldn't burn in hell for joining them at their church.

⁓

Friday afternoon, Maxine and I were sitting on her bed with copies of *Chatelaine* magazine. I was trying to read an article called "Men Don't Want Clever Wives." Maxine was filling out one of those personality quizzes and annoying me by reading all the questions aloud.

"Number one. Are you typically late for appointments or work?" She made a mark in the magazine with her pencil. "No."

"Number two. What is your favorite color? *Raspberry red.*" She wrote it in.

"Number three. What words do you tend to overuse?" She paused. "What words do I overuse, Bridge?"

"All of them," I muttered, flipping a page in my own magazine.

We laid the magazines aside when Mrs. Ross walked in carrying a green dress.

"Bridget?"

I looked up at her smiling face.

"It occurred to me that you might be the same size as our Ruthie."

I looked at Maxine, not understanding.

"My sister," Maxine said. "She was sixteen."

I'd forgotten about Maxine's sister. I turned back to her mother.

"Would you like to try this on? If it works for you, you could have it. If you like. I think it would look wonderful with your red hair."

I didn't know what to say. No one had offered me anything so beautiful in my life. The dress was velvety and grown-up looking, and it clearly had been made for someone much slimmer than Maxine.

I stared at the lovely garment. "Oh, I . . . I couldn't."

"We'd be honored," Mrs. Ross said. Her head nodded, and her eyes glistened. "Really."

"Try it on," Maxine said.

So I did. When I saw my reflection in the mirror, I was convinced it was someone else's at first. The dress was a perfect fit, falling below my knees with a gentle flare. The elbow-length sleeves and lacy collar made me feel feminine in a way I never had before.

"Oh, Bridget!" Maxine gushed. "It's perfect for you! You're beautiful!"

I smiled and did a little twirl, admiring my reflection. But when I saw the tears on Mrs. Ross's cheeks as she stood smiling at me, I knew I couldn't do it. I was not part of this family, and no dress was going to change that. I looked back at my image and frowned.

"Thanks, Mrs. Ross. I appreciate the gesture, but this isn't really me. And it's a little tight."

"Not *you*? What do you mean, not you?" Maxine's voice rose half an octave. "Look at yourself!"

"Besides, where would I wear it?" I asked.

"Well, for starters, to church tomorrow night!"

I shook my head. "No. Thank you. I . . . can't."

Maxine was about to protest again when her mother raised her hand to quiet her. "Maxine. It's all right."

I slipped out of the dress and handed it back to Mrs. Ross, who carried it away gently without another word. Maxine pouted and stopped talking to me, but within half an hour she couldn't stand it anymore.

"Personally, I'm going to wear my red blouse and black skirt. Or should I go with that royal blue dress? It would look great with the new string of beads Dorie gave me. Well, not new, exactly. New to me. Right? What do you think?"

I guessed all was forgiven.

~

The two church experiences were a study in contrast, but as Mr. Ross had reminded us at the supper table before we left the house, "We're all celebrating the birth of the same Savior." The earlier service at Pinehaven Fellowship featured lively singing of "Joy to the World" and "Hark! The Herald Angels Sing." The children, dressed in bathrobes and towels, acted out the Nativity story, and the pastor talked about God's love, so great that he sent his son so we could be called children of God. Afterward, some men handed out bags of peanuts and candy to all the children and even the teens.

Midnight Mass was more subdued but felt just as meaningful. The glow of the candles and the voices of the nuns' choir harmonizing on "Adeste Fidelis" stirred something inside me as we made our way inside.

I attentively observed the congregation and followed their patterns of sitting and standing, awkwardly aware that the Ross family was looking to me for guidance. Arnie had been right. It *was* mostly in Latin, and the little bit of Latin Miss Johansen had taught us was just enough for me to recognize words like "Christus" and "Dominus." It didn't matter. It was a beautiful setting, and a feeling of awe and a reverent sense of majesty filled my heart as I surveyed my surroundings.

That night, after Maxine's words finally faded into snoring, I lay awake a long time pondering all I'd seen and heard and felt. The longings provoked by the softness of that green velvet dress on my skin. The peace in the Ross home, their voices raised in praise to their Savior— even as they grieved the loss of their dear daughter and sister. Vague memories surfaced within me of my mother kneeling by her bed with her rosary. For the first time in years, I felt something deep in my heart beginning to awaken. If God really loved all of us as the Ross family believed, then that included me.

I fell asleep hoping desperately that it was true.

Chapter 12

The Monday after Christmas, Maxine and I boarded the train and returned to Winnipeg. We'd been in such a rush when we left town before Christmas that I hadn't taken time to look around at Union Station. Now I stood gawking like a little kid at the tiled floor with a circular pattern that reflected the domed ceiling above—a magnificent display of architecture. How had they built such a thing? What held it up? People scurried past a gigantic Christmas tree that adorned the center of the station, everyone headed somewhere in a hurry. Everyone but me. I'd never seen such a big tree.

Maxine shouted at me from the front door. "Bridget! Hurry up, we'll miss our bus!"

But it was too late. The bus took off without us and we had to wait for the next one.

"Sorry," I mumbled, though I was secretly glad to have extra time to take in the sights around me.

Maxine sat on a bench and pouted. She'd been quiet on the train— unusual for Maxine. She was even more subdued as we climbed aboard the next bus and rode past the city sidewalks toward our home away from home. I enjoyed the peace and quiet until we had almost reached our destination. Yet the fact that something was bothering Maxine bothered *me*.

"I'm sorry I made us miss the bus."

"It's not that." She sighed.

"Then what?"

She shrugged and gazed out the window. "Our family's not the same without Ruthie."

I nodded. I could relate to the feeling, but I'd never told Maxine that I had lost a brother. Nor did I want to go into it now. "Seems like everyone's doing all right, though."

Maxine looked me in the eye. "Why wouldn't you accept Ruthie's dress? You know you wanted to."

I turned and watched the world go by on the other side of the window, trying to answer her question for myself. She was right. Part of me would have loved to keep that beautiful dress. But how could I make her understand that no part of me anywhere deserved such a fine thing?

"Bridget?"

"I don't know. I don't think your mother was really ready to part with it." I swallowed.

"It would have done her heart good to see you wearing it, Bridget. Mine, too." She sounded convinced, and convincing. "I mean, yes, it would have been hard. But it would have been a blessing all the same."

I couldn't bring myself to look at her. "I'm not your sister, Maxine."

"I know."

"Then maybe you should stop acting like it."

Maxine gazed at me until I had to look away again. "Why do you hold everyone at arm's length? It took a lot of courage for Mom to get that dress out of the closet—"

"Look, I'm sorry if I hurt your mother's feelings. But people lose people all the time. It's life. You just have to make the best of it."

We pulled to a stop in front of Weinberger Textiles. I brushed past Maxine to get off the bus ahead of her. My bag thumped against each seat as I stomped past.

"Bridget, wait up—!"

I heard Maxine call, but I hopped down from the bus—and then noticed a fancy car parked in front of it. To my horror, a little girl had climbed out of the car on the street side and stood in the road, right in the bus's path. She was so small, I feared the driver wouldn't see her. I dropped my bag and dashed toward the child as the bus pulled away. I swept her up and ran around the front of the car. I had deposited her safely on the sidewalk before I even realized what had happened. When I looked up, the tail end of the bus was passing us. Maxine stood frozen to the sidewalk, watching the whole thing. The little girl cried as a man in a swanky suit marched toward us.

"Cynthia!" The man scooped up the little girl. "Are you all right, precious?"

"D-daddy!" The girl pointed an accusing finger at me. "That lady grabbed me!"

"That lady *saved* you, Cynthia." He held her tight to himself. "Oh, thank God you're all right."

He turned to me.

"Young lady, are you all right?"

"Yes, sir. Mostly." I could feel myself trembling as the reality of what just happened set in. Maxine had picked up my bag and stood next to me.

"What's your name?"

I was nearly too stunned to speak. "B-Bridget. Sullivan."

"Do you work here, Miss Sullivan?"

I glanced at Maxine and back again. "Yes, sir."

The man set his daughter down and held tightly to her hand while he put out his other hand to shake mine. "How do you, Bridget

Sullivan. My name is Sol Weinberger. This is my factory. I want to thank you from the bottom of my heart for saving my daughter's life."

I'm sure my mouth hung open, but I felt powerless to move.

Maxine spoke up. "It's true, Bridget. You really did save her! I saw the whole thing! You were amazing!"

Mr. Weinberger knelt down to his daughter's height. "Darling, you must obey when Daddy says to stay in the car. You must never, ever climb out on the street side, do you understand?" The little girl nodded and her father hugged her to his chest again, then picked her up once more.

"You ladies come with me. Let's get out of the cold." He led the way up the steps and held the front doors open while we passed through. "Please come to my office, Miss Sullivan. Your friend can come, too, if you like."

Maxine and I exchanged looks but said nothing. We followed Mr. Weinberger past the reception desk, past Mr. Thompson's office, and past Miss Brenner's office, still carrying our bags. Mr. Weinberger pushed open a door with his name on it, and we followed him through. This, apparently, was simply his outer office.

A secretary took his coat and hat. "Good afternoon, Mr. Weinberger. Hello there, Cynthia!"

"Hi, Miss Pritchard. I almost got hit by a bus!" Cynthia said proudly.

The secretary raised her eyebrows and looked up at her boss.

"I'll tell you later," he said. "Please entertain Cynthia for a few minutes, will you?" He opened another door and turned toward us. "Ladies? Follow me, please."

His office was bigger than Mr. Thompson's, and his desk much tidier. The walls were covered with framed photographs of the factory, the sewing room, and smiling men posing together in various locations around the factory.

I could feel my heart pounding. I didn't understand what was going on, but Maxine was grinning like an idiot so I figured she must know something I didn't, and it must be good.

"Have a seat," Mr. Weinberger said. "Can I get you anything? Tea? A glass of water?"

"Oh, yes. Tea, please!" Maxine said. How could she be so bold? Had she lost her mind? We took the two wooden chairs facing his desk.

"I-I'll have a glass of water, if that's all right." My throat was parched.

Mr. Weinberger leaned through the doorway, one hand resting on the frame. "Miss Pritchard, please bring one tea and one glass of water." He walked around his desk and sat in the big leather chair behind it. He pulled a cigar out of a box on the corner of the desk and lit it.

"Now, then. How long have you been with us, Miss Sullivan?"

"Since last April, sir."

Mr. Weinberger counted on his fingers. "So, eight months. Have you received a raise in that time?"

"Yes, sir. At my six-month date I was raised to seven dollars a week."

"Do you like this job, Miss Sullivan?" He blew a long puff of cigar smoke toward the closed window.

"Yes, sir. I do. I'm very grateful to have it." I looked down at my shaking fingers and then at Maxine, who grinned like a chimpanzee.

Mr. Weinberger studied my face a moment. "No higher aspirations? Quite content to keep working here, sewing seams day after day?"

"Well. I haven't really thought about it much, sir. I suppose it's not what I want to do forever. But with the economy and all—"

I could have died when Maxine jumped in. "She's really good, Mr. Weinberger. She's smart and catches on fast and sews a straight seam and she's got loads of other talents, too. Why—"

"Excuse me. I didn't catch your friend's name." Mr. Weinberger was still looking at me, but Maxine stood and stretched out a hand toward him.

"Maxine Ross, sir. I'm from Pinehaven. Bridget came home with me for Christmas and we're just now getting back—"

The secretary interrupted us by bringing in our tea and water. I took a long, slow sip and kept the glass in my hands, not sure where I should set it.

"Thank you, Miss Pritchard." Mr. Weinberger turned to me again. "Do you know how to cook, Miss Sullivan?"

What kind of crazy question was that? "Well . . . a little, sir. I used to cook for my father and myself. Eggs and potatoes and Irish soda bread, mostly. Garden vegetables in summer. Venison when my father could get it."

"I'd like to reward you for saving my little girl, Miss Sullivan. Our cook's helper just left us to get married. Mrs. Cohen is an excellent cook, but she gets downright surly when she doesn't have any kitchen help. My wife is growing weary of her complaints. I can offer you free room and board in our home and ten dollars a week."

"Ten dollars a—!" Maxine caught herself and clamped a hand over her mouth. "Sorry." She looked at me, eyes like two giant spindles sticking out of a sewing machine.

I couldn't quite take in what was happening. The man was offering me a better job with more pay. In an actual home. What was the catch?

"You'll have Saturdays off for Shabbat and a half day on Sunday."

Shabbat? "Sir, I'm Catholic."

The man flicked his wrist. "So what? You think I'd give my staff Christmas off if I cared about all that? My family and I only go to synagogue on holidays. Sometimes not even then, if we're on a trip somewhere."

"But sir, I wouldn't know how to cook for you—"

"—and I haven't eaten kosher since I was a kid. The last girl we had was a Mennonite, if you can believe that. A *Mennonite*! She sure could cook." He chuckled and took another long drag from his cigar. "Mrs. Cohen will teach you all you need to know. What do you say?"

Miss Pritchard poked her head in the door. "Charles Lipton on the line, Mr. Weinberger. Do you want to take it?"

"Excuse me a moment, ladies." Mr. Weinberger picked up his phone and swiveled his chair away from us. "Charles! How was your Christmas?"

I was still stunned. I looked at Maxine, who nodded her head like a fool. "You have to do it, Bridget!" she practically hissed. "Do you know how long it will take you to earn ten dollars a week if you stay here? And you'll get to live in some big fancy mansion!"

I frowned at her.

"What's the matter with you? This is your big chance!"

"If Mr. Nilsen comes around with my necklace and doesn't find me here—"

"I'll be here, Bridget. I'll tell Mr. Thompson to find me if Mr. Nilsen comes looking for you. You have to do this."

"Promise?"

Maxine nodded. "I promise." I could tell by the look in her eye that she didn't believe for one second Mr. Nilsen would ever come looking for me.

Mr. Weinberger hung up the phone and stubbed out his cigar into a big ashtray. "Well? Do the Weinbergers have a new kitchen maid?"

I swallowed hard. "Yes, sir. I guess you do."

Chapter 13

I knew I was staring again, but I couldn't help it.

Mr. Weinberger was bringing me to his home in his big fancy car with its plush leather seats. He sat up front with the uniformed chauffeur, while Cynthia sat quietly beside me, casting occasional glances my way as though I couldn't be trusted. All my possessions had been stuffed into two bags and stashed in the trunk. I'd hardly had a chance to say goodbye to Maxine, which was fine with me because her big teary face was getting on my nerves. The most annoying lump stuck in my throat as we drove away and she stood on the sidewalk, waving. Eventually, I swallowed it down and turned my attention to the wintery city sights outside my window.

When we first pulled up to a big black iron gate on Wellington Crescent, I wondered if I'd been duped and was being hauled off to prison for some reason. Then I saw the house at the end of the winding driveway. The Weinberger residence. I tried to maintain my composure, but all the while I was wondering: *How can this be someone's home? How many people live here, anyway? And how on earth am I gonna fit in?*

Of course, I didn't ask any of those things. I just gawked. The house was three stories high and all white, including the two towering pillars in front. Hefty double doors under a covered porch were flanked by marble pots planted with evergreen shrubs. Massive bay windows graced the first and second stories on either side. So many windows sparkled everywhere, I couldn't help wondering who cleaned them all and who kept the curtains inside dusted. No wonder the Weinbergers were short-staffed. It would take an army just to maintain this place!

A butler greeted us at the front door, and Mr. Weinberger introduced him simply as "Stevenson." Was that a first name or last? I didn't know, and didn't think it appropriate to ask. Mr. Weinberger explained my presence and disappeared up the stairs with Cynthia.

Stevenson led me through a vast entryway where I got a quick glimpse of a gigantic glittering chandelier. A double-width staircase split in two directions, gracefully curving to the bottom like twin sisters in matching ball gowns with long satin trains. A hallway led to the biggest kitchen I'd ever seen, and I felt as if I had accidentally been delivered to a hotel.

A middle-aged woman stood at a stove that would have filled our entire kitchen in Bleak Landing.

"Mrs. Cohen," Stevenson said. The woman turned but kept stirring something in a large stock pot. "This is Bridget Sullivan. Mr. Weinberger has hired her as your new helper. It seems she's some sort of heroine." He pivoted and left the room without once lowering his nose to a normal level.

"Finally," the woman said. She walked toward me, wiping her hands on a big white apron that covered her ample midsection. "Heroine, eh? What'd you do?"

"Um. Well, I . . . nothing anyone else wouldn't have done, ma'am. Grabbed the little Weinberger girl and lifted her out of the path of a bus. Sort of a fluke, really."

"Well, I like your honesty. Can you cook?"

I told her the same thing I'd told Mr. Weinberger. And added an apology for not having more experience.

"Not to worry. I prefer helpers who don't think they know it all. Means I can train you to my liking." Mrs. Cohen pulled an apron down from a hook on the wall and held it toward me. "Here, put this on and wash your hands at that sink. I've got vegetables you can chop. Set your bags down there until we've got dinner underway, and then I'll show you around." I piled my bags, coat, and purse in an empty corner.

"And don't worry about Stevenson. He's a big snob but he's got a good heart. Wouldn't hurt a flea."

I spent the next half hour cutting carrots, potatoes, and onions. Mrs. Cohen added these to her pot along with some herbs she carefully selected and snipped from a windowsill container that overlooked a snow-laden, postcard-perfect yard. The stew smelled fantastic and my stomach rumbled. Once the contents of the pot were simmering, Mrs. Cohen placed the lid on top with a firm clunk.

"All righty, then. Grab your things and follow me."

She led me two flights up a narrow back staircase to the third floor, explaining that these were the only stairs I was allowed to use. A long hallway stretched before us with doors on each side, but we stopped at the first. "Since the cooks are the first ones up in the morning, our rooms are closest to the kitchen," Mrs. Cohen explained. "The good part is, you get a room all to yourself, for the same reason. This one's mine and you'll be right across the hall."

She opened the white wooden door opposite hers to reveal a room about twelve feet square. Plain white curtains hung over two narrow windows overlooking the pretty backyard. The single bed was draped with an olive-green bedspread. A wooden nightstand held a lamp, and a four-drawer bureau stood waiting for whatever I might wish to place in or upon it. The walls stood bare except for several hooks from which one could hang clothes. A simple wooden chair, painted the same green as the bedspread, and a braided oval rug in shades of olive and gray completed the room.

I stood perfectly still on the rug and tried to grasp the concept that all this was for my own personal use. How was it possible? Suddenly, I didn't care how hard I might have to work or how early I would have to rise. Even the thought of redeeming my mother's necklace took a backseat as I contemplated the wealth that was mine to enjoy.

"Bathroom's down the hall. C'mon, I'll show you." Mrs. Cohen headed back into the hall. I set my things on the floor and followed.

Along the way, Mrs. Cohen named the people who occupied the rooms, waving her hands toward each doorway as we passed. "Rita and Hannah share this room, they're housemaids. This is Evelyn's, she's a lady's maid to Mrs. Weinberger, and next to her is Edith—lady's maid to *Miss* Weinberger."

"Cynthia?" I asked, frowning. Why would such a little girl need a lady's maid?

"Oh, no. Miss Caroline Weinberger. She's seventeen."

"Oh."

Mrs. Cohen kept marching down the hall. "Dolly and Dorothy share this room, they're sisters. Both housemaids as well. They all take turns serving at meals." My head was spinning already, but Mrs. Cohen continued. "This is Miss Cuthbert's. She's the nanny."

"How many children do the Weinbergers have?" I asked.

"Well now, I already mentioned Miss Caroline Weinberger. She's Mr. Weinberger's daughter from his first marriage. Her mother died in childbirth, God rest her soul. Mr. Weinberger's older son, Carlton, lives here sometimes, when he's not off on adventures."

She waved another hand to her right. "Here's the women's bathroom."

I poked my head in to see a room very much like a public washroom but with showers at one end.

We reached a door at the end of the hallway.

"The male staff live on the other side, and this door stays locked. In addition to Stevenson, whom you've already met, there's the chauffeur,

Logan. He brought you home. And two younger fellows whose names I can never keep straight. Reggie and Robert, maybe. Anyway, they keep the grounds mowed and the pool clean in summer. In winter, they shovel snow and keep the furnaces running. Whatever's needed. And they eat. A *lot*."

She kept up the flow of information as we retraced our steps. "After Mr. Weinberger married the current Mrs. Weinberger in 1928, they added Sol Junior and Cynthia to the family. They are eight and five. Miss Cuthbert would normally have been watching over Cynthia today, but she's still away on her Christmas break. Fortunately for Cynthia, God sent you along." She smiled at me. "Like a guardian angel!"

No one had ever accused me of being sent anywhere by God, and I had no idea how to respond. I wondered how angelic she'd find me if she knew I'd run away from home.

We descended the stairs to the second floor, where Mrs. Cohen led me down another hallway. This one had doors on one side only, all of them closed. The other side featured a white railed balcony that overlooked the entryway below. From it, I got a closer look at the fancy giant chandelier I'd seen earlier. Even though it wasn't lit, the hundreds of tiny crystals shimmered in the late-afternoon sunlight pouring in through the windows. I'd have stood mesmerized by the reflected light for hours if not for Mrs. Cohen.

"This will probably be the only time you're ever on this floor," she said. "It has the family bedrooms, the nursery, and guest rooms. The housemaids take care of all this. You and me, we don't leave the kitchen."

She led me back down the servants' stairs. She stopped in the kitchen to stir her stew pot and looked up at a huge clock on the wall. "We've got time for a quick tour of the main floor, and then we really need to finish dinner preparations." I'd have rather stopped for a bowl of that stew, but I followed obediently. I hadn't eaten anything since breakfast in Mrs. Ross's kitchen, but it wasn't the first time I'd skipped a meal.

Mrs. Cohen led me swiftly through a sitting room; a den; a library; a study—I hoped no one would ever ask me the difference between all these rooms—a dining room already set with gorgeous china and crystal, fresh flowers, and candles; and a grand ballroom. My mind was completely boggled that one household could be so wealthy during such lean times. Though the rooms were filled with fancy upholstered chairs and couches, solid tables, and artwork in gilded frames, they were devoid of people. I wondered where everyone was, even though I wasn't likely to meet them any time soon.

When we returned to the kitchen, Mrs. Cohen instructed me to set the table.

I hesitated, confused. "In the dining room?"

"Oh, my. You do have a lot to learn, don't you?" Mrs. Cohen shook her head. "No, dear. Only Stevenson sets the family table. *You'll* set the servants' table. Over there." She nodded toward one end of the kitchen, where an arched doorway opened into a room containing a large table with benches and a hutch filled with pewter plates. "There'll be twelve of us. You and I serve the others at six. While they eat, we put the finishing touches on the family's meal and, if there's time, grab a bite ourselves. Then they serve the family at seven. After that, you'll be in here with me for the rest of the evening, cleaning up and preparing for tomorrow."

I hadn't realized the stew was for the staff, while the family and their guests would be dining on prime rib. Nor that I'd have to wait even longer to taste that stew.

As I served the other staff members, I listened intently to their conversation around the table. I was surprised to realize they were all immigrants from one country or another. Their varied accents interested me as they chatted through the meal. For the most part, they ignored me. I didn't mind. I had no desire to tell them my story, though I was curious to know each of theirs.

The two lady's maids, Evelyn and Edith, captured my attention more than the others. They held their heads higher, spoke more genteelly, and clasped their spoons with more grace. As I watched them, I found my chin automatically lifting a little, too. I wondered what it might take to become a lady's maid and whether getting such a job was possible for someone like me.

When Mrs. Cohen finally gave me the go-ahead to sit down with a bowl filled for myself, I ate it with gusto.

The family dinner hour felt like being in a wild beehive, with uniformed servants constantly coming and going with various dishes and trays. I followed Mrs. Cohen's orders as best I could, and after dessert was sent out, she insisted the two of us sit down for a cup of tea while the other servants dispersed.

Tea was followed by one hour of washing dishes that felt like fourteen. Then Mrs. Cohen had me break eggs and chop onions for breakfast the next morning. When the day was finally over, I climbed the two flights of stairs feeling wearier than I had ever been after a day at the garment factory and thankful that I still had plenty of hand cream. The cozy little room to which I fled already felt like home. I curled up in bed with a glad heart. Was it really only this morning that I'd woken up in Maxine's bedroom in Pinehaven? Now, here I was in an entirely new life. How could it be?

As I drifted off to sleep, Mrs. Cohen's words about me being a guardian angel returned to mind, and I replayed the incident with Cynthia on the street. That bus could have easily hit us both. What if we had both been killed? An entire city would be in mourning for the child of a wealthy, influential family, while an unknown factory worker would be quietly laid to rest in a pauper's grave.

Chapter 14

*V*ictor Harrison sat at his mother's kitchen table flipping through an outdated copy of the *Winnipeg Free Press* his father had brought home. His little brother, Bobby, sat at the other end of the table with the funny pages. The paper had already been passed around the community, and his ma had said the coffee stains, rips, and cut-out coupons gave it character. Much of the news Victor already knew, like the Chicago Blackhawks defeating the Toronto Maple Leafs and taking home the Stanley Cup—to his immense disappointment.

More and more, the headlines blasted news about Europe, where the National Socialist German Workers' Party was making itself famous for its mistreatment of Jews. Meanwhile, Frederick Blair, the director of Canada's Immigration Branch, was making *him*self famous for his determination to keep the Jews away. In a letter to Prime Minister King that became public, Blair had bragged, "Pressure by Jewish people to get into Canada has never been greater than it is now, and I am glad to be able to add that, after thirty-five years of experience here, it has never been so carefully controlled."

Where would it all lead? Most of the people Victor knew were too busy trying to feed their families to worry much about the rest of the world. But the news articles troubled him. Was there another war brewing, as rumors suggested? His father had served in the Great War. While Pa rarely shared any specific experiences, Victor would never forget that day in the barn when the topic had come up.

"A man who is spared the horrors of war will never be a real man, Vic. And it's just as well," Pa said, hefting a pitchfork of manure. "You and your generation are such pansies, you'd surrender at the first threat."

As much as Victor would have loved to prove him wrong, Pa was probably right. The thought of going to war terrified him, and it wasn't just the idea of dying. Dying he could handle. The afterlife, he could handle. Though he'd done his share of troublemaking, he'd always believed the words his parents taught him from the Bible, that Jesus had died for his sins and that he could trust God for eternal life. "To live is Christ, to die is gain," and all that.

It was the possibility of surviving that worried Victor. Surviving and having to live another fifty or sixty years with wounds, visible or invisible. With memories of things too horrific to speak about stuck in his mind, images that could never be erased. War did awful things to people. And yet the God to whom he wanted to remain faithful instructed men to defend the defenseless, to stand up against injustice. What on earth did that look like for an almost eighteen-year-old farm boy in Manitoba, thousands of miles from Germany? He didn't even know any Jews!

His buddy Bruce had finished high school and was off to university in Winnipeg, working to become a lawyer. Victor figured maybe guys like Bruce could make a difference in the world. Education was influence, people said.

Victor's mother disagreed. "Whoever holds the most hope carries the most influence, Victor," she told him. "Don't forget that."

It was one of her favorite things to say, and in her little world, it seemed to be true. It wasn't that she was perfect. She had her moments. But she was probably the most hopeful person he knew, given the way she trusted God for things and managed to be kind to almost everyone. Still, he figured her influence in Bleak Landing, where she'd taught Sunday school to nearly every kid he knew, was small potatoes. Her prayer territory didn't extend beyond the four square miles surrounding the Harrison farm. Did it?

His mother still prayed faithfully for Bridget O'Sullivan, though the girl had disappeared well over a year ago. Victor didn't know what disturbed him more, Patrick O'Sullivan's apparent lack of interest in finding his daughter or his steady decline into drunkenness. He'd become the town lush, a pitiful sight even in this sorry little community. Ma called him a sad, hurting man with a painful past and hoped his daughter had found a better life for herself somewhere. Victor hoped so, too, but feared that might not be the case. He'd heard about the desperate things girls sometimes did to survive. As much as Bridget had gotten on his nerves with her stubborn meanness, he wouldn't wish that awful life on anybody. Either way, the thought of her freckled face and her flaming red hair still brought a smile to his lips.

Rebecca Olsen brought a smile to his lips, too. They'd been dating for three months now, and Victor knew Rebecca was already looking at magazines filled with pictures of wedding dresses. Not that he was anywhere near ready for that. Still, it felt fantastic to have a pretty gal like Rebecca interested, and he reckoned he probably would marry her when the time was right.

"Are we ready to throw this paper in the fire, Ma?" he asked after he'd scanned the last page.

"No, Mr. Berg hasn't seen it yet. Can you please take it over to him?" His mother held out her hand, and Victor spotted two dimes and a nickel in her palm. "Here. I want you to bring home as nice a chunk of ham as he'll sell you for that. And then come straight back."

Victor ran the errand as requested, carrying home a piece of smoked meat that smelled so delicious he would have delved into it all by himself if he hadn't feared the wrath of his family.

When he walked into his mother's kitchen, he nearly dropped the ham.

Bruce Nilsen was seated at the table, and Victor's parents and sisters filled the other chairs. Bobby stood watching from the living-room doorway. *What on earth?*

"Bruce? I didn't know you were home! It's the middle of the week!"

Bruce and Mr. Nilsen often rode home to Bleak Landing together, but only on weekends and rarely more than once a month. Bruce had just been home the previous weekend.

Bruce glanced up at Victor, then stared at the center of the table. Everybody looked deadly serious, and his ma was wiping her eyes with a hanky.

"What's going on?" Victor laid the meat down beside the sink. "Ma?"

When Bruce remained silent, Victor's mother spoke up. "Bruce has come home because he's had some bad news. Very sad news." She paused, but Bruce still didn't speak. "His father has passed away."

Victor felt frozen to the floor.

"Girls, Bobby, let's go to the other room," Ma said. They filed out to the living room, where Victor could hear Ma still speaking softly. Already organizing some sort of support for Bruce's family, he supposed.

"I'll leave you two alone," Pa said, giving Bruce a pat on the shoulder and heading outside. "Give your ma our sympathy, son."

Still Bruce said nothing, and Victor hadn't moved from his spot in the middle of the room. He cleared his throat. "Aww, man. I'm so sorry, bud. What happened?"

Victor had rarely seen Bruce as anything but Mister Confidence, ready to tackle the world. It felt strange to see him like this, hunched over and fragile looking. He stepped over to Bruce and placed a hand on his shoulder. Bruce looked up.

"I found him."

Victor knew Bruce had been sharing a boarding room with Mr. Nilsen in Winnipeg, but between his university classes and his part-time job at a gas station, Bruce spent little time at the boardinghouse except to sleep. Victor took a chair and leaned toward his friend.

"He died in bed, and I found him. I didn't know what to do, Vic. I didn't know if he was dead or alive. I didn't want to touch him, but I . . . I finally did. He was already cold." Bruce paused. "I'd been on a date. A date, Vic! I could have gone straight back to our room from my work shift, but no, I had to go and let some stupid girl distract me. Now my father's dead, and it's my fault."

"Whoa. Bruce, it's not your fault, bud. You couldn't have known."

Bruce sat quietly for the longest time. Finally, he let out a sigh. "They say it was his heart. We had no idea. Ma's devastated."

Victor nodded and tried to imagine what it would be like to suddenly lose his father. "I'm sure you all are."

Bruce sniffed and wiped his cheeks with his sleeve, then stood. "Well, I just wanted you to know. The funeral's on Saturday. I hope you'll come."

"Of course. We'll all come, Bruce. I'll support you any way I can."

"Actually, Ma and I were wondering if you'd read the eulogy. Can't believe I almost forgot." He fished for something in his pocket.

"Me?" Victor felt he hardly knew Lars Nilsen. The man had been around so little.

"I know what you're thinking—you weren't really acquainted with my pa. But that's just it, nobody was. You were in our home more than anybody else over the years." He pulled out a sheet of paper. "And you read well. We've got it all written out."

When the paper came out of Bruce's pocket, something else did, too. The object fell to the ground with a quiet *clink*, and Bruce bent quickly to retrieve it and stuffed it back inside. Victor caught only a brief glimpse, but it looked for all the world like a necklace. And not just any necklace. A locket. A silver Celtic knot surrounding an emerald shamrock.

He realized this was not the time to bring it up with Bruce, but he recognized that locket. He'd seen it around Bridget O'Sullivan's neck so many times, he'd know it anywhere.

Chapter 15

Winnipeg. Autumn 1938

*M*axine hugged me so hard I had no choice but to hug back. We'd both been so busy, we hadn't been able to see each other in ten months. We'd written several letters and even managed a few telephone calls, and now at last she'd made her way to the big house. She stood at our kitchen door, hugging the stuffing out of me.

"Oh my goodness, look at you!" she gushed. "Bridget, you look so much older and more sophisticated!"

I didn't think I should tell her she hadn't changed a smidge, so I said nothing. I suppose she was making note of my uniform and new hairstyle. I'd been promoted to housemaid just two weeks earlier, when Hannah left, and now wore a crisp black dress with a white collar and frilly white apron. I filled it out much better than I would have last time Maxine saw me, thanks to the abundance of food available to me. Bruce Nilsen wouldn't call me a skinny stick now. I'd even figured out how to put my hair up in a French twist by watching Evelyn, Mrs. Weinberger's personal maid.

"You're beautiful, my friend!" Maxine wiped her feet on the welcome mat. "Am I too early? Are you off duty?"

"I just got off. Come in."

I showed Maxine around the place as if it were my own, enjoying her gasps and sighs at the opulence of it all. I even sneaked her up the grand staircase, which I was now allowed to use as long as I was in uniform.

"I can't believe you get to live here!" She ran her gloved hand along the shiny banister as we ascended. At the top she gazed down at the entryway with its sparkling chandelier, and I thought she'd pass out. "It's so marvelous! How can you stand it?"

"Well," I said, "you get used to it pretty fast when every little thing you see is something more to be cleaned. I have personally spent an entire morning on top of a stepladder, cleaning all those crystals. That's why I'm hoping to work my way up to lady's maid." We continued on to the third-floor room I now shared with Rita, who was still on duty. This room was like my first, right down to the color scheme of olive green and gray. It was just bigger and had two of everything, including windows.

"Really? Oh, tell me all about it! Have you gotten to know the family? What are the other staff like?" Maxine pumped me with questions while she waited for me to change out of my uniform. I pulled on a navy skirt and lilac sweater set I'd bought the first payday after my promotion.

"Now that I help serve meals, I see the Weinbergers almost every day. But the only one I've gotten to know is Caroline, their older daughter. She's our age and very nice." I hung up my uniform and ran a brush down its front and back. "I've only met her brother Carlton once. The little kids, Sol Junior and Cynthia, are bratty, but they're with their nanny most of the time, so they don't bother me. Can you believe I've only spoken with the lady of the house once? She seems nice. But she leaves everything to the butler, Stevenson."

"Ooooh, a butler! Bridge, you simply must find me a job here." She flounced from my bed to the window and back to the dresser, where she played with my brush and mirror set and admired her own reflection.

"You were born in Canada, Max. I honestly think they hire only immigrants for the house. I don't know why."

"Maybe I could fake an accent." She put on her best cockney. "I'm just goin' down the apples an' pears to get a cuppa tea for the lads."

I rolled my eyes. "You also have to know how to stay very quiet to work here, Max."

"What are you trying to say?"

I pushed my feet into my black Mary Janes and kept silent.

She hurled a pillow at me and laughed. "It's okay. I know, I get it. I don't shut up. I wouldn't fit in. And you know what? It's all right. Really. God made me a talker. Now, what do you want to do? *Boys Town* is playing at the Roxy. Wanna go?"

"Sure."

All the way to the theater, Maxine proved my point.

"You know I'm still planning to become a hairdresser and even run my own shop one day, right? It's gonna happen, Bridge. Until then, I'll keep practicing on the girls at the factory. I cut Yvonne's hair real short. Do you remember her? Oh, maybe she came after you left. Ooh, did I tell you Rosa is engaged? I wanted to introduce her to Arnie, but I guess there's no point now. Did I tell you Arnie and Billy both plan to sign up for military service? Much to our mother's horror. They're convinced war is imminent. I pray it's not true. It would destroy Mom to lose another child."

I told Maxine more about my hopes of becoming a lady's maid. "If I can move from kitchen maid to housemaid in only nine months, I figure I can move up again by next summer. Edith is leaving to get married then, and Evelyn is teaching me what I need to know. Of course, a lot of the job is taking care of clothes, and I can already sew a fine stitch—thanks to the factory."

"You'll do it, Bridge. You already talk different. No trace of that old Irish."

Maxine, always eager to encourage, had to know that was exactly what I wanted to hear.

"Really? You mean it?"

"Oh, yes! You sound like a proper lady already."

I gave her a playful shove. "Like you'd be able to hear the difference."

She only laughed and shoved back. "Now *that* was most unladylike."

~

We paid our dimes at the Roxy and settled into our seats with popcorn. Maxine's commentary included her opinion that Spencer Tracy was much too handsome to play a priest and Mickey Rooney was simply the cutest—too bad he was so short. But she grew quieter as the story of Father Flanagan unfolded. His belief that "there is no such thing as a bad boy" motivated him to battle indifference, the legal system, and often the boys themselves in order to build a sanctuary for kids like Whitey Marsh. Much as I had the previous Christmas, I felt something stir inside me. This was different than the experience at church, though. This felt more like a conviction: that one committed person with the right motives could make a real difference in the world, and in the lives of those less fortunate.

I'd been fortunate, that much I knew. I'd managed to escape a dismal world and become something better than I'd been. I'd had help along the way from Mr. Nilsen, from Mr. Thompson and Mrs. Huddlestone at the factory, from Mr. Weinberger, from Mrs. Cohen, and now from Evelyn. But I wondered: Was I *really* any better? Did I show care to others who were in the same situation as I? When I thought about it, I really hadn't. Some of my coworkers struggled desperately just to learn English well enough to hold down a job in Canada. They had experienced much tougher times than I had. For a while, I'd tried to help Natasha, the new kitchen maid who replaced me and was still fresh from Russia. But it was a halfhearted attempt at best. I had become so focused on improving my own lot in life, changing my own mannerisms, that I barely heard the stories Natasha tried to share in her broken English.

The picture ended on a triumphant note, but Maxine and I left the theater subdued. Too full of popcorn to think about supper, we decided to walk through the park and say our goodbyes at her bus stop. The warm fall day was rapidly turning to evening, and we stopped and sprawled on the carpet of leaves, gazing up at the sky like two little children.

"I want to do something meaningful," I blurted.

Maxine waited for more, but I didn't elaborate. "You mean, right now?"

"I mean like Father Flanagan."

"You want to tame a bunch of wild boys?" Maxine tossed some leaves into the air.

"No, silly. I just . . . I want to do more than just live. More than just try to make a better life for myself." Surprisingly, Maxine remained quiet, so I kept going. "I look at people like Caroline Weinberger, who's got it all . . . *has* had it all, since she was born. But she lost her mother when she was little, like me."

"You said her stepmother was nice."

"She is. But still. It must have been difficult." I watched a flock of geese overhead, their *V* shape pointed due south. "Then I look at people like Mrs. Cohen and Natasha who struggled so hard all their lives just to survive."

"Also like you?"

I didn't respond. I'd told Maxine little about my former life and still wasn't comfortable talking about it. I sat up and gathered leaves around my knees, my legs straight out in front of me. "The point is, everybody has it tough in some way. Some are happy and some are not, and it doesn't seem to have much to do with the hardness of a person's life." I watched a young mother pushing her toddler on a swing. "Maybe I should be a nun."

"A nun?" Maxine rolled onto her side, bending one elbow to rest her head in her hand. "Are you kidding me? Never get married?"

"Boys are stupid. Why would I want to marry one? And I don't need children. I'm not sure I like them all that much."

Maxine sat up. "It's different with your own."

"How would you know?"

She shrugged. "That's what they say. Anyway, you don't have to be a nun to do good things in the world."

"I know." I sighed. "I'd be a terrible nun, anyway. They're all good and kind and unselfish."

"Well, maybe not *all*." Maxine lay back down. "I used to not believe in God, did I ever tell you that?"

I looked at her.

"It's true. When I was twelve, I decided I didn't believe what we learned at church and what my parents taught. It all seemed too far-fetched. Then my sister died. And I saw my parents lean on God like never before, and it wasn't just a show. It was real. They showed me Jesus."

I stood and brushed the leaves out of my clothes. Maxine followed suit. We meandered toward her bus stop, and for once, she had nothing to say.

"I think *you've* shown *me* Jesus," I said softly.

Maxine turned in surprise. "Me?"

I nodded. "In tons of little ways. You befriended me from the start. You're the one who has worked to keep our friendship going even though I've brought nothing to the table."

"Oh, I don't think that's true," she protested.

But I kept going. "Your family welcomed me and accepted me just as I was. Now you've made the effort to visit me, and you cheer me on even when I don't return the encouragement."

We walked the rest of the block without speaking. "Well, if that's all true . . ." Maxine paused. "Then what you said just now is the most inspiring thing you could ever say to me." She gave me a hug as the bus pulled to a stop in front of us. "I love you, Bridget."

She climbed aboard with a wave, the door closing behind her. I watched the bus pull away and whispered words I couldn't remember ever saying before.

"I love you, too."

Chapter 16

Spring 1939

"*M*axine, I can't believe I let you talk me into this."

We stood in the rain amid the throngs as we waved miniature Union Jacks and waited for the royal cavalcade to appear. King George VI and Queen Elizabeth were in Winnipeg, and Maxine insisted this was a once-in-a-lifetime opportunity to see them. It seemed the rest of the world agreed, and we practically had to keep our arms linked to avoid losing each other in the crowd. Folks had traveled by car and train all the way from the United States just to get a glimpse of Their Majesties.

"We live right here! How could we not go?" Maxine said. "Especially since Mr. Weinberger gave everybody street car fare."

"But it's raining."

Maxine laughed. "That's why God invented umbrellas! C'mon, Bridge. This is the first time a reigning monarch has visited Canada, and on Victoria Day to boot! We can't miss it, you silly goose."

So we stood on the sidewalk along Broadway Avenue. Manitoba's legislative building rose up in front of us, the Golden Boy faithfully holding his pose at the top of the dome. I pictured him with an umbrella in his hand and chuckled.

"What's so funny?" Maxine asked.

I turned my chuckle into a low growl. "Nothing. I'm standing here in my best outfit, cold and wet, waiting to see someone who won't even notice me. I could be using my afternoon off to study my correspondence courses on my warm, dry bed. So, no. Nothing is funny."

"Spoilsport. You need a break from your studying." Maxine was unfazed by my grumpiness. "Just wait. You'll see. One day, you'll be telling this story to your grandchildren."

"So they'll know what a fool their grandmother was?"

"Would you rather tell them you missed this because you were scared of a little water?"

Truth was, most people were thrilled with the water. Even the city dwellers understood how desperately the prairies had needed rain in recent years. Now the drought had ended and farmers were producing again. I wondered if Bleak Landing had ceased to look so parched, but couldn't imagine it any other way.

A roar went up at one end of the crowd.

"They're coming!" we heard people cry out. And as the motorcade made its way down the street, I had to confess that Maxine might have had a point. Though I'd never admit it to her, it felt wonderful to be caught up in something so big and so full of happiness. The rain continued, but we barely noticed it. We cheered and waved our flags and even caught a glimpse of the king and queen as they rode by.

"Look!" Maxine pointed. "They've lowered the roof of their car. If the king and queen can get wet, so can we."

⁓

By the end of the afternoon, we'd stood through speeches by Prime Minister Mackenzie King and Winnipeg Mayor John Queen—with everyone talking about how this unlikely combination of names would be a source of laughter for years to come. Maxine and I sang "God Save the King" along with the crowd.

I found myself growing strangely detached as we listened to a high school choir.

That could be me.

Not that I was much of a singer, but the kids in the choir were my age. If I were one of them, my life would look so much different. Most of them probably lived at home with both parents and brothers and sisters. They didn't need to worry about earning a living or keeping a boss happy so they'd have a roof over their heads and food to eat. They could spend their evenings studying in front of a cozy fire and their weekends socializing. They'd soon be graduating. The idyllic picture I painted in my head might not have reflected complete reality, but I still listened to their cheerful singing with envy in my heart.

Hours later, we warmed up in my room, drinking hot tea from Mrs. Cohen's kitchen. Maxine sat at the foot of my bed while I flopped across the head.

"I want a hat like that." Dressed in my bathrobe, Maxine pulled her knees into a cross-legged position. Her clothes were draped over the radiator.

"A hat like what?"

"Didn't you see the queen's hat? It was perfect! She's so beautiful!"

I shrugged. "I thought she'd be wearing a crown."

"No, silly. Crowns are for official portraits and such."

I pulled warm socks onto my feet. "I want a crown. It doesn't seem fair that one person should get to wear a crown just because they're born into a certain family. It should have to be earned. It should be something anybody can aspire to, anybody with enough gumption and grace."

"Like you?"

I threw a pillow at her, and her tea sloshed out of her cup onto my bed. "Hey! Watch it." Maxine tucked the pillow between herself and the wall and leaned against it. "I'm a princess."

I let out a snort and tugged a comb through the snarls in my damp hair. "And I'm a unicorn."

"No, I mean it. You're a princess, too. Or you can be, if you want. Want me to comb out your hair?"

"No, thanks. What do you mean, I can be a princess?"

"I'm a child of the king," she said.

"Max." I tugged on a tangled clump of hair until it yielded to the comb. "I've met your parents. They're lovely. But your dad is no king. Sorry to break it to you."

Maxine pulled a pencil and notebook from my table and began doodling. I wanted to yell at her for wasting paper, but I knew how much I'd enjoy looking at her drawing after she left. She wasn't a bad artist.

"No. It's the name of a hymn we sing at church, and at home, too. It's a reminder that because our God is the King of Kings and we are his children, we are royalty. And rich beyond measure."

Then she actually sang:

My Father is rich in houses and lands,
He holdeth the wealth of the world in His hands!
Of rubies and diamonds, of silver and gold,
His coffers are full, He has riches untold.

I'm a child of the King,
A child of the King:
With Jesus my Savior,
I'm a child of the King.

I didn't know what to say to this. I felt torn between bugging Max about her corniness and asking her to tell me more.

"Where's your Bible?" she asked. "I'll show you all about how God calls us his children, out of his deep love for us. How he adopts us."

I stared at her. "When have you ever seen me with a Bible?"

She looked around. "I guess I haven't. I just thought everybody—"

"How long have we known each other? Two years?" I shook my head in disbelief.

"Sorry, Bridge. We should remedy that soon. Anyway, it says 'Behold, what manner of love the Father hath bestowed upon us, that we should be called the sons of God.' Daughters are implied. Like I said, *princesses*." She told me how her family had sung this hymn with gusto all through the Depression years, when they never knew whether they'd still have a roof over their heads the next day.

As she described her family, gathered around the piano and singing about how rich they were, I wanted to scoff. But I respected Maxine enough to let her go on. If that's what worked for them, if it got them through, fine.

Besides, for them it probably *was* true. God probably *had* adopted them all, and one day they'd be living in some mansion with him forever. I couldn't expect her to understand that I was destined for hell, that my father was nothing but a drunken bully who would steal from his own child, or that I'd traded the only thing close to rubies or diamonds I'd even known to gain my freedom. Any aspirations I had for a better life, I'd have to realize through my own ambition. I couldn't wait around for some magic daddy-king in the sky to shower me with riches.

"If you're a princess, why are you slaving away at the factory, saving up for beauty school? Someone else should be doing *your* hair."

Maxine just kept humming the tune as she drew a sketch of the queen's hat. When she was done, she rested her head against the wall with her eyes closed, as if she was trying to remember something. She started singing again. Her next words made me stop my combing and stare at her.

A tent or a cottage, why should I care?
They're building a palace for me over there;
Though exiled from home, yet still may I sing:
All glory to God, I'm a child of the King.

Exiled from home? Had I heard her right? The words jabbed at my heart, but Maxine only kept doodling and singing. An argument broke out in my head. I hadn't been exiled. I'd left home of my own free will. And I could go back any time I decided to. Right? I had merely decided not to.

"It's a dumb song," I said, not caring about my friend's feelings.

Maxine stopped humming and looked at me, clearly hurt. For once, she didn't say anything. I climbed off the bed and straightened the books and papers on my makeshift desk. "I really need to get some work done," I said. "Want me to walk you to the bus? Looks like the rain has stopped."

"My clothes aren't dry yet. And you said you were caught up on your assignments."

"I am, but exams are next month. I should study." I held out my hand to take the notebook and pencil from her.

She reluctantly handed them over and started putting on her damp clothes. I felt guilty, but Maxine's royalty talk had made me squirmy. I sat at my table and randomly opened my history book, but it seemed there was no escape. Spread out before me—of all things—lay a chart depicting the kings and queens who'd ruled England over the years. I slammed it shut.

"You don't need to walk me to the bus," Maxine said, her hand on the doorknob. "But thank you for today. I'll never forget the day I saw the king and queen, and I'll never forget who I was with. Princess

Bridget. You're like a sister to me. Even when I'd like to wring your neck, and especially when you'd like to wring mine."

I stared at her shoes. "You say the weirdest things."

"One day, you'll discover who you really are, Bridge. And it won't seem weird at all. 'Bye. Call me next week?"

I nodded and she left, closing the door firmly behind her.

I looked down at the sketch of Queen Elizabeth's hat and saw that Maxine had added the words "I'm a child of the King" in a fancy cursive across the bottom of the page. Below that, she'd signed her name and added the date: May 24, 1939. I tacked the drawing to the wall over my desk and stared at it for the longest time.

Chapter 17

Summer 1939

I hurried past a sidewalk newsstand, giving the *Winnipeg Free Press* only a cursory glance. The headlines about Europe were ominous. British Prime Minister Neville Chamberlain was saying that Britain would intervene on behalf of Poland if hostilities broke out with Germany. Just that week, I'd overheard Mr. Weinberger telling Stevenson that he'd managed to bring his entire family to North America years before, except for one brother who stubbornly remained in Poland.

Not that any of it mattered to me. I welcomed the brilliant sunshine on my face and relished the blue sky as I marched away from the Department of Education offices with a thick package under my arm. I'd already completed Grade Ten correspondence courses and was now registered for Grade Eleven. All of this was done with the Weinbergers' approval, along with their stipulation that I must continue to perform my duties and not disturb my roommate. They didn't realize my roommate slept like a corpse and I could study late into the night. I had determined that I would finish high school "by hook or by crook," as Pa used to say.

The thought of my father made my stomach queasy. More than two years had passed since I left Bleak Landing. Had Pa bothered to look for me? Given me up for dead? Had Mr. Nilsen gone back and told him where I was, only to be met with the words "Good riddance"? Part of me longed to know, but I couldn't risk the cost of making contact. I was moving up in a world Patrick O'Sullivan played no role in, and I would not allow him to stop me. Soon I'd be lady's maid to the rich and sophisticated Caroline Weinberger. And in a couple of years, thanks to the miracle of correspondence courses, I would become a high school graduate. Who could say? I might go on to study even further than that. One thing was certain: I was *never* returning to Bleak Landing, and if I ever so much as passed through it on my way to somewhere else, nobody there would recognize me as the skinny, bedraggled woodpecker I used to be.

I caught the bus back to the Weinbergers' home and carried my course materials up to my room. Both my room and my duties were about to change. The next day would be Edith's last, and after a brief interview, Miss Caroline had agreed to take me on as her lady's maid on a trial basis—six weeks, she said. If things didn't work out, I was welcome to stay on as a housemaid, no hard feelings. It was difficult to imagine that there'd be no hard feelings in that case, at least on my part, and I suspected I wouldn't be the one to decide whether things were "working out." But I'd already found Miss Caroline to be a lovely person, and I had every intention of giving my best effort.

"Between you and me, ladies' maids are on their way out," Evelyn said as she demonstrated proper use of a curling iron on Edith's hair. She and Edith were the real deal, trained in Britain and brought over by Mr. Weinberger to serve his wife and daughter. "He hired us because he has something to prove," she said, "having worked his way out of the gutter. Word has it his own parents served in a wealthy home and he saw so little of them, he vowed to make a better life for himself and his family, whatever it took." She handed me the curling iron and nodded for me to make the next curl. "But Edith and I are the last of our breed, mark my word. I hope this isn't a profession you hope to practice for a lifetime."

Of course it wasn't. But for now, it was perfect. Having this job meant that most mornings I could sleep later than the rest of the staff, as long as I was up before Miss Caroline. Once I'd helped her with her hair, makeup, and outfit, I might not see her again until late afternoon. After I finished tidying and airing out her room and taking care of her clothes, my time would be my own until she needed me to help her dress again for dinner—new attire and usually a new hairdo, too. My last duties of the day would be to help her prepare for bed and, one last time, to tidy her room.

"There shouldn't be so much as a stray thread on the carpet or a trace of soap scum left in her tub," Evelyn instructed. "And if she's in the mood to chat, you listen. But never share." If she needed me to accompany her on an outing, whether for an afternoon or a week, that, too, is what I was to do. Who knew what adventures I might have or where I might get to travel? Why, just last month Miss Caroline had taken the train all the way to Minneapolis to visit her brother Carlton. Edith went along and, in her free time, shopped for her own wedding dress!

On Edith's last day, I shadowed her in order to learn the ropes, even though she and Evelyn had already been coaching me and letting me practice on their hair. Miss Caroline insisted that I do her hair this day, under Edith's supervision.

"All of this just seems silly, doesn't it?" she said as I arranged curls around her face. "None of my friends have lady's maids except for Irene Beauregard, and she's the biggest snob. She's not even my friend, really. Our fathers are friends."

I took my cue from Edith and listened without comment. *Agree with the positive; ignore the negative* was the rule. *Don't volunteer anything from your personal life, and never express a political opinion, even if asked.*

Miss Caroline dabbed some perfume onto her wrists. "It's Katherine and Olivia I adore and would rather spend time with any day."

"And I'm sure they adore you as well, Miss," I said. Edith gave a slight nod, and I knew I'd responded appropriately.

"They think I'm the luckiest girl alive to have all this help. I suppose they're right, but at least they know how to do their own hair. Father says it's our duty to provide employment for as many as we can."

"And we appreciate it, Miss," Edith replied from where she stood by the closet. "How do you feel about this green dress for today?"

"It's perfect. You always make the right choice. Thank you, Edith. I'm going to miss you. You must be so excited about your wedding!"

I laid the hairbrush down, and Miss Caroline fluffed her hair with one hand. "Thank you, Bridget. Well done." She moved toward the closet to dress. I began cleaning brushes and combs and tidying the vanity while Edith answered Miss Caroline's questions about the plans for her simple wedding, taking place in only a few days' time. When Edith abruptly stopped talking, I looked up to see her looking at me, her eyes as round as the hubcaps on Mr. Weinberger's Cadillac. She shook her head at me and glanced at Miss Caroline, whose back was to me. Suddenly, I realized my error.

How could I have forgotten a cardinal rule? *All cleaning and tidying must wait until your lady is out of the room. Timing is everything.*

I quickly laid the brush back on the vanity and stood still, awaiting my next instruction. I'd been doing so well, but now I felt nervous.

"I can't remember how we accessorized this dress last time, Edith. Can you?" Miss Caroline was admiring her reflection in a full-length mirror. "The locket?"

"The white pearls, Miss. But the locket would look beautiful with this dress." She straightened the seams on the back of Miss Caroline's stockings. "Bridget, in the bottom right drawer of the vanity you'll find a black Birks-Dingwall box."

I opened the drawer to see a variety of small jewelry boxes, most covered with velvet. Only one was from the prestigious Winnipeg jeweler Birks-Dingwall. I lifted it out and closed the drawer with care. When I pulled the hinged lid open, I gasped. The Celtic locket inside was so similar to my own, my hands felt frozen in place. Miss Caroline's, of course, was new. Mine had been in my family for two generations, at least.

"You can put it on Miss Caroline," Edith said. But I stood frozen, staring at the locket. "Bridget?"

I gave my head a little shake. I hadn't thought of my locket in weeks, and this was not a good time to be reminded. I lifted this one from its satiny bed with shaking hands, but when I undid the clasp, it slipped through my fingers and dropped to the floor.

"Bridget!" Edith charged over to where I stood and bent to retrieve the necklace.

"I'm so sorry!" I knelt as well. "I can do it, Edith."

"What's the matter with you?" she whispered angrily.

"It's all right." Miss Caroline came back and sat on her vanity stool, holding her hair up so I could fasten the necklace. "It's not as fragile as all that. And neither am I. Really. Go ahead, Bridget."

With my shaking fingers, it took three attempts to fasten the clasp. I was immensely relieved when I finally centered it on the back of Miss Caroline's neck and saw the reflection of the locket resting on her breastbone. It did, indeed, look beautiful with the green dress, and I found myself once again longing to be reunited with my own.

Miss Caroline went down for breakfast, and Edith scolded me as we threw open windows, hung clothes, and made the bed together. "I recommended you for this job, Bridget, but you are not making a good first impression. Cleaning her brushes is excusable, but dropping her locket?" She picked up a wicker laundry basket and rested it on one hip. "Care to explain?"

I merely shook my head.

Chapter 18

Spring 1940

*T*he snow outside my window was melting as I flung open the curtain to welcome a new day. Another winter had passed, and I'd spent another Christmas with Maxine's family. This time, they had presented me with my own Bible and I'd given each of them a warm crocheted scarf. I'd also survived my trial period as Miss Caroline's lady's maid and completed two modules each of English and math. None of this left much time for letter writing, though I longed to fill Maxine in on my progress and learn of hers. When I reread her most recent letter, I could almost hear her voice:

> *Only half a year left, Bridget! In six months, a new course starts at the Beauty Academy and I plan to be one of their students. I intend to be their top graduate at the end of ten months of study, and to start working at my dream job the very next week. In time—my own shop! Maybe then you'll finally let me do your hair?*

> *Are you reading the Bible my parents gave*
> *you for Christmas? Want to come home with me*
> *for Easter? I was home last weekend and Arnie*
> *and Billy were most infuriating. All they can talk*
> *about is the war.*

War had officially broken out in Europe on September third, and Canada had declared war on Germany just a week later. The occupants of the Weinberger household, both family and staff, talked about it constantly. I tried to tune the news out, but it was everywhere. Even in Maxine's letters.

> *My brothers insist they're going to sign up and*
> *it scares me, Bridge. If they go off to war and*
> *come home maimed—or not at all—well, I just*
> *don't see how our family could survive. I know*
> *it's selfish to think about it this way—and you*
> *know I love those two knuckleheads—but I don't*
> *want to be the only surviving child! The only rea-*
> *son I've had the freedom to go off and earn money*
> *for school is because Billy and Arnie have stayed*
> *behind to help with the farmwork. Does that make*
> *me terrible?*
>
> *Dad says the Lord is in control. I hope he's*
> *right. It's hard to look at what's going on overseas*
> *right now and see anything as being under control,*
> *except for all the places where the Nazis are con-*
> *trolling things.*
>
> *I need to see you, Bridge. I'm proud of you for*
> *the way you've applied yourself to your studies*
> *and for how quickly you're working your way up*
> *in the world. But I miss you!*

I missed her, too. But it was increasingly difficult to make time for socializing. The Weinbergers had recently announced their plan to host a house party, and I'd been asked to help serve along with the housemaids. Evelyn assured me this was an honor and that I'd be rubbing shoulders with Winnipeg's most elite. It seemed to me a strange time to be throwing a party, but perhaps it was the Weinbergers' way of staying optimistic and showing their patriotism.

Sure enough, a box of Union Jacks arrived the day of the party. Evelyn and I strung the flags around the ballroom while the kitchen staff bustled about preparing hors d'oeuvres and the housemaids polished silver. A local band showed up midafternoon to set up on the small stage, and a florist delivered two massive arrangements of red and white carnations garnished with navy-blue ribbons and more Union Jacks. I'd never been part of such festivities and found myself energized by the excitement.

When it was time to help Miss Caroline dress for the party, I pulled out the new dress she'd brought home from "The Bay." I had accompanied her on that shopping trip, and it had taken great effort for me to keep my composure when I got my first glimpse of the massive store's interior. A dozen elevators were arranged in two banks of six, each door facing another in a concave arrangement. Immense murals depicting historical scenes of the Hudson's Bay Company decorated the lobbies. When we walked into the ladies' fashion section, I did my best to act nonchalant, though I was squealing with glee on the inside. After she'd tried on several dresses, Miss Caroline chose an appropriately patriotic red one with matching red shoes. I watched in awe as the salesgirl wrapped the dress in fine tissue paper and placed it in a special box.

Now I ran my fingers over the silky fabric. The dress seemed to shimmer and change shades in the glow of the bedroom's lamplight. I'd heard that ladies sometimes gave clothes to their ladies' maids after they were through with them. This hadn't happened to me yet, even though

Miss Caroline and I wore the same size. It was hard to imagine myself in this magnificent dress, but I can't say I didn't try.

Not my color, anyway. I shrugged the idea off. *Redheads shouldn't wear red. Everyone knows that. And where would I ever wear it?*

The anticipation in the air was palpable as I helped Miss Caroline dress. From her room, we could hear the band tuning up. My untrained ear tried to discern the sounds of the saxophone, clarinet, and trombone I'd seen being hauled in along with drums and a big bass. Spicy aromas wafted up from the kitchen. I wished Maxine were with me. I could just imagine the running commentary she'd provide, the thrill she'd derive from the hustle and bustle of the household in which I was fortunate enough to find myself.

I spent the evening in the black-and-white uniform I'd moved to the back of my closet when I graduated to lady's maid, knowing I'd still need it on occasions such as this. There wasn't a moment that night when I didn't have a tray in my hands, laden with fine flutes of champagne or dainty tidbits Mrs. Cohen created. She'd made us memorize their names so we'd know if guests asked. I found it a challenge to keep the "angels on horseback" and the "devils on horseback" straight, especially since neither of them looked particularly appetizing to me. Stevenson made sure the staff ate a substantial supper before the party so there'd be no growing faint and little temptation to sneak treats off the party trays. We kept the food and drinks flowing all evening, remaining available to the guests yet keeping ourselves virtually invisible, as we'd been taught, and taking our laughs in the kitchen when we returned to restock our trays.

We were all caught up in the gaiety. Even Reg and Rob were recruited to help inside after they finished parking cars. They added a fun dynamic to the household staff, and their humor was contagious. Several of us had gone to see Judy Garland in *The Wizard of Oz* together. Now we joked that everything in the Weinberger kitchen was black and white, but when we crossed the threshold into the ballroom, it was like stepping into the Technicolor of Oz. The room sparkled in the light of two massive chandeliers. The band's repertoire of upbeat tunes seemed endless, and the dancers were draped in a glorious array of bright fabrics and glittery jewelry.

Mayor and Mrs. John Queen attended, along with several prominent businesspeople, a university president, and loads of friends from the Weinbergers' synagogue and social circle. Miss Caroline was constantly surrounded by a gaggle of chums, both male and female. Her brother Carlton, who'd come home for the affair, arrived fashionably late, descending the magnificent staircase dressed in a black tuxedo with a red carnation tucked into his lapel. He seemed to have no shortage of friends and followers of his own, and he mingled with confident ease and danced with oodles of pretty partners.

But it was also Carlton who brought the celebratory mood to a halt. At ten o'clock, he walked over and spoke to the bandleader, who promptly directed the music to an unsatisfying resolution. Carlton stepped to the microphone, cleared his throat, and called for everyone's attention. I looked at his parents to gauge their reaction. They appeared surprised. As did Miss Caroline.

"I'd like to make an announcement," Carlton said.

From those few words, I gathered that the heir to the Weinberger throne had consumed a few too many glasses of champagne. Not that I'd had much opportunity to hear him speak before. The slight slurring of words was simply a sound I recognized from my childhood.

"I'd like to announce that today I enlisted in the Royal Canadian Air Force." The room grew quiet as all eyes turned toward Mr. and Mrs. Weinberger and then back to their son. "That's right. You are looking at one of His Majesty's loyal and most honor-bound subjects, prepared to serve king and country come what may. I'd like to thank my parents for this fabulous party, though they had no idea when they planned it that it would be my glorious send-off. Thanks, Mom and Dad. I ship out next week. Carry on! God save the king!"

He stepped away from the microphone and promptly missed the step down to the dance floor, landing face down on the gleaming hardwood. He scrambled to his feet, laughing and brushing off the assistance offered by the bandleader, who clearly didn't know whether he should pick up his instrument or wait for further instructions from Mr. Weinberger. A lone pair of hands clapped together, and soon everyone picked up the cue and gave Carlton a round of applause. Mr. Weinberger made his way to the microphone and raised his glass.

"Here's to a swift end to this war," he said with a quiver in his voice I'd not heard before.

"Hear, hear!" someone shouted. This was followed by more clapping as Mr. Weinberger walked over to his son and patted him on the back. As the applause faded, the band began a subdued rendition of "Over the Rainbow." The Oz analogy was complete. Couples waltzed slowly, but the festive mood had disappeared as completely as if it had been picked up by a tornado and carried far away.

Chapter 19

December 1940

Fresh from boot camp, Victor Harrison and the rest of his company waited to board the train from Winnipeg to Halifax. They scratched at their newly issued wool uniforms and tugged on the field service caps that did not sufficiently protect their freshly shorn heads against the cold of a Manitoba winter.

He'd spent the previous night in his own bed back home. With two days' leave to spend, Victor had returned to Bleak Landing to celebrate Christmas with his family, and to say goodbye. His mother and sisters treated him like he was some kind of celebrity, waiting on him hand and foot. He'd sat beside them in church, singing "It Came Upon the Midnight Clear." When they reached the third verse, Victor had to stop singing. He stared at the hymnbook he shared with Bobby and listened to the voices around him as they raised up the words:

> *Yet with the woes of sin and strife the world has suffered long;*
> *Beneath the angel-strain have rolled two thousand years of wrong;*
> *And man at war with man hears not the love-song which they bring;*
> *O! hush the noise, ye men of strife, and hear the angels sing.*

That evening, when they sat down to Christmas dinner, Ma prayed for a swift end to the war and offered up a special prayer of protection over Victor. His father added a loud *Amen.* The next morning, when Victor stepped off the platform to board his train, Pa clapped him on the back and spoke the words Victor had dreamed of hearing all his life:

"Proud of you, son."

But the praise fell flat. For more than two years, Victor had carried a secret he'd done nothing about, and the weight of it was crushing him. He was convinced the locket he'd seen Bruce Nilsen drop the day after his father died belonged to Bridget O'Sullivan. Yet he'd never confronted Bruce or asked if he knew anything about Bridget's whereabouts. He'd never told his parents. Never gone to Mr. O'Sullivan to tell him what he knew.

What am I so afraid of? He had sat in church every Sunday, riddled with guilt, unable to answer his own question. He'd done everything to avoid thinking about it, throwing himself into the farmwork and helping out neighboring farmers when he could, working for only a meal. Most people were just getting back on their feet after the Depression and didn't need the added burden of paying for help. Victor had even volunteered to teach Sunday school, taking on the older boys that his mother found more challenging. They seemed thrilled to have him as their teacher, but he knew their hero-worship would dissolve if they knew what a coward he really was.

Is it that I don't want to risk Bruce's friendship? Or am I afraid to learn some horrible truth about Bridget? The questions tormented him in his bed each night, yet every time he made up his mind to confess to someone what he'd seen, the words refused to come.

His mother had noticed the change in him. "You've been so sullen, Victor. Ever since Mr. Nilsen passed."

She tried to diagnose his melancholy. "Are you worried you could lose your own father? Because he's healthy, you know. And even if such a thing happened to us, our family would be all right, son. The responsibility for the family wouldn't be on your shoulders alone. We'd pull together, and God would provide. He always has, always does."

When this didn't bring Victor around, she tried a new tactic a few weeks later.

"Are you worried about this war? You know, Prime Minister King has promised Canada will not resort to conscription. You needn't worry about getting called up."

This, too, failed to lighten Victor's mood. Eventually, Ma gave up trying to pry anything out of him.

She would never know that she was the one who planted the idea. It was the perfect solution, the just penitence. If Victor signed up for service, he figured, he could make up for his failures. He could learn to be brave, he knew it. He mulled over the idea for weeks. Other fellows in the community were signing up. Victor secured a brochure and kept it under his pillow, reading it at least twice a day. By the time a recruitment officer visited Bleak Landing and set up shop at the community hall, Victor's mind was made up. Once he'd signed and submitted the forms, there was no turning back.

His parents said little about his decision, though Victor could hear his mother crying after they all went to bed the night following his announcement. Though her tears added to his guilt, he knew she would support his decision and keep praying for him. And if it took death or a maiming to make him a man, then so be it.

"You're crazy." Bruce Nilsen had shaken his head when Victor told him. "Completely crazy. You know what could happen to you? I'm not joining you, I've got an education to finish."

"I'm not asking you to join me," Victor said. "A little support would be nice, though."

Victor thought back to the childhood years he'd spent with Bruce. They'd had so much fun, getting into mischief and creating happy memories. He'd always figured he and Bruce would remain lifelong comrades. But it seemed life was pulling them in different directions now, and maybe he didn't know his old friend as well as he'd thought.

Then Bruce surprised Victor even more. "Besides, sometimes I think you'd be fighting on the wrong side. If you ask me, the Nazis are onto something."

Victor stared at him, hoping he was joking. But the set of Bruce's jaw matched the conviction in his voice.

"Now who's the crazy one? I can't believe you're still hanging on to your father's old-fashioned attitudes." They clearly ran deep. But so did Victor's loyalty to his old friend. "I would have thought life in the city would have shown you a broader perspective. Opened your eyes to what's going on."

"Maybe I'm not the one who needs my eyes opened." Bruce sighed. "You really figure this is something you need to do?"

Victor nodded. With any luck, he'd come home a new man. A *real* man. And if he didn't make it home, it wouldn't matter anymore what he was.

"Then I'll support you all I can," Bruce said, clapping Victor on the shoulder. "From here. Try to come home in one piece."

~

Victor did just fine at boot camp. Years of rising early, slinging hay bales, and mucking out the barn had built strength and stamina into his nineteen-year-old muscles. Pa's training had taught him how to respect his superiors and follow orders without question. And his mother's prayers had showed him how to rely on God's power when his own strength failed.

Now the training was behind him and he'd soon be faced with real battles. While the other guys covered their nerves with joking and jostling, Victor sat quietly and looked around the exquisite domed rotunda of Winnipeg's Union Station. A gigantic Christmas tree adorned its center, and at least half the people bustling about were dressed just like he was: as soldiers, either headed out or coming home.

Then he saw someone he had thought he would never see again.

At least he thought it was her. Maybe the constant strain of guilt over Bridget O'Sullivan was finally making him nuts. Maybe he'd be imagining he saw her in random places for the rest of his life. But the more he watched, the more convinced he became. Two young women had just entered the station from the tracks on the east side and were swiftly headed across the lobby to the street on the west side, carrying their bags. One was tall and blond and was talking in an animated fashion to her companion. The companion was a dead ringer for Bridget. Oh, she looked a little older than last time he'd seen her, and definitely more sophisticated. She had more meat on her bones and a healthier glow to her face. But that hair! It *had* to be her. Didn't it?

Victor watched the pair cross the lobby. He studied the redhead. Had Bridget ever carried herself with such confidence and poise? Maybe it wasn't her. But the resemblance was uncanny. He had to know, but if he didn't hurry, they'd be gone. Just as he stood to follow them, an announcement came over the public-address system.

"Harrison, we're boarding!" one of his buddies hollered.

Victor kept walking toward the young women. Instead of exiting through the main doors, they stopped in front of the ladies' room.

"Harrison, c'mon! Where you going, man? It's this way!"

Bridget—if it was Bridget—went into the ladies' room while her friend took a seat on a bench, their bags by her feet. Victor had no more time to waste. He rushed toward the woman, ignoring the calls to board with his troop.

"Excuse me, miss." The blonde looked up at him through pale blue eyes. "Sorry to bother you, but my train is boarding and I only have a minute. My name's Victor Harrison. That other girl with you, the redhead. Is her name Bridget? Bridget O'Sullivan?"

The young woman scrutinized his uniform before she spoke. "Not exactly."

Not exactly? What kind of answer was that?

"Harrison! We have to go!" His buddy called out again. "Now!"

"It's just—if it's her, if it's Bridget . . ." Victor stumbled over his words. "We're old school chums. She went missing. Years ago. I need to know if she's all right. Please, if it's her, tell me."

The woman glanced back toward the door to the ladies' room. "Want me to get her for you so she can tell you herself?"

"Private Harrison!" Victor recognized the voice of his commander. "You will board this train *now*."

Victor pleaded with the blonde even as he backed away from her. "I have to go. Please, just—just tell her you saw me. Victor—Victor Harrison. She can write to me in care of the armed forces." He jogged back to join his group and threw his duffel bag into the pile with the others being loaded. He was the last to step aboard, but managed to claim a window seat. The train was about to pull out when he heard rapping on his window. He turned to see the blond girl on tiptoe, reaching as high as she could. He pushed the window open. The girl held a slip of paper toward him, and as the train began to chug away, he reached out and took it. She waved, and Victor gripped the paper tightly, waving at her with it. He pulled it inside and read what appeared to be a label of some kind.

It said **BRIDGET SULLIVAN**, followed by a Wellington Crescent address.

Victor tucked the slip of paper deep into his shirt pocket while his traveling companions hollered at him to shut the window against the winter air. He slid the window closed with a glance up at the December sky. *Thank you, Lord.*

Bridget was alive. And by all appearances, she was thriving. As the train picked up speed, two other words resonated in Victor's head. Though he never imagined he'd apply this description to this particular girl, the thought persisted with the rhythms of the rails as he closed his eyes and rested his head on the back of the seat.

Bridget O'Sullivan was stunningly beautiful.

Chapter 20

$\mathcal{M}$axine and I had enjoyed another memorable Christmas with her family, and I was still replaying certain developments in my mind when I visited the ladies' room at Union Station. The biggest change was, Maxine's plan to start beauty school had been postponed. The course had been canceled, thanks to the war. Though tearful at first, Maxine agreed with her parents that it would be smart to keep her job at Weinberger Textiles, which now produced uniforms for the Canadian military. Once her initial disappointment passed, her happy attitude returned, to my amazement. "The Lord has already mapped my life out for me," she said. "As long as I stick with him, I won't get lost."

What a knucklehead.

The war had a dampening effect on Christmas, too—not the least of which was, folks could get a seat on a train only if it wasn't needed by a serviceman. As a result, Maxine and I had been delayed in Pinehaven by a day and should have been back at work by now. We'd managed to catch this morning's train back to Winnipeg and would now ride separate buses to our respective workplaces.

When I left the ladies' room, I couldn't believe my eyes. Our bags still sat by the bench where we'd left them, but Maxine was nowhere in sight. Even her purse lay abandoned. Had she followed me into the ladies' room without my noticing and left our belongings unguarded? If she needed to go that badly, why hadn't she said so? I dropped onto the bench with an unladylike plop and scanned our bags to make sure nothing was missing. Maxine was going to get a piece of my mind!

Suddenly, I heard her, roaring in like a hurricane. A train was pulling away from the station, and she was running in through the east doors.

"Bridget!" she yelled. "You're not going to believe this in a million years!"

I swear every eye in the place was tracking her as she flew across the lobby. My face was probably turning fifteen shades of red. When would that girl learn that she didn't have to be so exuberant about *everything*? She ran toward me, her unbuttoned coat flying behind her like a magic cape. She stopped in front of my bench, trying to catch her breath.

"Victor," she said, panting.

"Huh?"

"While you were in the loo." She took a big gulp of air. "A soldier came over and asked me if your name was Bridget and I didn't know what I should tell him, so I offered to go get you so you could talk to him yourself, but his train was leaving and he had to run but he said his name was Victor Harrison and he recognized you and he said you went missing." Finally, she took another breath.

I was glad I was sitting down. *Victor Harrison? A soldier?*

"And Bridget, he wanted to know if you were all right, and he said you could write to him! And you'll never believe this. He thought your name was O'Sullivan. With an *O*. It's not, is it? Have I had it wrong all this time?"

I must have blinked fifteen times, trying to absorb what I was hearing. "Well, I—"

"And Bridget, he's *so* handsome! Why haven't you ever mentioned this Victor guy before?"

"Victor." This time, I managed to actually form the word. Maxine was nodding and grinning like an idiot. "What did you say to him?" I asked.

"Nothing," she said. "I swear. Except—well, I sort of gave him your address."

"You *what*?"

"Well, he was running off. There was no time to wait for you. He would have missed his train. But I didn't think I should just let him get away, so I pulled the label from your suitcase and ran after him. He was already on board. But then I spotted him through a window—and oh my gosh, Bridget, he's dreamy!—so I knocked on the glass and he opened it and took the label from my hand just as the train was pulling out, and he yelled *thank you* at me. At least, I think that's what he said. I had to read his lips over the train whistle. Isn't it the most romantic thing you've ever heard of?"

I looked down at my bag. Sure enough, the transparent slot where my address used to be was now empty.

"Well, you're right about one thing," I said. "I don't believe it."

Maxine sat on the bench beside me. "Well, I'm not making it up. How could I when I never heard of Victor Harrison before today? Why does he think you're missing? This is so romantic, Bridge! He's going off to war with your address in his hand. You know he's going to write to you, don't you? And you'll write him back and he'll cherish your letters and they'll sustain him through the mud and the muck on the battlefield—"

"Maxine, please." I rolled my eyes and gave her my most earnest *stop talking* face.

"So who is he to you? Were you really just school chums, like he said, or was there something more?"

"I'd hardly use the word *chum*." *More like mortal enemies.* "He locked me in the outhouse and I've never forgiven him. Never will, either."

To my horror, Maxine laughed. I wanted to sock her one.

"Locked you in the outhouse? When was this, when you were six?"

"Twelve."

"Oh, believe me, princess. If you'd seen him looking all handsome in that army uniform, you'd have let go of your grudge in a heartbeat!"

"I doubt it. Look, if we don't get out there and catch our buses, we're going to be waiting here all day." I picked up my belongings and headed for the door. "I doubt I'll ever see or hear from Victor Harrison again, so I don't see what difference it makes."

Maxine followed me. "Bridget's got a boyfriend," she singsonged, like an eight-year-old. Suddenly, she switched gears. "Oh, I wonder if I made his uniform? I could have, you know. How dreamy would *that* be?"

I was glad to be getting rid of her for a while. My bus pulled up first, but before I could board it, Maxine stepped in for a hug. "Thanks for coming home with me for Christmas. And you better call me the minute you get a letter from that Victor. The very minute! And if you don't want him, can I have him?"

I couldn't help grinning as I pulled out of her embrace and stepped up into the bus. "Right about now," I called over my shoulder, "I'd say *he* can have *you*!"

I waved to Maxine through the window as my bus pulled away. On the short ride home, my thoughts turned to Victor Harrison. I tried to picture him in a soldier's uniform, but my memory of the skinny kid with straw for hair just didn't fit. I wondered what he'd thought when he saw me in the lobby. Was I easy to recognize? Did he still see me as the gawky little carrot he'd always called me? I was glad I was wearing the quality woolen coat Miss Caroline had passed along to me. It was a gorgeous shade of cobalt blue and fit me even better than it had fit her. I brushed the thought aside. Did it matter what Victor Harrison thought?

I wondered how his mother was handling her son going off to war. It was not the first time Mrs. Harrison had crossed my mind since I left Bleak Landing, although I supposed she had forgotten me long ago.

~

As I approached the Weinbergers' house on my way back from the bus stop, I looked forward to seeing Miss Caroline again. She'd become almost a friend to me—as much of a friend as she could be, given the nature of our relationship—and had confided that she was anticipating a marriage proposal from her beau, Captain Rodney Phillips. I expected I'd be coming back to exciting news on that front.

As I approached the house, though, an ominous feeling nudged out my optimism. I slowed my pace. What was different? The sky was overcast and daylight was waning on this late afternoon, yet no lights appeared through the windows. Though the Weinbergers didn't celebrate Christmas, their home typically gave off a warm and welcoming glow all its own through the winter. Now it stood quiet and gray, looking almost deserted. The front walk had not been shoveled, though several sets of footprints had mashed the snow down in spots.

I thought of the horrible stories I'd read about Jewish families being forced from their homes in Europe, gathered into ghettos, their belongings taken by the Nazis. For one brief moment, I wondered if the same thing had begun here in Canada. When I stepped in through the side door, the kitchen was empty, and I smelled none of the appetizing aromas that had always been present before. I climbed the servants' stairs and noticed the door to Mrs. Cohen's room was ajar. I rapped lightly on it.

"Yes?"

"It's me, Mrs. Cohen. Bridget." I pushed the door open and saw her seated at her desk, writing.

"Oh, Bridget. Good. You're back. Come in." I set my bag down in the hallway and entered her room.

"What's happened, Mrs. Cohen?"

She waved toward her bed, and I sat on the edge, unbuttoning my coat.

"I'm afraid the family's received some crushing news. A telegram came December twenty-fourth. Carlton is missing in action."

Chapter 21

March 1941

Spring was approaching, but the Weinberger household showed little sign of life. There had been no word about Carlton, and with every passing day, the likelihood of his death increased. Mrs. Weinberger rarely emerged from her bedroom, while Mr. Weinberger seldom came home from work. The house was draped in sadness: no music played, no parties were hosted, no meals were served in the dining room. Occasionally Rabbi Nebowitz stopped by to check on the family. Sometimes Mrs. Weinberger would agree to see him, and other times she refused.

I didn't know what to do, so I just kept working on my studies. Miss Caroline hardly needed my services. She had no social life to speak of and chose to spend her days writing letters to the Department of National War Services in an attempt to find information about her brother. This led to her involvement in volunteer efforts that were cropping up all over the city. I accompanied her on these trips. We joined other women in organizing salvage drives and preparing packages for the military. Before long, this became a full-time occupation. We spent long days working shoulder to shoulder, bundling up clothing, bedding, bandages, and other hospital supplies to ship overseas. On more enjoyable occasions, we assembled care packages for the soldiers. We packed together things like coffee, tea, sugar, milk powder, dried fruit, canned meat and fish, jam, chocolate, and soap. Most of the packages would go to prisoners of war. Miss Caroline confided to me that she imagined each one she packed ending up in her brother's hands, sustaining him through whatever hardships he faced.

Working side by side like this quickly changed the essence of our relationship. Caroline no longer stood out in a crowd, and she seemed to prefer it that way. She was just one of many women committed to helping us all survive the war in whatever way we could. Prime Minister King had assured us through his radio messages that the roles each person played made an important difference. The government was urging women to seek employment. We were needed to fill the holes left in the workforce and take on new positions created to provide munitions, uniforms, and other supplies for the war effort. It was as if our lives suddenly had a new and completely different focus. I'd never seen people rally together like this before.

Suddenly, it seemed our country was wealthy. Everyone who wanted to work could. Sure, the government had set limits on wages and restrictions on changing jobs. It also encouraged workers to put their money into Victory Loans and savings programs. Shortages and rationing of food and other products increased. But what a difference from the awful Depression-hounded dirty thirties! If it weren't for the awful realities of the war and the frequency with which families received those terrible telegrams—as well as the constant dread felt by those who feared they would—it might have been the most exciting time to be alive.

Miss Caroline took to eating with me and the rest of the staff in the kitchen rather than dining alone. Her parents were too distracted to notice, or if they did, they hadn't the energy to stop it. Perhaps their loss had made them realize the futility of maintaining class separation.

Or maybe they simply understood that their daughter needed things they couldn't give her—like friendship.

At the end of a long day at the Red Cross volunteer center, the two of us arrived home hungry for whatever we had smelled as we walked up the sidewalk and through the front door. The day's mail lay on the hall table, and Caroline sifted through it as I hung up our coats.

"You've got a letter, Bridget," she said, her eyebrows raised. "And not from Maxine."

I took the letter from her hand. Had Victor Harrison written after all? Wouldn't Maxine just relish this chance to say *I told you so?* But when I looked at the return address, I was even more surprised. Written in the corner was "Ingrid Harrison, Bleak Landing, Manitoba."

Victor's mother had written to me?

Preferring to read it in private, I hung on to the letter until we'd eaten our supper and Caroline had assured me she could draw her own bath. In my room at last, I sat on the bed and opened Mrs. Harrison's envelope. The letter was short, but it sounded so like the woman I remembered that I could almost hear her voice:

Dear Bridget,

I do hope it's okay that I'm writing you. We've received our first letter from Victor, who I'm sure you know by now spotted you at the train station and acquired your address from your friend. He wrote from England and as far as I know, he is still there. Although disappointed that he didn't get the chance to speak with you, he was immensely relieved to see that you are alive and well. I am so pleased, Bridget. This community has all but given you up for dead, I'm afraid. I'm writing to ask you two things.

The first is on Victor's behalf. He would like to write to you and would love to have you write to him as well. May I tell him that would be all right?

Secondly, may I please tell your father you are alive and well? I won't reveal your where-abouts if you ask me not to, but Bridget, no parent should have to endure the anguish of not know-ing whether their child is dead or alive. I know I couldn't bear it, and I would gladly ease your father's pain if I could. It's clear that up until now you have not wanted him to know you're alive or you would have contacted him, so if you wish to keep this secret, I will respect your wishes. But perhaps you simply don't realize how dreadful a thing this not knowing is. One day, if God grants you children, you will understand.

I ask this for the good of your father only. He is not well, Bridget. I hope that you can find it in your heart to contact him, or at the very least let me know that I can, on your behalf. I do hope Victor's conclusion that you are well is indeed the case. I would dearly love to hear from you.

Sincerely,
Ingrid Harrison

P.S. I don't know whether you're aware that Bruce Nilsen also lives in Winnipeg. He is com-pleting his law degree at the university. Perhaps the two of you could travel together should you ever wish to come visit. You'd be most welcome in our home if you prefer to stay here. I will try

> *to track down Bruce's address or telephone num-*
> *ber for you if you like. He returns to Bleak Land-*
> *ing infrequently—but more often since his father*
> *passed away.*

I dropped the letter to the floor. *Bruce's father passed away?*

My hands began to shake, and I felt heat rising from my body to my face. When I closed my eyes, I pictured Lars Nilsen's sickening grin as he took my mother's locket from my hand and tucked it inside his jacket. Stifling the urge to roar out my rage, I stomped out into the hall-way, leaving my door open wide. I clattered down the servants' stairway to the kitchen and marched straight out the back door without a coat. A pile of split firewood was stacked against the garage, for use in the household fireplaces. I picked up one of the pieces, gripped it tightly, and began flogging the backyard trees with all my might, yelling and crying and not caring who heard me.

How dare he die? How dare he take the only piece of my mother I had and then die?

How dare his son blissfully go to law school when the whole world is turned upside down?

How dare Victor Harrison tell his mother where I am?

How dare Maxine give Victor my address?

How dare Mrs. Harrison assume I would ever want to return to that stupid, worthless town or care whether my father died of a broken heart? He broke mine more times than I could count!

How dare my mother die and leave me with that miserable wretch of a man?

And where was God in it all? How dare he call himself a king and a good father when he couldn't even keep track of one little locket belonging to a lonely girl from a stupid, stupid little town called Bleak Landing?

Chapter 22

I have no idea how many times I hit that tree with the firewood or how many bad words I used in the process. But once my anger was spent, I hurled the wood as far as I could with one last cry of pain and crumpled to the still-frozen ground, sobbing. I knew I should feel cold, but I couldn't seem to even move from my spot. Nor could I stop bawling. All at once, every tear I'd never shed throughout my childhood rose to my eyes. Every time I thought I was starting to catch my breath, I pictured my mother's lifeless body stretched out on that tiny bunk in our ship's cabin. And when I'd howled out my pain over that, I remembered the sting of my father's willow switch on my backside and legs. I heard his voice as he told me he wished I'd died instead. I recalled his reminders that I was headed for hell. And I remembered that he'd gambled away my honor in a card game.

My violent outburst frightened me more than anything. I was no different than Pa.

"Bridget."

At the sound of my name, I became aware of my surroundings again, and my wails turned to sobs. Mrs. Cohen crouched beside me. How long had she been watching?

"Whatever is the matter, dear? I know you've had a letter. Have you lost someone in this dreadful war?"

I couldn't speak. I couldn't move. In the darkness, I saw another form running toward me and finally recognized it as Rob, one of the yard boys. He was probably the one who'd split the wood I'd used to beat on the tree.

"What's all the commotion?" he asked. "I was sound asleep when I heard someone yellin' and carryin' on."

"Rob, help me get Bridget into the house," Mrs. Cohen said. "Listen to me, darlin'. Your hands are bleeding and you're freezing. You need to come inside."

I allowed her and Rob to support me on either side and pull me to my feet, feeling like the biggest idiot of all time. After we walked through the door, they lowered me into a chair. Suddenly I could feel the sting in my hands. Mrs. Cohen got me to hold them out, palms up.

"Good gracious, girl. What have you done?"

I stared at my splintered and bleeding hands. What *had* I done? I'd never had an episode like that in my life. I'd never even cried before, not since I was little, anyway. What was wrong with me? It was that stupid letter, that's what it was.

"We've got to clean this before we can pull out the splinters," Mrs. Cohen said. "Can you come over to the sink?"

I followed her in silence and she gently ran warm water over my hands. "Fetch Miss Caroline, Rob," she said over her shoulder.

I wanted to protest but didn't have the energy. I was back on the chair and Mrs. Cohen was pulling slivers from my right hand with a pair of tweezers when Rob returned with Caroline.

"We can handle it from here, Rob," Mrs. Cohen said. Rob took one last look at my face and left the kitchen, still wearing a look of bewilderment.

"What's happened, Bridget?" Caroline took the warm washcloth Mrs. Cohen handed her and dabbed at my face.

I turned my head away. "I'm all right. I can wash my own face. I just—a little help with my hands and I'll be fine. I'm sorry for disturbing everyone. Really. I'm so sorry. A good sleep, that's all I need. A hot bath and a good sleep."

Mrs. Cohen and Caroline looked at each other. Mrs. Cohen applied ointment to my hands. "The bleeding has stopped. I think you might be better off without bandages overnight. Let the air get to these scratches and cuts. We can check again in the morning to see if I've missed any slivers. We don't want anything to fester."

Caroline followed me up the servants' stairs and into my room, closing the door behind her. I picked Mrs. Harrison's letter up off the floor, crumpled it, and hurled it into a wastebasket. I sat on my bed and noticed the envelope still lying there. I picked it up and stared at the return address. *Bleak Landing* indeed.

Caroline watched me from a chair in the corner. "Want to tell me what that letter said?"

I felt so embarrassed by my behavior that I wanted to disappear. "Really, it's nothing."

"Has someone died?" Caroline asked softly as she took a seat on the chair.

I didn't know what I should tell her. "Well . . . yes. Someone died. But not someone I was ever close to. And not even recently. I don't know why I reacted like that. Really, I'll be fine."

She waited patiently for more, but that was all I was prepared to divulge. "Perhaps you're overtired. I know you've been burning the candle at both ends, volunteering with me all day and working on your studies at night." She stood and moved toward the door. "I'm leaving instructions that you're not to be disturbed in the morning. Sleep as long as you need to."

She gave me one more concerned look and quietly left the room. I glanced over at the wadded letter in my wastebasket before I went down the hall for a bath. When I returned, dressed in my robe, I pulled the letter out and without rereading it folded it and stuffed it back into its envelope. I shoved it into a dresser drawer, turned off the light, and went to sleep.

⌐⌐

The next thing I remember, daylight was penetrating my consciousness. I squinted into the unusually bright March sunlight. My head and hands hurt. I wondered if this was what a hangover felt like. The memory of the previous night's breakdown flooded my mind, along with a distressing wash of humiliation. What had I done?

"Good morning, Bridge."

I just about jumped out of my skin.

I looked over and saw Maxine sitting on my chair, reading a book. "Maxine! What on earth are you doing here?" I wondered if I was still dreaming, but my croaky morning voice told me I was awake.

"Got instructions from Mr. Weinberger early this morning to come directly here—in his chauffeured car, no less—and to report straight to Miss Caroline. She told me you'd had a bit of a to-do last night and thought it best that I wait in your room in case you need someone to talk to. What's going on, Bridge?" She gasped. "Look at your *hands*!"

I forced myself to look. My palms appeared as bad as they felt—raw, puffy, and all scratched up.

"You should see the other guy," I muttered, pushing myself up and swinging my legs over the side of the bed. "I'm fine, really. This whole thing is just silly. What time is it?"

"Nearly ten. And it's not silly. What's going on?"

"What's going on is, I got a little exhausted and blew some things out of proportion. Now I've slept, and as soon as I go to the loo, get dressed, and eat a bite, I'll be right as rain."

She stared at me.

"What?" I said.

"Bridget. Look . . . at . . . your . . . hands."

"I did! They'll be fine." This was getting annoying. "Go back to work, Max."

I grabbed my robe with a wince and wandered off down the hallway. But when I returned, Maxine was still there, laying out my navy skirt and a flowered blouse.

"This should be a good outfit for today," she announced. "I love this color on you, and the flowers are cheerful. Now, what do we need for undies?" She moved to my dresser and opened the top drawer before I could intervene. Sure enough, Mrs. Harrison's letter was the first thing to catch her eye, and she pulled it out.

"Give me that." I moved toward it and held out one of my sore hands. She did as I asked, but not before she'd read the envelope. I guess she figured I was in no mood for a wrestling match. I stuffed the letter under my pillow and got dressed, in a different outfit than the one Maxine had chosen.

She sat down again. "Look, I don't know what's in that letter, but I was told you were crying a lot last night. By the look of you, it was more than just crying. Do you want to talk about it or not? Because if not, I should get back to the factory. I really don't think they're paying me to be here."

I pulled a brown dress over my head. I supposed I owed her some kind of explanation, and since she already knew the story of my bartered necklace, I figured I should say something. But while I was still trying to figure out what to tell her and how to say it, Maxine surprised me with a deduction of her own.

"Who is Ingrid Harrison?" She gasped. "Victor's *wife*? Is Victor married?" Her eyes looked as round as Mrs. Weinberger's good dinner plates.

"No, dummy." I sat on the edge of the bed to pull on my stockings. "She's his mother."

"Oh. Well, is Victor all right?"

I hung up the clothes Maxine had pulled from the closet. "Far as I know."

"So what did she say, then?"

With a sigh, I turned around and faced her. "Remember Mr. Nilsen?"

"The one who has your necklace?"

"Yeah." My gaze went to the window. "He's dead."

Chapter 23

July 1941

*M*r. Weinberger had turned both his factory and his home into war machines. The factory workers, who were now creating uniforms for the Canadian forces, increased their efforts, and even more people were hired to man more sewing machines. At the mansion, staff who used to spend their days polishing silverware or cars now organized metal drives, assembled packages for prisoners of war, wrote letters, grew vegetables, and distributed posters and pamphlets. The magnificent ballroom that once hosted elegant ladies and gentlemen now resembled a factory itself, having been set up with rows of long tables where goods were organized and packed for delivery. Even Miss Cuthbert, the nanny, spent her days working alongside us until the children began their break from school. Now that it was summer, she put them to work part of the day, too, helping with the vegetable garden.

Mrs. Cohen and Natasha still kept the meals coming, but it was much simpler fare these days. Now everyone ate the same thing, regardless of their rank. Family members and staff worked as one team. I never knew from one day to the next whether I'd be folding sheets or brochures, washing dishes or clothes, delivering sandwiches or letters.

The motivation behind all the effort was the missing crown prince. Carlton Weinberger had not been found. His father and sister worked diligently, around the clock it seemed, to increase the odds of his being brought home and of the war coming to an end. But the more time passed, the more their efforts embraced the cause in general. They quit hounding the war offices and stopped insisting that Carlton be located.

Mrs. Weinberger remained sequestered in her room, and Evelyn continued to play the role of lady's maid on top of contributing to the war activities.

I overheard a conversation between Evelyn and Miss Cuthbert one day when I was carrying a stack of clean towels to the family bedrooms. Their exchange was not meant for my ears, but I stopped to listen anyway.

I could hear the genuine affection in the nanny's voice. "The children miss their mother more than anything."

Evelyn made a humming sound in agreement. "Have you spoken to their father about it?"

"Yes. He says only that she's not ready to see them and that it's best if they not see her like this."

Evelyn didn't answer, but she must have nodded because Miss Cuthbert said, "It's that bad, then, is it?"

"She's wasting away. Refuses to eat. Won't see anyone. She ignores me for the most part, although she'll submit to being bathed."

"How can a mother grieve so for one child—a son she didn't even give birth to—and ignore the ones who are right here under her roof, her own flesh and blood?" I could hear the frustration in Miss Cuthbert's voice.

"You don't know the full story, Miss Cuthbert. Mrs. Weinberger was best friends with the first Mrs. Weinberger from the time they were children. They were inseparable. She was the sandek at Carlton's brit milah."

I was just familiar enough with the terms to know that a *sandek* is a little like a godparent. Mrs. Weinberger had probably promised her friend she'd help raise her son.

"Then when Caroline was born, her mother died giving birth," Evelyn said. "Mrs. Weinberger started caring for those children long before she became the second Mrs. Weinberger. You could say she was their first nanny. She legally adopted them when she married their father."

Miss Cuthbert sighed. "And now she feels she's let her friend down."

"She hasn't said as much, but I suspect that's a big part of it. Mr. Weinberger tries to encourage her, of course. But he's not around much."

"He could spend more time with his children, too. They're practically orphans."

I coughed, quietly at first and then louder, to warn them of my presence as I came around the corner.

"Oh, Bridget." Evelyn took the towels from me. "Thank you, I was just going to fetch these."

Miss Cuthbert carried on down the hall and, with a nod to Evelyn, I retreated back down the stairs with their conversation echoing in my head.

Caroline was just emerging from her father's den. "Bridget, I need you to take this packet of papers to Father at the factory. I just spoke with him on the phone, and he needs them as quickly as possible." She handed me a bundle. I took it, raising my eyebrows at her in an unspoken request. "And by all means, find Maxine while you're there. Have lunch."

I smiled at Caroline's kindness. She knew I appreciated any opportunity to run errands to the factory and possibly spend a few minutes with my friend. Besides, it was a beautiful summer day and I hadn't been anywhere in ages.

On the bus ride, I made an effort to focus on my surroundings, but I could not push the conversation regarding Mrs. Weinberger's deteriorating condition from my thoughts. I recalled Mrs. Harrison's words about how my father suffered, not knowing my whereabouts. The unlikely comparison almost made me laugh.

It's not the same thing, I argued as the bus turned the corner onto Main Street. *My father would just as soon I'd died. He could have found me easily by now, if he cared. Mrs. Weinberger loves her son. And he's not even her natural-born son!*

I delivered the papers to Mr. Weinberger's secretary right at noon and hurried to the cafeteria. It wasn't hard to find Maxine, who was in the middle of an animated story and surrounded by eager listeners.

"Bridget!" She rushed over and embraced me right in front of everyone. "You here for lunch? Get some food and come join us!"

I grabbed a sandwich and a glass of milk and took a seat beside Maxine. None of the other girls looked familiar to me. One by one, they finished their meals and left the table.

"I only have a few minutes, Bridge. Catch me up!" Maxine curled her hands around a cup of coffee.

"The house is looking more and more like this place," I said. "Like a busy factory, only fancier." I told her about Mrs. Weinberger's behavior and the conversation I'd overheard.

Maxine's face registered immediate compassion. "Oh, that poor woman. If only she could muster the strength to join in on the war efforts. It would help her feel better, I'm sure."

"Here's the thing, Max. She's not even Carlton's real mother. I don't get it."

Maxine looked at me a moment. "Define *real*," she said. "She adopted him, right?"

"I suppose. But she's got children of her own that she's neglecting . . ." My voice trailed off.

"I'm going to pray for her. For all of them." Maxine took a swallow of her coffee. "I'm ashamed that I haven't been doing so already. I mean, I've prayed for Carlton to be found, but I haven't really thought about what all this was doing to his family."

I wasn't sure what good Maxine's prayers would do, but I didn't argue. I knew she prayed for me, too. She'd prayed that my hands would heal up without scars, and they had. She'd prayed that I would pass my difficult mathematics exam, and I had. She even prayed that I'd write back to Victor's mother.

I had not.

We talked of other things until she needed to get back to her sewing machine, and I caught the street car back to the house.

That evening in my room, I could hardly believe my eyes when I read my next English composition assignment: *Write a letter to someone, alive or dead, who has influenced your life—for better or for worse. The assignment will be returned so you can send it if you choose, but doing so is not a requirement for this course. Allow your words to flow freely and honestly as you express any thoughts you may have kept inside.*

I wanted to laugh out loud but just shook my head. *Maxine.* I could picture her grinning that stupid grin, insisting this was God's answer to her prayer. Well, maybe I'd just show *her*. The assignment didn't mean I had to write the letter to Victor's mother. I could name plenty of people who'd influenced my life either for better or for worse—including Maxine Ross herself, though at the moment I wasn't entirely sure which category I'd put her in. I began a mental checklist.

My mother. I had only three vague memories of her; braiding my hair and humming a lullaby were two of them. The other was of her lying sick on a wretched ship until she died, her locket still around her neck. The way she'd influenced my life most was by leaving it.

My father.

Miss Johansen. She'd believed in me, encouraged me to study. Showed me I was smart in spite of everything. She deserved a letter of appreciation.

My father.

Mrs. Harrison. There should be a sketch of her next to the word *kindness* in Mr. Webster's big old dictionary. She was the very definition of the word. At least, she *had* been until she so rudely interfered in my present life.

My father.

Mr. Weinberger. I owed the man a debt I could never repay. Though we rarely spoke, he had created every opportunity that led me to the life I had now, had opened doors for me that I could never have pushed open on my own.

With a sigh, I picked up my fountain pen and began to write.

Chapter 24

February 19, 1942

e'd been warned it was coming, but it was still the most disturbing day of my life.

Winnipeg's Victory Loan committee chairman, John Draper
Perrin, had organized a mock German invasion of the city. The idea
was to frighten folks into forking over their cash for Victory Loans or
bonds so the federal government could increase its war spending. The
premise was "What would it be like if the Nazis invaded Winnipeg?"
Hence the name: "If Day." We laughed about it ahead of time, wondering what good a bunch of play actors could do since we all knew the
whole thing was a hoax.

But as the rest of the Weinberger household and I listened to the
local radio station over breakfast, our laughter faded. "Nazi forces" were
moving across the city from the west end. At six, air-raid sirens sounded
and a blackout was ordered. Determined not to let the silly exercise
interfere with our day, Caroline and I headed out the back door to run
some errands we'd planned.

As we made our way downtown, the sights unfolding before us were
horrifying. Giant swastikas had been unfurled from flagpoles where

the Union Jack had always flown. Guns on vehicles fired antiaircraft rounds at fighter planes overhead, and tanks rolled down the street. Even though I knew it was all blanks and make-believe, I felt as though I'd walked into a war newsreel. Troops in Nazi uniforms goose-stepped down the street, arms raised in the famous Hitler salute. We retreated to the relative safety of the garment factory to be closer to Mr. Weinberger.

Inside, public service announcements blared over the radio. Casualties were reported, and locations were given for dressing stations set up to treat the wounded. By nine o'clock, it was reported that the city had surrendered, and we thought maybe the game was over. But at lunchtime, we suddenly heard yelling and heavy footsteps coming down the hallway. Soldiers barged into the cafeteria, a frightened and roughed-up-looking Mr. Weinberger between them.

"Do not resist," Mr. Weinberger told us. He sounded weak and apologetic, and it all seemed very real. My heart was pounding.

In between their shouts at us in German, the soldiers helped themselves to the food from our trays and demanded warm coats. They tacked posters onto the walls and then left the factory and marched on down the street, taking Mr. Weinberger with them. We gathered around to read the posters:

ANKÜNDIGUNG

IT IS HEREBY PROCLAIMED THAT:

1. This territory is now a part of the Greater Reich and under the jurisdiction of Col. Erich Von Neuremburg, *Gauleiter* of the *Fuehrer*.

2. No civilians will be permitted on the streets between 9:30 p.m. and daybreak.

3. All public places are out of bounds to civilians, and not more than 8 persons can gather at one time in any place.

4. Every householder must provide billeting for 5 soldiers.

5. All organizations of a military, semi-military or fraternal nature are hereby disbanded and banned. Girl Guide, Boy Scout and similar youth organizations will remain in existence but under direction of the *Gauleiter* and Storm troops.

6. All owners of motor cars, trucks and buses must register same at Occupation Headquarters where they will be taken over by the Army of Occupation.

7. Each farmer must immediately report all stocks of grain and livestock and no farm produce may be sold except through the office of the *Kommandant* of supplies in Winnipeg. He may not keep any for his own consumption but must buy it back through the Central Authority in Winnipeg.

8. All national emblems excluding the Swastika must be immediately destroyed.

9. Each inhabitant will be furnished with a ration card, and food and clothing may only be purchased on presentation of this card.

10. The following offences will result in death without trial

a) Attempting to organize resistance against the Army of Occupation

b) Entering or leaving the province without permission.

c) Failure to report all goods possessed when ordered to do so.

d) Possession of firearms.

NO ONE WILL ACT, SPEAK, OR THINK CONTRARY TO OUR DECREES

published and ordered by the Authority of (signed) Erich Von Neuremburg

At home that evening, we learned that the soldiers had charged into some school classrooms as well, and I felt sorry for the trauma-tized young students. Notices had been posted on churches, forbid-ding worship services, and the German troops arrested some priests who objected. Copies of the *Winnipeg Tribune* appeared on doorsteps, renamed *Das Winnipeger Lügenblatt*—The Winnipeg Lies Sheet—and the front page was written almost entirely in German.

Of course, by now we realized that Mr. Weinberger had been part of the plan all along. He'd agreed to allow the invasion of his factory and was released by supper time. He returned home to address his household.

"I'll tell you what I told my factory staff," he said after he'd gathered us all around in his den. "What happened here today, and much worse, is really happening in Europe. My family and I would be prime targets if we still lived there. That is why I felt compelled to participate in If Day." He cleared his throat and pressed his lips together before going on, his voice a raspy whisper. "May you all rest well in the safety of this home tonight."

I called Maxine. Having left her factory job to start beauty school in September, she'd been spared much of the day's drama. But she planned to keep a copy of the fake newspaper to show her children one day. Typical Maxine.

I thought I'd never get to sleep that night. I kept thinking I heard the air-raid sirens or planes flying overhead. The event was truly sobering, and it was all anyone could talk about for the rest of the week. In the months to come, we learned that it had also been a grand success, as the sales of Victory Bonds rose through the clouds like those fighter planes I'd never forget.

Chapter 25

Summer 1942

*M*axine's parents sat beside me: Mrs. Ross in a summer dress with pink flowers, Mr. Ross looking uncomfortable in his suit and tie. When it was Maxine's turn to walk across the platform and receive her hairdressing certificate, I clapped and cheered as loudly as they did. With her brothers still overseas, I felt like an only sibling. Maxine had finally achieved her dream, graduating from beauty school and securing a job at Renee's Hair Boutique downtown. I felt genuinely proud and happy for Max, but I couldn't help wondering how it would feel to walk across a stage and have someone shake my hand. I had graduated, too, though without the fanfare. Finishing my high school work and the typing and shorthand courses that came with it felt like a shallow victory. With no desire to remind anyone that I hadn't graduated before this, I'd said nothing the day my diploma arrived in the mail.

Besides, the timing of my coursework completion had coincided with Miss Caroline's marriage to her captain. I hadn't wanted to infringe on her show. The wedding was a quiet, small affair in consideration of the war and her missing brother, by now presumed dead.

Mrs. Weinberger had recovered from the loss only slightly. While she did appear in public now, she rarely spoke and never smiled.

Caroline expressed no desire to take me or any of the household staff with her to her new home, preferring the modern way of things. I wondered if she also wanted a clean break from the sadness that engulfed the house. Mr. Weinberger pulled me aside, saying he was reluctant to let me go and that he recognized my abilities. He asked me to work in his office at the factory, which I was happy to do. But living in their home felt awkward now.

All through school, Maxine had shared a third-floor apartment with another student, but her roommate was taking a job across town and moving out. So I wasn't surprised when she started badgering me to move in with her.

"It's not like you work at the big house anymore," she said. "You're practically Mr. Weinberger's secretary now. My place is much closer to the factory."

She was right about that, but I hadn't given her an answer yet. It seemed like a big step, knowing I'd have to budget my earnings for rent and food. But the idea of being independent appealed to me.

After Maxine's graduation, Mr. and Mrs. Ross took us to an Italian restaurant, where the four of us shared a booth. While we waited for our pasta, Max talked to her parents as if everything was already decided.

"Bridget's moving in with me," she announced. "Just think of the fun we'll have!"

"That's a fine idea." Mrs. Ross smiled at me and then turned back to her daughter. "Did you still want those old green curtains from your room at home?"

"No, thanks. Too old-fashioned." Max talked around a mouthful of food. "Our place is going to be the cat's meow when we're done with it, won't it, Bridge?"

"No wild parties, now," Mr. Ross teased. "You sure you two can get along?"

Part of me wondered how well we actually *would* get along once we were sharing our living space. But we'd be apart all day, at our respective jobs. I loved the idea of eating or showering when it suited me instead of following the strict routine at the Weinbergers'.

When the meal was over, Max opened her graduation gift from her parents, and the deal was clinched for me: a brand-new radio! We could listen to whatever we liked, whenever we liked, at whatever volume we liked. Her proposal was sounding sweeter by the minute.

"It's a combination graduation and housewarming present," Mrs. Ross said. "So that means it's for you, too, Bridget."

"Don't burn all the tubes out in the first week," Maxine's father cautioned with a grin.

So it was decided. Since Maxine's parents were still in town through the next day, I packed up my belongings that night so they could help me move. Not that I owned any furniture or anything. I'd acquired a large collection of nice clothes, though, and I packed them carefully in boxes for the car ride over.

As I was emptying drawers in my dresser, I found something I'd forgotten about: the letter I'd written to Victor Harrison's mother for the English composition assignment nearly a year before. I scanned it quickly. Feeling suddenly carefree and adventuresome, I scrawled a quick note to add to the letter. I stuffed both in an envelope and addressed it to Mrs. Harrison in Bleak Landing. Before I could change my mind, I added a stamp, carried it downstairs, and left it in the outgoing-mail basket by the front door.

I spent the next morning hanging my clothes in the closet and settling in at Maxine's place. Except now it was *our* place! Her mother threw together some sandwiches, and the four of us ate lunch in our little kitchen. The new radio, installed on the counter, played classical music on CBC. After Maxine's parents said their goodbyes and headed back to Pinehaven, she and I switched to swing jazz and had our own little dance party.

To celebrate, we went to see a new movie called *Bambi*. Giggling like little kids, we munched our popcorn and laughed at the little fawn sliding around on the ice. But when the hunter shot Bambi's mother, I was livid. What kind of stupid children's story was this? I looked over at Max, and she had tears rolling down her face.

"Let's go," I whispered.

"No! We need to stay and see how it turns out."

I really wanted to leave, but as usual, Maxine got her way. With a huff, I settled back into my seat and stewed through the rest of the idiotic movie. As we headed down the sidewalk afterward, I was still angry. "Why would they do such a horrible thing?" I ranted. "Poor little guy needed his mother. They call this entertainment? Are they trying to scare little kids? Mark my words, Max. *Bambi* is going to be nothing but a big flop."

Maxine cheered me up with her best impression of Thumper, which didn't really require much alteration of her personality. It was well past midnight when we finally collapsed on our beds. I fell asleep right away, which was a good thing. Being independent was splendid, but I knew Mr. Weinberger could easily replace me. And I figured that if I showed up late for work in the morning, he might do just that.

Chapter 26

Bleak Landing, October 1942

Victor's father didn't say much the day he and Victor's ma met their son's train in Winnipeg, but while she wrote down the army nurse's instructions about how to care for Victor's stitched-up leg, he thumped his eldest on the back. Clearing his throat, he said, "Good to have you back in one piece, son. Real good. You did just fine."

Somehow, hearing those words wasn't as satisfying as Victor had always imagined it would be.

The three Harrisons agreed that before boarding the train to Bleak Landing, a side trip to Wellington Crescent was in order. Victor gave the cabdriver the crumpled scrap of paper with Bridget's address on it. He'd been carrying it around for nearly two years. He knew Bridget had moved up in the world, but he was not prepared for the sight that met him when the car stopped in front of the mansion. He could feel his palms sweating.

"Why don't you let me go to the door?" his mother asked. "That way, if she's not home, you'll save yourself some unnecessary steps."

"No, I'll go." He swallowed. "You and Pa wait here."

The iron gates stood open. As Victor hobbled up the sidewalk toward the imposing white house, he felt more nervous than he had since boot camp. An older gentleman answered the door. Victor asked for Bridget, explaining that he was an old friend.

The man sized up Victor and his crutches without moving his head even a fraction. "She doesn't live here anymore."

Victor pressed further but got no more information. He wasn't sure whether the man didn't know or wouldn't tell where Bridget had gone. "What about her friend—a blond girl?" he asked.

"I'm sorry, I have no idea."

Lord, Victor prayed as he walked back to the cab, *if it's not meant for me to see Bridget, why did you put her in my path that day? Where is she?*

He and his parents rode back to the station in silence. On the train ride home, Victor talked about his war experiences. The story of his getting shot while helping a wounded private had reached Bleak Landing long before, and a group of supporters had gathered to welcome him home. His sisters had baked a cake and hung a banner across the living room. Conspicuous by her absence was Rebecca Olsen, who'd written Victor a Dear John letter as soon as she learned of his injury. He knew it was just as well. Whatever feelings he'd once had for Rebecca evaporated the day he spotted Bridget O'Sullivan's flaming red hair across the expanse of Union Station.

Life was back to a new normal now, and Victor wanted to be a contributing member of the household—and eventually, of the community. He swallowed the last of his milk and rose from the kitchen table. He picked up the crutches that leaned against it. "Sure have missed Bessie's milk. The only thing worse than that canned stuff is the powdered stuff." He started toward the door.

His mother smiled from the sink, where she was scrubbing the last of the garden carrots. But when she realized he was heading outside, her smile turned to a frown. "Where do you think you're going?"

"Gonna give Pa a hand."

"Victor. Anna and Bobby are helping your father, and Nancy will be back from town soon. Sit down."

"Those squirts? Some help they are. I figure the Lord allowed me to get wounded when I did because he knew I'd be needed here at harvest time. I aim to help."

His mother pressed her lips together. "Then come over here and scrub these carrots. You can't risk getting dirt into that wound until it's completely healed."

"Ma. I'm going nutty in here. Do you realize how long I've been cooped up?"

Two months had passed since Operation Jubilee. The horror he'd witnessed in Dieppe never escaped Victor's mind for long, especially if he closed his eyes. The whole raid had turned out to be a miserable failure. Over half the men who made it ashore had been killed, captured, or wounded. He considered himself fortunate to have been only wounded. And, by God's grace, evacuated.

But now that he was home, he couldn't bear to sit around watching his younger siblings work alongside Pa while he did nothing. His oldest sister, Peggy, had left home to work as a telephone operator in the city and was engaged to be married. He'd been shocked by how much his parents had aged in the time he was gone. But then, they'd said the same about him—except in a positive way.

"Three days," his mother answered. "You've been home three days, which is nothing."

"It's been *two months* of hospitals, Ma. With hardly a breath of fresh air all that time."

"Then we'll set you up on the front porch and you can breathe all you want. If you're lucky, Mr. Berg will be spreading manure and you can get yourself a good whiff."

Victor chuckled. For as long as he could remember, the odors drifting over from their neighbor's pigs had exposed the weak spot in his mother's otherwise gracious temperament. It really was good to be home.

"Here." She grabbed his jacket from a hook by the door and helped him into it while he shuffled the crutches from hand to hand. "It's getting nippy out there. Take a seat and I'll bring you a tub of clean carrots to slice for canning."

When Victor stepped out onto the front porch, he saw Nancy walking toward him with a grocery bag in one hand and a letter clutched in the other.

"Ma!" she called, waving a white envelope in the air. "You've got a letter. From Bridget O'Sullivan!"

Victor gaped at his sister and turned back to his mother, who still stood in the doorway. She was staring at Nancy, too. He watched her take the envelope and look at it in wonder. She grabbed a ratty old sweater from a hook behind the door and moved slowly to her porch rocking chair. Nancy disappeared into the house with the grocery bag.

Victor watched as his mother pulled her sweater on and slowly opened the envelope.

"You get letters from Bridget?" He couldn't believe Ma hadn't mentioned it before.

"First one," she said softly. "It's been well over a year since I wrote to her, with no word back. I've wondered whether she even got it." She read silently while Victor lowered himself to the porch swing and braced his crutches against the wall behind him. Bingo immediately jumped to his lap and rested a whiskery chin on his hero's knee. Victor scratched behind the dog's ears and waited impatiently while he surveyed the familiar farmyard and soaked up the crisp fall air. The bright sunshine emphasized the brilliance of the few orange and yellow leaves clinging to the poplars and Manitoba maples, and his mother's multicolored dahlias still danced in the gentle breeze. He turned his eyes to his mother and tried to gauge her response to the words she was reading.

Victor knew she still prayed for Bridget regularly. In fact, the evening he'd arrived home, they'd gathered in the living room, where Pa read from the Psalms and Ma led the family in a tearful prayer of thanks for

Victor's return. She'd also offered up petitions for a full recovery of his wounded leg, despite the doctor's prediction that he'd always limp. She'd prayed for each of his siblings, too, of course. Then the O'Sullivans: for Bridget's safety, and for the Lord to watch over her "wherever she was," and for God to soften her heart toward himself. And for "that poor man, her father," that God would bring him deliverance and healing.

Victor had never understood why his mother's heart held such a soft spot for Bridget. With three daughters of her own, it wasn't as if she had an empty place that needed filling by a girl. He'd asked her about it once, and she'd said only that "God has a tender spot for each and every one of us, and he doles out to us compassion for others in bite-size chunks that we can handle. Otherwise, we'd never survive the pain of it."

He guessed his ma's "bite-size chunk" was for the O'Sullivans, for some unexplainable reason, and wondered if perhaps he'd inherited the same chunk—at least as far as the daughter was concerned. He'd prayed for Bridget, too, though never in a way that anyone else could hear.

Ma finished reading. One hand clutched the letter; the other swiped at tears. Victor was dying to know what Bridget had written.

"Bad news, Ma?"

His mother shook her head and let out a big sigh, wiping both cheeks with the sleeve of her old sweater. She stood and handed the letter to Victor. "No. It's not all I was hoping for, but it *is* evidence of answered prayers. It is that." She picked up a broom from the corner of the porch and began sweeping leaves off the floorboards into the flower beds below.

Victor pushed Bingo's nose away from the two-page letter so he could see it clearly. It appeared to be two separate letters, the first page more of a brief note, written recently.

Dear Mrs. Harrison,

I was sorting through my belongings as I am packing to move to a new home, and came across

171

*this letter I wrote for an English composition
assignment over a year ago. I thought you might
like to have it. I'm sorry I didn't respond to your
letter or send this one sooner. That was rude, and
you deserve better. Here it is now. My instructor
gave me a C on the assignment and said it could
have been more heartfelt. I received my high
school diploma last spring. If you ever see Miss
Johansen, you can tell her. Everything I said in
the letter about my father still holds.*

    Bridget

Victor flipped to the other page, dated July of 1941. He'd been
overseas when Bridget wrote this, fighting battles bigger than he'd ever
imagined could be fought and cherishing every word he received from
loved ones back in Canada. Wishing every day for a letter from Bridget.
What sort of battles had she been fighting at the same time?

Dear Mrs. Harrison,

*Thank you for your letter and for your concern
for me. My friend Maxine says God places angels
in charge of us, and sometimes I think you were
always a bit of an angel in my life when I was
growing up. I never ever told anyone, but I used
to wish I could belong to your family, and it
was because of you. Even though we only saw
each other when I came to collect eggs, your
kindness and gentleness spoke to me in ways I
can't describe. I'm sure you guessed that I didn't*

experience that sort of thing in my own home, which brings me to your question about my father.

The household in which I now find myself is carrying deep grief for a beloved son missing in action. I am witnessing firsthand the devastating effect on the parents, and I have been burdened with guilt. Still, I am not prepared to contact my father, and if you knew my reasons, I think you'd understand. But if you wish to tell him I am alive and well, you may do so. Yes, it was me Victor saw in the train station that day and my friend Maxine who gave him my address.

Maxine reminds me of you. I mean, she's boisterous and talks way too much—which is very unlike you. But she seems to know God the same way you do. She talks to him all the time, and she talks to him about me. Her family has shown me love as well, and gave me a Bible of my own. I intend to read it one day soon.

I trust that your whole family is well. I see no reason to write to Victor or to hear from him, but I do hope for his safe return and wish him well.

Thanks again for the positive influence you have been on my life.

Bridget

Victor checked the return address corner on the envelope. Clearly, Bridget had no desire to be pursued. She had written only her name, and her last name was definitely missing its *O*.

Chapter 27

*M*axine and I were arguing. Again.

"This was a dumb idea, Max. We used to be able to go to the movies or buy a Coke now and again. Now we can't even keep up with the rent and food. And now that winter's here, we've got to pay our share of the heating—and we're not even warm!"

"Quit your grumbling," Maxine said, rolling her eyes at me. "You got so used to living in that fancy-shmancy house, you've forgotten how the rest of the world lives."

"I have not! I just know I was better off before this big idea of yours."

Maxine's plan for us to share an apartment had once seemed like an excellent opportunity to become more independent. Now I wasn't so sure.

"Remember the fun you promised?" I challenged her. "I'm still waiting for the fun to *start*. We both walk to work to save bus fare, slave away all day, trudge home after dark, open a can of soup for supper, and bundle up in blankets to listen to a scratchy radio. Half the time, we can't even count on hot water for a bath. And our neighbor across the hall has bedbugs!"

"Oh, he does not." Maxine folded a blue sweater into her suitcase.

"Well, he stinks."

"He's just a sweet old man! And it's hard for him to climb all those stairs. You should be nicer to him." She closed the lid on her suitcase. "Anyway, we're getting out of here for a few days. Once we get home for Christmas, you'll quit being so surly. Think of all the yummy things we're going to eat in Mom's kitchen. She said she has enough sugar rations saved up for us to bake shortbread cookies."

I sighed and closed my own bag, not knowing whether to feel warmed or resentful that Maxine referred to *home* as if it were mine as well as hers. This would be my fourth Christmas with the Ross family. They always treated me like I belonged. It was I who felt otherwise. I knew I didn't deserve their acceptance, no matter how much I longed for it.

Maxine's usual chatter had given way to silence by the time we reached Pinehaven. It was going to be the first Christmas with both of her brothers overseas. They'd been conscripted for home defense only, but both had volunteered to fight.

I studied my friend's face as she peered out the train window to see who would come to meet us. "It'll be all right, Max," I said. It wasn't much to offer, but I could tell she was nervous. She'd said the same words to me more times than I could count.

She looked at me and smiled. "I know." She turned back to the window. "They're both here."

Sure enough, Mr. and Mrs. Ross were waiting on the platform. While her father picked up our bags, Maxine's mother embraced her daughter first, then me. It seemed to me she hugged me a lot more tightly than she had the year before.

"So good to have you girls home," she said, swiping a tear from her cheek. "You and I have some more crochet stitches to master, Bridget."

I walked with Mr. Ross so Maxine could have her mother to herself. They held hands and spoke softly—a definite contrast to Max's usual boisterous and annoying demeanor. But as we neared the house, she became more like her old self and greeted the family dog with all the enthusiasm his wagging tail inspired.

And she'd been right. Our argument was forgotten by the time we snuggled into a warm bed that night, our tummies full of Mrs. Ross's homemade bread and beef stew, Christmas carols still playing on the phonograph in the living room, and the warm smells of cinnamon and nutmeg lingering in the air. From their prayers around the table at supper, I could tell her parents felt every bit as much concern for their sons as the Weinberger family had felt for theirs. But nothing about the atmosphere was the same. I drifted off to sleep knowing that this home embodied something I wanted in my life more than anything. Though I couldn't completely identify that *something*, I was beginning to sense that it might have a direct connection to the baby whose birth we were about to celebrate.

Maxine and I spent the next day decorating the Christmas tree and baking shortbread cookies and gingerbread. As promised, her mother taught me to crochet some new stitches and, more importantly, how to follow written instructions to create patterns with the yarn. That evening, we attended a joint church service in the community hall. Pinehaven Fellowship had initiated a service that would bring its nondenominational congregation together with the Catholics and Lutherans to celebrate Christmas and to pray for the young men of the community who served overseas.

"Of course, there are some who refuse to participate," Maxine's father said, shaking his head. "Each group has those few who claim the other churches are doing the devil's work and say we should have nothing to do with them."

"But those few don't have sons off at war," Mrs. Ross countered. "They don't understand that we need all the prayer and unity we can muster."

I'd never heard of different religious groups cooperating like this before—not that I had much experience with such things. I'd noticed a marked contrast in styles when I'd visited two of these congregations in other years. I knew I could count on ritual and ceremony at the Catholic church, while the pastor at Pinehaven Fellowship talked like an everyday Joe and prayed in English instead of Latin. I felt drawn to both styles, but I had yet to enter the confession booth at the one church or walk to the front for prayer at the other. I hadn't been to the Lutheran church at all.

The service began with a short pageant presented by the children of all three congregations and organized by the Lutherans. Small shepherds and angels delivered their lines as a miniature Mary and Joseph laid a bundled-up doll in a wooden crate filled with hay. Adults smiled at the cuteness, and some wiped tears from their cheeks at the sight of their little ones learning the foundations of their faith and playing their roles with such sincerity.

Next, as the red-robed Catholic choir sang "Ave Maria," two boys in white robes lit dozens of tall candles held in curving candelabras, transforming the auditorium into a reverent sanctuary. The choir led us through the more subdued carols, including "Silent Night" and "O Come, All Ye Faithful." But it was when they began the beautiful harmonies of "Dona Nobis Pacem" that a holy hush fell over the big room. By the end of the piece, everyone had joined in singing, some with tears on their cheeks. In this frightening time of uncertainty and war, the meaning of the Latin words was not lost on anyone: *Grant us peace.*

After the singing, Pastor Collins from Pinehaven Fellowship delivered a brief message. He talked about how the birth of Jesus made God's presence with us possible; how one of his names, Immanuel, means "God with us." He told us we need never be afraid because God is always by our side. That God wants us to live every aspect of life together with him, but that he is also a gentleman who waits to be invited into our lives. How there is no greater "present" at Christmastime—especially in a world at war—than the ever-present God.

Immediately following the service, Maxine was swallowed up in a gaggle of her old school chums. I found Mrs. Ross and excused myself from the gathering, preferring to spend a little time alone. I headed toward the peace and quiet of their farm as the sounds of the community faded behind me until all I could hear was the crunch of my own boots on the snow. The stars, which I saw so rarely in the city, seemed to be putting on a particularly outrageous show just for me. I nearly tripped as I craned my neck to take in the magnificent country sky.

A warm red glow called to me from the Rosses' barn. I pushed the door open and went in. Mr. Ross had set up a heat lamp for a new calf that had been born out of season. I sat on a bale and watched the mother and baby resting peacefully in their corner stall, the mama chewing her cud and the calf sleeping. A gray-and-white barn cat jumped into my lap and instantly started to purr. I welcomed its warmth. I tried to imagine having a baby in such surroundings, as Mary had. The cozy children's pageant had failed to depict the reality of barn life, with its filth, odors, and discomforts. I wondered if I would ever be a mother, and couldn't imagine it. How would I know how to be one? Who could I use for an example?

Mrs. Harrison came to mind. I'd finally sent off the letter I'd written her for the school assignment, leaving off my new address. I hoped that with this act I would be closing the Bleak Landing chapter of my life once and for all. But all too often, thoughts of my past, and of my hometown and its people, still came to mind unbidden. It was becoming increasingly difficult to push them away. I wondered how Victor was faring. I shook my head to rid it of its wondering, placed the cat on the floor, and walked out of the barn.

Back at the house, I left the lights off and lit the candles Mrs. Ross had placed in the living room. Something in me wanted to re-create the solemn moments I'd experienced in the church service. Mrs. Ross's favorite recording of Christmas carols performed on harp and guitars still sat on the phonograph, so I switched it on. I studied the painting of the Good Shepherd hanging on their wall: Jesus carrying a lost lamb in his arms. How long I stood staring at it, I'm not sure. Maybe it was just because I was still cold from the outdoors, but I found myself desperately longing to enter the picture frame and become that little lamb. The Ross family Bible sat on the coffee table, a tall candle on each side. I approached it the way I used to do with Mr. Webster's dictionary and randomly flipped it open.

"God," I said aloud, "if you really do care about me, I need to know it. I need peace. I need to know my life matters for something, and whether or not I'm headed for hell like Pa said. I need to know it makes some kind of difference whether I'm here on this earth or not."

I read the words before me and my heart did a flip.

The first thing I read was Jesus telling his disciples a story about a lost sheep, and about how the shepherd called his friends together to rejoice when he found it. He used the story to illustrate that there is marvelous rejoicing in heaven when one sinner repents.

He went on to tell about a woman who loses a precious coin and, after much searching, finds it again and rejoices. Immediately, I thought of my locket. In my case, it wasn't so much lost as it was stolen—which made the pain even deeper. Would I ever see it again? Would I call people over to celebrate with me if I found it someday? The scenario seemed impossible, but what if God were big enough to handle even little details like this one?

Next, Jesus told a story about a lost son who ran away from his father. I wanted to stop reading, but I couldn't pull my eyes from the page. The son rebels and wastes his inheritance until he's so desperate he has no choice but to return to his father. For that son, though, it is only a matter of swallowing his pride. The father who awaits him with open arms will not beat him or swear at him or threaten to sell him to the highest bidder or wish him dead. The father runs to his son, embraces him, and welcomes him home with a big party.

How would it feel to be loved like that? To know that no matter what you did, you were wanted, loved, celebrated? Maxine always told me God loved me that way, and I fiercely wanted to believe her.

I could hear her voice and her parents' soft responses drifting in from outside. The door opened, and I heard them stomping the snow off their boots. The light in the kitchen snapped on, and I quickly brushed tears from my cheeks and rose to greet them.

Chapter 28

April 1943

Spring had arrived in Manitoba, and with it came Canada geese, crocuses, and renewed hope. Maxine was taking me out to celebrate my twenty-first birthday. With a dozen or more quality dresses in my closet—cast-offs from Caroline Weinberger—I knew I'd look as sophisticated as any woman in the restaurant of the prestigious Fort Garry Hotel. I chose a peach-colored two-piece outfit with white collar and piping, a belted waist, and a flared skirt. Maxine looked pretty spiffy herself in a red chiffon dress her mother had sewn and given her for Christmas.

Four good-looking soldiers rushed up the sidewalk just to pull the door open for us. When they beamed at me with appreciative smiles, winks, and whistles, I knew I was no longer the awkward ragamuffin who'd arrived in town six years before. I held my head high and ignored their attention while we breezed through the door and let it fall shut behind us, the soldiers still gaping from the sidewalk. The maître d' welcomed us respectfully and ushered us to our table. I tried hard not to gawk at the glittering chandeliers that put even the Weinbergers' to shame.

We ordered the cheapest item on the menu—chicken breast supreme—skipping drinks and dessert. We'd come for the atmosphere, which did not disappoint, and ate slowly to make the meal last. A live swing band was on stage, and Maxine and I wondered if we might be asked to dance. I looked around the room to see if all the other diners were already paired off. Not that I was any great shakes as a dancer, but I did enjoy a nice beat. Besides, Maxine and I had practiced in the apartment while the radio played some of these same tunes. It would be a shame for all that effort to go to waste.

This band wasn't quite Glenn Miller's orchestra, but they did perform a scaled-down version of "(I've Got a Gal In) Kalamazoo" complete with whistling, just like Maxine and I had seen in *Orchestra Wives*. I half expected two male tap dancers to burst out and entertain us with fancy flips and splits, running partway up the wall just the way they had in the movie.

As I was surveying the room for possible dance partners, a guest seated on the opposite side of the dance floor made me do a double take. My body froze as I stared at the young man, who was engaged in conversation with another man and two women. Dressed in a nice suit, he looked much older than he had the last time I saw him, but I was certain I would recognize Bruce Nilsen anywhere.

"Maxine." I practically hissed her name.

She was so caught up in the music and watching couples on the dance floor, she didn't even hear me the first time.

"Max," I said louder, my voice cracking.

In my peripheral vision I could see her looking at me, but I still hadn't taken my eyes off Bruce. I was almost afraid he'd disappear if I did.

"What?" she said, but all I could do was stare across the room. She looked that direction and then back at me. "What is the matter with you? I don't know what you're looking at."

I turned toward her and she gasped. "Bridget! You look like you've seen a ghost. What's the matter?"

I leaned in. "It's Bruce Nilsen." I held up one hand to shield my other hand, which I used to point at Bruce's table.

Her jaw dropped. She looked in the direction I was pointing, then back at me. "Bruce Nilsen? The one who took your locket? I thought he died."

"No, that was Lars. Bruce's dad. Bruce lives in Winnipeg now. He's some kind of hotshot lawyer, or will be soon. Mrs. Harrison told me. I can't believe he's here."

Maxine drew in her breath with the kind of dramatic flair only Maxine could pull off. "You've *got* to talk to him, Bridge! Maybe he knows what happened to the necklace."

Part of me wanted her to be right, but the situation was so complicated! Bruce was my childhood bully, and I still hated him. I didn't want anything to do with anybody from Bleak Landing, and I certainly didn't want him reporting back to anyone there that he'd seen me. But what if he *did* know something about my mother's locket?

"C'mon, I'll go with you." Max was already standing and tugging on my elbow.

"Wait!" I pulled away and stayed seated. "I can't just march over there." The thought of Bruce humiliating me in front of Maxine was unbearable. I felt as though my two worlds were about to collide and I'd die in the process.

"Why not?"

"I can't. I just . . . can't." I felt like I might pass out.

"He's an old schoolmate, isn't he? What's the big deal?"

"You don't understand." How could I explain all the years of being addressed as *Carrots* and *Woodpecker*, the stench of that outhouse, the sight of that taunting grin that crowded in on me until I thought I'd suffocate? It was as if someone had dropped me in the middle of a snake pit and I dared not move.

Maxine finally registered my distress and changed her approach. "Bridget. You can do this. I'll go over there with you. Who knows when or if you'll ever get another chance?"

I let out a big puff of air and tried to breathe normally. I knew Max was right. I needed to do it. I'd been watching him long enough to have seen him glance our way once without showing a hint of recognition.

"His father died," Maxine said. "You could offer your condolences, for one thing. Right? Isn't that what people do?"

"Sure," I said. *Normal, healthy, mature people. People who weren't trying to escape their past.*

"What's the worst that could happen?"

My heart could vibrate its way right out onto the floor.

I followed Maxine to the table where the foursome sat talking and laughing together. They all glanced up at us with expectant expressions. I looked at Bruce. His eyes darted from Maxine to me and back again.

"Yes?" he finally said.

Maxine nudged me, but not one word would come out. What was wrong with me?

Max came to my rescue with a bright smile.

"Hello there, I'm Maxine Ross. This is my friend Bridget Sullivan."

We both waited for some response from Bruce, but all he said was "Good evening." This was followed by an awkward round of *good evenings* from his companions.

Max was looking at me again, but before I could say anything, she jumped in. "The two of you went to school together." Maxine waved her hand between Bruce and me.

"I . . . I'm afraid you're mistaking me for someone else," he said. "I would definitely know it if I'd gone to school with you, Miss . . . I'm sorry, what was your name again?" His friends chuckled and nodded as if they were in on a good joke.

I stood in my spot like a statue.

"Sull-i-van," Maxine said slowly. She looked back at me with a disgusted look that said she'd completely given up on me. She turned back to Bruce. "You *are* Bruce Nilsen, right?"

His companions twittered.

"Yes."

"Then you must remember Bridget."

"I do. I remember a girl with a similar name, but she's dead. Trust me; this isn't her." He turned to me. "You, young lady, are not the Bridget I knew, and you can thank God for that. You're much too pretty and much too quiet."

Young lady? We were practically the same age!

He turned back to Maxine. "Now, I don't know how you know my name, miss, or what kind of game you're playing. But I'm not falling for it. Goodnight."

I grabbed Maxine's elbow and tried to pull her away, but she shook me off. She leaned into Bruce's face and spoke in a voice his friends would have had to strain to hear.

"We need to know what you can tell us about Bridget's locket."

Bruce frowned. "Her *what?*"

"Her locket. Your father stole it from her, six years ago."

I wanted to holler *"To the day!"*

Bruce either truly didn't know anything about my locket or was an awfully good actor. "My father is dead."

"We know." I couldn't believe Maxine was still talking! I pulled on her arm again, but she would have none of it. "And we're sorry for your loss. Bridget knows what it is to lose a beloved parent, and that locket was all she had of her mother. She deserves to get it back."

"Well, I'm sorry for her loss, too," he said, sounding truly sincere. "But I have no idea what you're talking about, and even if I did—this person is a fraud. Does she even speak English? Does she speak at all?"

Finally, I managed to spit out three words. "Maxine, let's go!" I gripped her wrist as tightly as I could and pulled without looking back. As we walked away, I could hear Bruce muttering to his friends.

"Do I look like someone who would fancy a girl's locket?" They all laughed, and I kept pulling on Maxine's arm until we reached the ladies' room.

"What on earth is the matter with you?" she said as I pulled her inside. She was angry, but so was I.

"I don't know!" I released Maxine's wrist. "I don't know, okay? You didn't have to badger him like that!"

"Badger him? I wouldn't have had to say *any*thing if you'd stood up for yourself and just talked to the guy." She ran water in the sink and dabbed at her face with wet hands. "Honestly, I just don't understand you sometimes."

With a heavy sigh, I sat on a bench upholstered in red velvet. "Sometimes I don't understand me, either."

"Are you sure it's him?"

"Positive. Anyway, he admitted to his name." I pulled a handkerchief from my purse and blew my nose.

"Couldn't very well deny it with his friends right there. Do you think he really didn't recognize you?"

I thought about this awhile. All I had wanted when I fled Bleak Landing was a new life. I'd changed my name, hoping for a new identity. I'd worked hard; developed skills. I'd dropped all traces of an accent—for all the good it had done me tonight. I had learned to imitate women I admired, hoping I could become a new person. Had I actually succeeded?

"In a way, I hope he didn't," I said.

"But Victor Harrison recognized you."

"True. But that was over two years ago."

Maxine sighed and shook her head, studying me. "You're a puzzle, my friend. I feel like you know *me* better than I know myself. But sometimes I wonder if I will ever truly know *you*."

When we left the ladies' room, Bruce and his friends were gone. We paid for our meal and carried on down the street to a theater playing *Casablanca* with Humphrey Bogart and Ingrid Bergman. As we watched the film, I tried my best to forget about Bruce Nilsen. How could I have been so stupid as to let him get away? The chances of him knowing what had become of my necklace were slim, but Maxine's words replayed in my head: *Who knows when or if you'll ever get another chance?*

I'd failed my mother again.

Chapter 29

October 1943

As I made my way to work, the crisp morning air and overcast sky told me another uneventful summer was gone for good.

I arrived at Mr. Weinberger's office early, as usual, and took a moment to scan the headlines as I placed the *Winnipeg Free Press* on his desk. Italy had switched sides, declaring war on the Nazis and joining the Allied forces. But with so many Germans already occupying their country, could they make a difference or were the Italians doomed?

We all wanted it to be over. Surely some kind of end would come soon and things could return to normal. The newsreels at the movies could go back to showing the latest gossip from Hollywood instead of footage of men firing at one another and planes dropping bombs. There would finally be young men for Maxine and me to dance with when we went out on Saturday nights. Japanese Canadians could leave their camps and return to their lives. And Weinberger Textiles could stop turning out military uniforms and go back to making suits and overcoats.

I walked over to my desk, where a stack of paperwork waited. When I heard Mr. Weinberger's footsteps coming down the hall, I rose to take his coat and hat from him as I always did just before fetching his coffee from the cafeteria. But when he appeared, I was shocked by the grave burden I saw etched on his face. Had he finally received word of his son's fate? Instead of handing me his hat, he hung it on the stand himself. He turned to me and fished something out of his coat pocket.

"A telegram came for you, Bridget," he said, concern in his voice. "To the house."

A telegram? For me?

"I thought it simplest to sign for it and bring it here myself—I hope you don't mind. It's terrible news, I'm afraid."

I waited in silence.

"I think you should sit down."

I slid into one of the chairs meant for visitors and looked up at my boss. Who on earth would send me a telegram? Who knew I'd ever resided at the Weinbergers' house? I took the typed card from his hand and saw the words *Canadian National Telegraphs* in large lettering across the top. I read the type below:

REGRET TO INFORM YOU PATRICK
O'SULLIVAN DIED OCTOBER 9, 1943. BURIAL
TO TAKE PLACE BLEAK LANDING CEMETERY
OCTOBER 12 1500 HOURS. PLEASE RETURN
TO BLEAK LANDING TO ARRANGE ESTATE
MATTERS.
    VICTOR HARRISON

I read the message twice, then just stared at it. Pa was dead.

I tried to focus on the thought, to sort out what I should feel, but all that came to me was curiosity. How had he died? Who found him? What was Victor doing back in Bleak Landing, and why was he the one sending me notice? I looked up at Mr. Weinberger, who stood watching me.

"I'll give you leave, of course." He paused and sat with one hip on the corner of my desk, his hands folded on his lap. "Bridget, the fella who delivered the telegram said our house was the last known address the sender had for you. He had little hope that it would reach you. Why have you not kept in touch with anyone back home?"

I stared at the floor. If Victor didn't expect the telegram to reach me, he wouldn't be expecting a response, either. I could completely ignore it if I wanted to. And why shouldn't I? The man who died was nothing to me, and I was nothing to him. As far as the so-called estate, what on earth would I want with a tumbledown old shack on the wrong end of a worthless little town I'd vowed never to return to? Let them keep it, if it was even still standing. For all I knew, the place had burned to the ground around my father's drunken body.

"Leave won't be necessary." I looked up at my boss again.

"Nonsense. The burial is tomorrow. You can probably get there today, but if not, catch the first train tomorrow morning and take as much time as you need." He pulled a five-dollar bill out of his pocket and held it out. "This will take care of your fare. Miss Brenner can cover for you here."

I stared at the money, then slowly took it from his hand. Maybe I *would* take some time off. Without a word, I put on my coat and hat, shoved both the telegram and the cash into my pocket, and pulled on my gloves.

"Take care, Bridget," Mr. Weinberger said as I walked through the door. I managed to mumble a "thank you, sir" before the door closed behind me.

Fall leaves swirled around my feet as I headed down the sidewalk. Where should I go? Maxine would still be at the apartment getting dressed for work, and I wasn't ready to face her. I wandered to a little park halfway between work and home and found a wrought-iron bench to sit on. A small pond had attracted a flock of Canada geese so loud their honks drowned out the traffic noise. I listened to their strange committee meeting and watched with longing as they took off in groups of four or five, eventually forming a lopsided V, their necks stretched toward the south.

Oh, how I wished I could join them! I pulled my coat tighter against the cool breeze and shivered as the sound of the geese slowly faded. What would it be like to soar above it all, to escape a Canadian winter and bask in warm sunshine, surrounded by others just like oneself? To head in the opposite direction of Bleak Landing?

I wouldn't go back. I couldn't. I'd take a few days off work, let Mr. Weinberger assume whatever he wanted. I could spend my work hours shopping or going to the movies, and Maxine would never know the difference. It would be just a nice holiday, my little secret. The bell on city hall gonged ten o'clock, and I knew Maxine would be at work by now. My mind made up, I stood and hurried toward home.

Outside our apartment building, a vagrant rested on the bus-stop bench. I'd seen him around before but generally averted my eyes. This time, I slowed my steps and approached the bench, waiting to make eye contact. He looked up at me with a watery gaze.

"Spare some change?" he asked.

From just those three words, I could tell two things: First, that he didn't expect a positive reply. And second, by his dark complexion and speech patterns, that his people had been in this country far longer than mine—or any white man's.

I paused only a moment.

"Yes," I said. "I can." I reached into my pocket and pulled out Mr. Weinberger's five-dollar bill and held it out. "What's your name?"

The man looked at the money with disbelief, then at me. "George," he said.

"Like the king," I said.

George's mouth turned up in a lopsided half smile, revealing gaps in his teeth. I waved the money closer to him. "Here. Take it."

His expression turned incredulous as he held out a trembling hand and accepted the money. I pulled from my purse the sandwich I'd packed earlier and held that toward him, too. "Do you like peanut butter and jelly?"

George took the sandwich. "Thank you, miss."

"You're welcome, George." I turned toward my building. When I looked back over my shoulder, he was shuffling down the sidewalk. I hoped he'd get himself a decent meal and a room for the night.

—

When Maxine walked through the door eight hours later, she saw the table set for supper.

"How did you have time to do all this?" She stood wide-eyed, taking in the sight and breathing in the aroma of the corn chowder and biscuits I'd prepared—two of Mrs. Cohen's specialties. "It smells wonderful! Did you get off early?"

I nodded. "I thought having the oven on would take the chill off."

Maxine kept up her usual enthusiastic chatter, filling me in on the quirks of her hair clients and the stories they'd shared with her that day. I wondered how some of them put up with her, and whether she actually let them speak or just made up the stories they supposedly told. Either way, I was glad to let her talk tonight. The less I said, the easier it would be to maintain my charade.

It was only later, as we lay in our twin beds in the darkness, a dim beam from the streetlight outside our window falling across the floor, that the truth settled upon me like a damp, heavy cloak.

My father was dead. I was alone in this world without a single known relative, at least not in this country.

"Max?" I finally whispered.

She responded with a low murmur and rolled over to face the wall. I sat up and swung my legs to the floor, pushing my feet into the pink slippers she had given me last Christmas. With my blanket wrapped around my shoulders, I tiptoed out to the living room and sat in the darkness awhile, trying to think about *anything* but the fact that my father was dead.

My Bible lay on the coffee table. I'd been reading it off and on, trying to get through the books that described Jesus's life. Trying to decide whether to believe what it said. Jesus had done such crazy, impossible things! But if the stories were all lies, how could there have been so many witnesses to write them down? I turned on the lamp at my elbow and picked up the book, turning to where I had left off.

In the story, two sisters, Mary and Martha, were grieving the death of their brother, Lazarus, from an illness. Jesus hadn't healed him, and Lazarus's friends couldn't understand why not, when he had healed so many others. Then Jesus said to Martha:

> "Thy brother shall rise again." Martha saith unto him, "I know that he shall rise again in the resurrection at the last day." Jesus said unto her, "I am the resurrection, and the life: he that believeth in me, though he were dead, yet shall he live: And whosoever liveth and believeth in me shall never die."

Where was my father now? I wondered. Had he been reunited with my mother and baby brother? And if so, did I truly want to join them someday?

I laid the book aside, wandered to the window, and looked out. A few flakes of snow twirled about, and I wrapped the blanket more tightly around myself at the sight. I saw someone asleep on the bus-stop bench and knew it was George. Why hadn't he found shelter for the night? Had he spent the money on a bottle? A hundred questions swirled around in my head. What was George's history? Had he always lived in the city? Did he have a daughter like me somewhere? A daughter who was warm and fed and sober, but who didn't care whether he lived or died? A daughter who had traded her most treasured possession just to escape him?

I felt a drop on my collarbone and in a moment of confusion took it for one of the snowflakes that were just inches from my face, on the other side of the glass. Then I realized it was a tear, as more of them came running down my cheeks. I didn't know whether I was crying for George or for Pa. Or neither. I tried to stop, but the tears kept coming. In that moment, I realized I was weeping not so much for what I had lost, but for what I'd never had. And for what I knew could now never be.

Though I tried to stop them, the tears turned into huge, gulping sobs. George remained undisturbed on his bench, but I gradually sank to the floor and tried to muffle the sound of my crying with my blanket. It didn't work.

"Bridget?"

Maxine stood in the doorway to our bedroom. She rushed over and knelt beside me on the floor.

"Bridge, whatever's the matter?" She let out a little gasp. "Did you lose your job? Is that why you came home early? Oh, Bridge, I'm so sorry! I didn't even ask you how your day went. Please tell me what's going on."

She rubbed my back, begging me to speak, but I could hardly catch my breath. Finally, I looked into her worried face and whispered the words that had been haunting me all day.

"I'm an orphan."

Chapter 30

"*B*ridget, you have *got* to go. He's your father. You'll regret it for the rest of your life if you don't."

Maxine had been all motherly love the night before, making me tea, tucking me back into bed, and even saying a prayer for me. She was still hovering when I fell asleep. But now that daylight had arrived and I'd informed her I had no intention of going to Bleak Landing, she'd turned into the Wicked Witch of the West.

"I don't *have* to do anything!" I argued, still lying in bed.

Maxine spoke through the sweater she was pulling over her head. "Look, I don't know what your father did or neglected to do, but he's still your father. He can't hurt you anymore, and you're hurting nobody but yourself by being so stubborn."

I flopped over onto my side, my face toward the wall. "Stay out of my business!"

"Bridget! I care about you!"

"Then you know I don't owe that old man anything."

"You're not going for him. You're going for *you*." She yanked my blanket down to my feet, and I quickly grabbed it and pulled it back up.

"No I'm not, because I'm not going." I pulled the blanket right over my head.

"You can still make it to the burial if you get up and hurry."

"They'll manage fine without me."

"Well then, think about the estate settlement." The *zip* of Maxine's skirt zipper punctuated her words.

I let out a snort. "Oh yeah. That eyesore will be worth a real fortune."

"Maybe not, but it's got to be worth *some*thing. You could sell it and use the money."

"I don't want anything from that man." I heard Maxine throw the window shade open and closed my eyes against the light filtering through my blanket.

"Then give it away. Use it for something important to you. How many times have I heard you talk about the struggles of immigrants coming over here and trying to make a go of things? You could help someone. Maybe you could do some good in the world instead of—"

She paused.

I lowered the blanket to my chin. "Instead of what?"

But she only sighed, then changed her tone. "I'll go with you."

"I've got just enough money in the bank for my share of the rent. I can't afford one ticket, let alone two." I didn't bother telling her about Mr. Weinberger's gift or my regifting it to George.

She dragged a brush through her hair. "I'll buy my own ticket."

"And take time off work? You'd lose your job."

"No, I won't. They just promoted me to assistant manager, remember?"

"You're not going because *I'm* not going. End of discussion." I pushed my bedding aside and swung my feet to the floor. "Thank you for ruining a perfectly good day off."

Maxine's face was turning red with exasperation. I quickly headed toward the kitchen.

"Bridget, one of these days you are going to have to grow up and do the right thing!" she hollered, following me.

I swung around to face her. "Well, aren't you just little Miss Missionary, doing good deeds and taking care of sad little Bridget, the poor, sorry immigrant girl who doesn't know which way is up." I saw Maxine's eyes grow wide, but I didn't stop. "You've been butting into my business from the day we met. Maybe it's time you found some new flunky to boss around."

And in that moment, I knew I had gone too far. Maxine stared at me, her lips clamped shut. She blinked hard, but tears welled up anyway. I knew I'd hurt her feelings. But it was bound to happen, eventually. I'd known all along that sooner or later she'd get sick of me. If this is what it took to arrive at that inevitable point, then so be it. I figured I might as well drive the stake in all the way, for good measure.

"You even talked me into moving out of a luxurious mansion to come live here with you in this dump. Now we're stuck here. Why did I ever listen to you?"

"Well, if you hate it so much, why don't you just move out?" She stomped over to where her coat hung on its hook and yanked it off, pushing her arms through the sleeves so hastily she might have been escaping a fire.

"Well maybe I just will!" But even as I yelled the words, a picture of George asleep on the bus-stop bench popped into my mind. Where would I go?

"In that case, you can forget about coming home with me for Christmas this year!" Maxine stepped through the door and slammed it behind her.

There was no way I was going to let her get away with the last word. I ran to the door, flung it open, and leaned out as Maxine's back disappeared around the corner of the hallway that led toward the stairs. I hollered loud enough to wake the neighbors. "Hallelujah! I thought you'd *never* un-invite me! Finally, I get a break from your stupid family and that sorry excuse for a home."

I waited, certain she would return the attack, but I heard only the scrape and the click of the door at the bottom of the stairs. I rushed to our living-room window and looked down at the street below. Maxine's bus was just pulling away, and though she tried to flag down the driver, he kept going. She kicked a stone clear across the street, barely missing a passing car, then stomped swiftly down the sidewalk and never looked back.

I ran back into the hallway where I'd seen the neighbor's copy of today's newspaper lying outside his door. I scooped it up and backed into our apartment, closing the door and pulling the chain across its plate. I spread the *Free Press* quickly on the table, certain I could peruse the classified ads and return the paper before it was missed.

I scanned the ads, running my finger down the page until I saw "Rooms for Rent." Jackpot!

Available immediately: furnished bedroom in clean boarding house, shared kitchen and bathroom. No children or pets.

The rent was less than my share of our apartment. I grabbed a pencil and paper and jotted down the address and telephone number. A second ad with similar wording and pricing showed up farther down the page and I wrote that one down, too. Either of them would be a simple streetcar ride from work, taken in the opposite direction from Maxine's. I returned the newspaper, dressed quickly, and left the apartment without breakfast.

The first house was a narrow three-story wedged tightly between two others. A pot of red geraniums clung stubbornly to summer in the chilly October air, and I thought I smelled chicken cooking even though it wasn't yet ten o'clock. The lady who came to the door informed me kindly that the room was taken but she hadn't managed to telephone the newspaper office before it went to print.

Disappointed but still determined, I went on to the next address. This house was similar to the first but more rundown. I knocked on the door and looked around while I waited for someone to answer. No flowerpots or cooking smells here. In fact, I spotted a busted pane of glass on the third floor and a broken board at the bottom of the front steps. Finally, the door opened and the smallest woman I'd ever seen looked up at me.

"Yes?" she said around the burning cigarette dangling from her lips.

"Hello, ma'am. I'm here about the room for rent?"

"Got references?" The woman didn't open the door any farther or smile.

I needed to think quickly. "I work for Weinberger Textiles, ma'am. I'm Mr. Weinberger's secretary, and I have lived in his family home. I'm certain he would be happy to talk to you."

The tiny woman looked me up and down. "First month up front."

"Uh—that would be fine. If I decide I want the room. I'll need to see it." I had just enough money in my bank account, though spending it all on the room would mean a stringent diet between now and next payday. It occurred to me that maybe I shouldn't have been so generous with George.

The woman opened the door and I was greeted by the meow of a geriatric tabby cat and the musty smell of an old, damp basement. While the cat sat on the bottom step of a narrow staircase, the woman led me past him up to the second floor, coughing all the way. I was surprised when she kept going to a third floor and more surprised to find it consisted of just one room. A narrow bed stood on the far side, under a dormer window. A rickety dresser with a cracked mirror completed the bedroom furnishings. Opposite, on the street side, a small table with one chair sat in front of the broken window I'd spotted from outside. Along the wall between them stood four cupboards and a counter. On top of the counter sat a hot plate.

"A hot plate?" I said. "I thought the ad mentioned a shared kitchen."

"You can share my icebox and sink," she said. "I don't want nobody cooking in my kitchen. And you'll share the bathroom on the second floor with two other boarders. You want it or not?"

Tempted to say something sarcastic, I bit my bottom lip. I had no time to lose if I was going to be gone by the time Maxine returned home from work. Which I had to be, if I wanted to teach her a lesson. Exactly what lesson that was, I wasn't sure. But I had no time to think about it now.

"I'll take it."

Chapter 31

Bleak Landing. November 1943

*M*ay the Lord bless you and keep you; may the Lord make his face shine upon you, and be gracious to you; may the Lord lift up his countenance upon you, and give you peace."

Victor pronounced the benediction knowing no more fitting words to bestow on his church family than these, based on the biblical blessing. He stepped down from the platform to a murmur of amens and walked down the aisle to the back of the church, no longer conscious of his limp. After much persuasion from the church board, he'd agreed to fill the pulpit until a new pastor could be found for their little church. Pastor Jorgenson had retired due to poor health but was instrumental in putting Victor's name before the board, much to the surprise of some church members.

"The war changed that young man," the old pastor told the congregation, in Victor's presence. "The war, and God. He knows his Bible thanks to the godly home he grew up in and all those years of Sunday school—even the ones when he refused to sit still and got himself in trouble every chance he had." This had been met with a polite chuckle from those gathered. "But now the Spirit's got hold of him, and that's a combination you can't beat. You'll find I'm right if you give him a chance."

Victor was shocked by the endorsement but reminded himself that with so many men gone to war, it was slim pickins and he would be replaced just as soon as they came home.

News stories offered some promise on that front. Adolf Hitler had issued Führer Directive Number 51, anticipating the Allies would invade Nazi-occupied France. He had transferred troops and reinforcements to Western Europe, surely having become nervous and less confident as the rest of the world rallied against him. It was only a matter of time before the Nazis surrendered. Victor prayed for this constantly, and leaned heavily on God to help him fulfill his new calling on the home front.

He stood on the church steps shaking hands with people as they stepped out into the frosty November air. While some hurried home on foot, others stood visiting on the sunny side of the church. The last to exit the building was Lars Nilsen's widow.

"Fine sermon, Victor."

"Thank you, Mrs. Nilsen." Victor shook her little hand.

"I have news from Bruce." She smiled up at him. "He's coming back to Bleak Landing and setting up his own law office right here."

"He is? Well, isn't that good news?" Victor couldn't imagine how Bruce could muster enough business in Bleak Landing to make a go of it, but since none of the surrounding communities had attorneys, either, perhaps they'd all come to him. "I'll look forward to seeing him."

"Victor!"

Five men approached from around the corner of the building. Victor recognized three from the church, along with Mr. Lundarson, who ran the general store, and Mr. McNally, who used to live next door to the O'Sullivan place.

The group appeared to be on a mission.

"Gentlemen," Victor said. "What can I do for you?"

"You can run for mayor!" Mr. Lundarson held up two sheets of paper. "We've got the nomination forms right here, and all the signatures we require."

Victor laughed. "That's a good one, Mr. Lundarson."

"We're quite serious, young man," Mr. McNally said.

"You think we'd go to all this trouble for a joke?" Mr. Lundarson pushed the papers into Victor's hand. "You've been home from the war over a year now. Long enough for us to see you've become a fine leader." In addition to his interim pastoring, Victor ran the Boys' Brigade club after school and had helped organize a metal drive for the war effort.

Mr. McNally chimed in again. "You're a hero around here, Victor. And we need a new mayor. You'd be a good one." Victor had bought McNally's property for a song six months earlier, after Mrs. McNally declared she needed a house on the right side of the tracks or she was leaving her husband for good. With his father's help, Victor had already torn down the McNallys' old house and hoped to start building a new one come spring.

"But Mr. McNally, I don't know anything about being a mayor."

"Nobody does when they start out, son. And you'd have a town council with some experience."

"Then why doesn't one of them—" Victor began.

Mr. Lundarson leaned in close enough to whisper. "The only councilor interested in the job is Hans Hansen. He's pushing eighty-five and stone deaf. Can't read, either."

Victor's father approached the group, and Mr. McNally welcomed him into the circle. "Tell him, Harrison. He'll listen to you."

Victor looked down at his feet. There was no way Pa would agree with the men. Even though they'd been farming together for the past year and Victor carried more than his share of the weight, his father would never see him as mayoral material.

But Pa surprised him. "I think it's a fine idea. He's proven himself on the battlefield, and he's doing a fine job on the farm." He turned toward Victor. "I'll even be your campaign manager, son!"

The men chuckled and thumped Victor on the back as though it was a done deal.

"I'll need to pray about it," he said, looking around to see whether one of them might finally own up to it all being a prank. But on the inside, his heart soared with the echoes of his father's praise.

Ten days later, while his sisters helped him put up their hand-painted election posters in the general store, Victor looked up to see Bruce Nilsen walking toward him.

"Bruce! Your mother told me you were coming. Welcome home!"

The two of them shook hands. "Thanks, Vic. Good to see you. Putting up the old campaign signs, I see."

Victor nodded. "Yeah. I'm not sure what I've got myself into, but they tell me running for office is a valuable experience even if you don't win."

"Well, I wouldn't know about that, since I intend to win."

Victor gave his head a shake. "You're running, too?"

Bruce grinned from ear to ear. "Just signed up this morning."

"But . . . didn't you just get back?"

"Been back a week now, and nothing's changed around here. I know everybody and everybody knows me. Except now I've got a law degree and a license to practice. Got my office set up just across the street." He nodded toward the former barber shop. "I'm on my way to Landeville right now to order my signage. Might dabble in real estate on the side."

"Real estate? Wow, Bruce. You're biting off a lot at once." Victor was still trying to grasp the idea of Bruce running for mayor. "Look, I had no idea you wanted to be the new mayor. Maybe I should just step down. If it's younger leadership they're looking for, there's no point in us both running and splitting the vote."

"Don't be silly," Bruce said. "A little competition is healthy. I think it's charming that you've thrown your hat into the ring."

Charming? Victor said nothing, but he could feel indignation rising in his chest. Along with, for the first time, a keen desire to win the election.

Bruce grinned. "Want to ride along with me to Landeville? We could catch up on the way, have coffee while we're there."

"Thanks, but my sisters need a ride home—"

"You mean to tell me these two fine young ladies can't drive a car yet?"

Victor hoped Nancy hadn't overheard, because she always jumped at the chance to drive. But she was at his side in a split second. "I can drive us home, Victor. Go ahead. I'll tell Pa you'll be home later this afternoon."

Victor looked at his sister and back at Bruce. "Um. All right, then."

They climbed into Bruce's car and, on their way out of town, drove past Victor's property.

"I hear you bought the McNally place," Bruce said. "Got plans for it?"

"Yeah. I hope to put a house on it—starting soon. I suspect it'll be a drawn-out project, but Uncle Bud's willing to work with me. And Pa, too."

"What's happening with the O'Sullivan place now that the old man's gone?" Both men turned to look at the sad little deserted shanty surrounded by tall weeds.

"I have no idea. I suppose it belongs to Bridget, wherever she is."

"You know how her pa got that place, right?"

Victor shrugged. "Bought it, I suppose."

"Nope. Cheated in a card game. By rights, it still belongs to the previous owner."

Victor wondered where Bruce got his information, but didn't question it. "Really? Well, probably serves him right. What kind of idiot gambles away real estate?"

Bruce grew strangely quiet for the rest of the ride.

~

Over pie and coffee at the Landeville Cafe, Victor tried to determine what was going on in his old friend's heart and mind. Bruce had avoided the draft after his father's death by declaring it would be too great a hardship on his family for him to serve. He'd finished law school and gave every appearance of being a successful attorney, yet he had returned to Bleak Landing and was currently living with his mother. And he'd immediately jumped into the mayoral race with apparent confidence, although Victor felt he knew Bruce well enough to suspect something else under the show of bravado.

"What made you come back to Bleak, Bruce?" Victor asked. "Most people never do."

Bruce's eyes darted around the room. "Opportunity, pal. Big fish, small pond. Here, I'm the only lawyer for miles around. Oh sure, maybe this town is just a hopeless little pimple on the landscape. But where else could a young guy like me be the mayor?"

Victor felt his hackles rising again. "You're not the mayor."

"I will be." Bruce lit up a cigarette and offered one to Victor, who shook his head. "No offense, Vic—but did you even finish high school?"

"You know I didn't. There are other ways of receiving an education."

Bruce blew a hefty dose of smoke off to the side. "Anyway, it's only temporary. This war will be over soon and when it is, I'll have enough dough squirreled away to leave Bleak Landing behind for good. Just a stepping stone, my friend. Just a stepping stone."

Victor cleared his throat. "Can I ask you something?"

"'Course."

"The day you came to our house to tell us your father had passed, I um . . . I saw a necklace fall out of your pocket. A lady's locket. It looked real familiar, even though I'd never seen you with it before."

Without a glance toward Victor, Bruce waved the waitress over to the table. "I'll get this." He pulled enough change out of his pocket to cover their bill and laid it on the table. He finally looked at Victor. "That necklace was in my father's hand when he died. It's been in my family for generations."

"Really." It wasn't a question. "I find it strange that a Celtic locket would be in a Norwegian family for generations. Don't you?"

Bruce rose to leave, blowing smoke in Victor's direction while he stubbed out his cigarette in the ashtray. "I don't know what you're insinuating, Vic. But whatever it is, you're wrong."

Chapter 32

Winnipeg. Christmas Day, 1943

It wasn't the *worst* Christmas ever. At least, that's what I kept telling myself. Memories of sitting home alone, knowing my father would come home drunk and mean . . . listening to his passed-out snore . . . dodging his angry blows . . . all qualified as worse than this. Here, I felt safe at least.

Sure, the room was frigid. But I'd stayed in bed as long as I could, bundled in a nightie *and* bathrobe *and* warm socks. I'd made tea and left the hot plate on just to have some heat. I'd stuffed a towel into the broken window and propped my door open so any warmth from the rooms below could drift in. Now I sat at my little table, dressed in two layers of clothing, sipping tomato soup and gazing out the window at the gray sky and deserted street. Darkness was falling, and a short red candle burned in the center of my table, providing ambiance.

Two months had passed since I packed up my belongings and moved into my own place. I had not contacted Maxine and could only imagine the look of shock on her face when she'd returned home that night. Somehow, the thought of it hadn't been as satisfying as I'd expected.

I'd returned to work two days later, dodging Mr. Weinberger's questions and nodding whenever anyone expressed condolences on the loss of my father. Though Maxine might not know where I lived, she could have contacted me at work if she wanted to. So far, it seemed, she hadn't wanted to. And I certainly wasn't going to be the first to make a move. I wondered if she'd found a cheaper place or if she now shared the apartment with a new roommate. Well, let some other poor girl listen to her nonstop nagging and blathering on about nothing. I didn't miss it.

You haven't done so badly for yourself, Bridget. I looked around the room. I'd picked up some spruce branches in the park and placed them in a mason jar on my dresser, decorating them with strings of popcorn and a loopy garland of crocheted red yarn. A Christmas carol played on the brand-new radio that sat on my counter. All right, so it wasn't exactly new. A thrift shop on my route to work had become my favorite store. There, I'd found pretty curtains to hang on both my windows, along with various household comforts like dishes and blankets. I'd brought home several woolen sweaters and had a nice little routine going. On Monday evenings, I listened to *Lux Radio Theatre* while unraveling sweaters and rolling the yarn into balls. The rest of the week, I'd listen to *The Happy Gang*, *Fibber McGee and Molly*, Jack Benny, and Edgar Bergen while I crocheted the yarn into mittens and scarves. At the end of the week, I dropped off the finished items at a nearby shelter where people needed such things.

I picked up my latest mitten project and stitched another row, remembering how patiently Mrs. Ross had taught me and how she'd kindly told me I had a knack for it. I could picture Maxine's family now, gathered around a twinkling tree in their warm living room, their tummies full of turkey or ham. Or maybe they were in church. Did they miss me?

I pushed the thought away. I could enjoy Christmas right here. I closed my eyes as I listened to the carol playing on my radio:

I heard the bells on Christmas day, their old, familiar carols play,
And wild and sweet the words repeat, of peace on earth good-will
    to men. . . .
And in despair I bowed my head: "There is no peace on earth," I
    said.
For hate is strong, and mocks the song of peace on earth, good-will
    to men.

I walked over to the radio and snapped it off. *Most depressing Christmas song ever.* Ironically, I'd no sooner turned it off than I heard church bells ringing. From my back window, I could see the steeple from which the clanging came. The church was an imposing stone structure I'd walked by many times, admiring the stained-glass windows. The thought occurred to me that the church would be warm inside, and before I could overthink it I blew out my candle; pulled on my coat, hat, gloves, and boots; and headed down the stairs with my purse.

I hustled down the sidewalk as the pealing of the church bells gave way to a discordant echo. The strains of a pipe organ took over as I ran up the steps and through the front doors. I identified the notes of "Joy to the World" as I dropped into the second pew from the back. It was definitely warmer in the church than in my apartment, but I kept my coat on anyway. The congregation was invited to stand. All eyes stayed focused on the front, where a music conductor led us through the joyful carol, then through two more.

When we sat down again, I prepared myself for the peaceful, fuzzy feelings that always filled me in Maxine's church. Instead, I found myself distracted. In contrast to the welcoming smiles I'd always received in Pinehaven, no one here seemed willing or able to make eye contact. I felt invisible. A couple of teenagers giggled in the row in front of me, and indignant scowls from the adults only increased their twittering. A siren wailed on the street outside, then another. This set off a chorus of crying infants, including one in particular who wouldn't be consoled and had the most mournful howl.

The pastor was talking about how he was convinced God would not allow the war to continue through 1944, predicting that we would soon be at peace and that victory would go to the Allied forces. Of course I hoped he was right, but I wondered how he could be so sure when the fighting had been going on so long already. I also wondered how he could concentrate on his sermon, what with all the ruckus inside and out. I could still hear intermittent sirens and several barking dogs who dared to compete with them. It was anything but the serene Christmas atmosphere I'd hoped to find.

When we rose to sing the closing song and I saw which one had been chosen, I snapped the hymnbook shut. They were ending with the same depressing carol that had made me switch off my radio an hour before. Not wanting to attract attention, I stood silently through the first two verses. Finally, I couldn't take it anymore. I'd come here for some warmth and hope. The last thing I needed was the despair of this horrible song. I slid out of the row and headed for the door.

That's when I realized the song had another verse, with a different message from the others:

> Then pealed the bells more loud and deep: "God is not dead, nor
> doth he sleep;
> The wrong shall fail, the right prevail, With peace on earth, good-
> will to men."

I paused, my hand on the door handle, and listened. The congregation sang one last verse.

*Till, ringing, singing, on its way, the world revolved from night
to day,*
A voice, a chime, a chant sublime of peace on earth, good-will to men!

I pushed the door open and faced a blast of cold air. *God, if you're not dead or asleep, show yourself to me,* I prayed. *Otherwise, I am pathetically and utterly on my own.*

Maybe God would hear. Maybe he would intervene and do something good for me, something that would turn my life around. I thought of the things I'd thrown away, the opportunities I'd taken for granted, the love I had not returned. The times I'd run away instead of facing my troubles. Why should God bother with me?

As I turned the corner, all thoughts of God dissolved at the sight of a fire truck and a police car on my street. A crowd of people had gathered. What was going on? Smoke rose from somewhere up ahead. I began to feel sick. Then I saw it.

My house was in flames.

I froze for only a moment. I ran toward the firetruck, pushing my way through onlookers and yelling, "I live here! Let me through!"

Two firemen held a hose aimed at the top of the house. A third approached me. "You live here?"

I nodded.

"Do you know if there was anyone else inside?" he asked.

"Anyone *else?*"

That's when I saw my landlady seated on the snowy curb, her cat clutched in her arms, a neighbor comforting her and wrapping a blanket around her shoulders. A police officer crouched in front of her, taking notes on a pad.

"I don't think so," I said. Two boarders lived on the second floor, but as far as I knew, both had gone away for the holiday. The place had seemed deserted when I left. Another vehicle pulled up, and a man I could only assume was the fire chief got out.

"Looks like it started on the third floor, Chief," one of the firemen called out. "This was all we could salvage. It was propping the door open." He held a black book out toward the chief.

And in that sickening moment, I understood two things.

I had left my hot plate on. And the only possession I had left in the world was the Bible Maxine's family had given me.

Chapter 33

*T*ime stood still as I waited on that sidewalk watching the firefighters do their work. The fire was out, but they continued to watch to make sure it didn't start up again. My landlady had gone home with her neighbor but not before giving me a withering look that said it all. I had destroyed her home.

"Do you have somewhere to go, miss?" A police officer stood beside me.

I stood there, clutching my purse and my Bible and thinking about the lost radio. Maybe if I'd used the radio to prop that door open, I'd still have it instead. It occurred to me that I was still wearing two layers of clothing under my coat. How lucky. I had a change of wardrobe.

"Miss?"

"Um . . . I . . . don't know." Where could I go? The factory was closed for the holiday, the dorms empty and locked up tight. It was too far to walk to the Weinbergers' home, and buses weren't running. And even if I wanted to go crying back to Maxine—which I didn't—she'd be home with her family in Pinehaven.

"Excuse me, officer?" An older woman approached from behind me. "I might be able to help." She turned to me. "Miss? We haven't met, but I volunteer at the shelter and I've seen you bringing donations. I was sitting behind you in church tonight."

Had I seen her before? Her gray hair was pulled into a tight bun, and she wore a striking red wool coat and jaunty hat. Nothing about her seemed familiar.

"I know this might sound odd, but when I saw you leave the church, I had a very clear sense that I was to follow you down the street. It took me a while to stop arguing with myself, but I knew I wouldn't rest tonight if I didn't obey. God tends to know what he's up to when he gives me these thoughts."

"God?" I muttered. Did she mean the god who refused to show himself to me when I asked? The same god who hadn't bothered to save my home?

"My name is Harriet Watson. I live just four blocks from the church, on the other side. If you have nowhere to go, you're welcome to come home with me. At least long enough to warm up and think clearly. You must be in terrible shock."

"I . . . uh . . ." was all that would come out.

"Do you recognize this woman, miss?" the police officer asked. I managed to shake my head.

"I served Christmas dinner at the shelter earlier today," the woman said. "Normally you could stay there, but they are bursting at the seams. There's space at my house, though."

I glanced at the police officer.

"I'm Constable Erickson. If you're not comfortable with that arrangement, I can take you back to the station with me."

"I'll go with her," I blurted. If my only other option was the police station where a bunch of drunks were probably sleeping off their Christmas binges, I'd take my chances with this lady. It was Saturday night, and Weinberger Textiles would open again Monday morning. Even though the dormitory was for sewing machine operators only, surely they'd make an exception for me until I could make other arrangements.

A wide smile broke across the woman's face. "Oh, good. Let's get you out of the cold."

I found it hard to keep up with her stride as she led me to a two-story brownstone and around to the back door. We walked into a warm kitchen where she put a kettle on before she even removed her coat. I took mine off as well, and she hung both coats on a hook by the door.

"Have a seat."

Before long, we sat drinking tea and eating oatmeal cookies at her cozy table. My purse and Bible lay on top of it.

"I know you're in shock, dear. You don't have to figure things out tonight. If you're comfortable staying overnight, you are more than welcome. You can sleep in my daughter-in-law's room. She stays here with me, but she had a chance to go home to visit her parents in Ontario for Christmas. She'll be back Monday."

I only half heard her as she explained that her son was overseas. All I could think about was my apartment in flames and the things that had been inside. I mentally took inventory of my losses. I thought about all the beautiful clothes Caroline Weinberger had given me and realized that, except for the two outfits I had on, they were all now in ashes. The little stack of mittens and scarves waiting to be delivered to the shelter were gone. My cherished radio, gone. The few books I'd collected, the letter from Victor Harrison's mother. Gone. I was trying to remember how much money was in my bank account and calculate what I'd need to set up housekeeping all over again.

"I'm glad they rescued your Bible, Bridget," the woman was saying, as though she'd known me for years. "The Word of God is powerful, and sharper than a two-edged sword."

I looked at the black book. "Bibles are replaceable," I said, picking it up and flipping through its pages. A faint odor of smoke wafted up to my nose.

"The printed page, yes." The lady refilled my teacup, pouring from a dainty china pot. "But God's actual words endure forever. They led me to you, and now you're here."

This woman was even weirder than Maxine. But her house was warm, and I was exhausted and in no position to argue. I flipped to the front page of the Bible, where Mrs. Ross had inscribed my name. I'd read her message more than I'd read any of the book's actual passages: *To Bridget. Merry Christmas, 1940. Remember, when you give your heart to God, he will cherish it—it doesn't matter what's going on inside it or how you're feeling. He loves you.*

That's when I saw it. I couldn't remember tucking Victor Harrison's telegram into my Bible, but there it was—still reminding me that somewhere in this world was a plot of land that was rightfully mine. A plan began to form.

⁓

Monday morning, I trudged to work carrying a small brown suitcase Mrs. Watson had given me. With her assistance, I'd washed all my clothes the day before. The case now held my one extra outfit plus a few things she'd supplied: a nightgown, a hairbrush, a few toiletries—even a simple dress she insisted no longer fit her daughter-in-law and said she'd be happy to part with. I gave her the most heartfelt thank-you I knew how to give, half expecting her to demand at the last minute that I pay her back. But when I suggested that I'd repay her kindness as soon as I was able, she merely told me to help someone else in need and said that would be payment enough.

In many ways, I felt much as I had the day I first arrived in Winnipeg. I wondered if I was destined to wander in circles for the rest of my life. But I reminded myself that I now had an education, a much better job, and experience. And I was a landowner, too, whatever that was worth.

My plan was to seek out Miss Brenner, explain my situation, and request a bed in the dormitory for a couple of nights while I used my off-hours to find a new boarding room. I figured I had enough money in the bank for a week—maybe two if I was really careful—and another paycheck coming in a few days. Then I'd buy a round-trip train ticket for Bleak Landing, claim my father's property, and put it up for sale. I had no idea how to go about any of that or how long it might take to sell the place or what I could get for it. Only one thing was certain: I wouldn't stay in Bleak Landing any longer than absolutely necessary.

I was early for work, so didn't expect to see many others around. But as I reached the front doors, I was surprised to find a dozen young women gathered on the steps. One of them recognized me and ran over.

"Miss Sullivan, what's going on? We've all returned from Christmas break expecting to go back to work. What's the meaning of this sign?"

One of the other girls was trying in vain to open the front door, while another peered through the window to see if there was anyone inside. A large sign was taped to the door:

WEINBERGER TEXTILES CLOSED UNTIL FURTHER NOTICE.
GOVERNMENT HAS CANCELED ALL ORDERS FOR MILITARY UNIFORMS.

Then, in finer print:

TO OUR VALUED EMPLOYEES: IF WE WERE UNABLE TO REACH YOU, WE APOLOGIZE
FOR THIS INCONVENIENCE AND TRUST IT DOES NOT CAUSE YOU UNDUE HARDSHIP.

That's all it said. By the time I turned around, another dozen people had gathered behind me, demanding to know what was going on. I assured them I'd had no idea this was coming and had not received a call or a telegram, either. I didn't mention I had no home at which to receive a call or a telegram. The only person here I recognized was Helen, who had been sewing for the factory since before I started.

"Well, well," she said as she approached me. And with those two words, I recalled the disdain she'd expressed for me the day we met. "Oh, how the mighty have fallen."

I studied her scornful face. "Excuse me?"

"It seems you've come full circle, *Miss* Sullivan. While some of us have stayed in our positions for years, you managed to somehow wiggle your way into Mr. Weinberger's house *and* office, and into his daughter's fancy clothes. Now you're in the same jobless boat as the rest of us."

I turned when another girl spoke.

"The government's confident the war will be over soon. They've stopped all orders. That's good, right? We can go back to regular production."

"Not that simple," said another.

I glanced around, hoping Mr. Weinberger would show up and set the record straight. What did "until further notice" mean? A day? Six months? My head was spinning. Clustered in groups of twos and threes, the others walked away in bewilderment and anger. I sat on the frozen steps to think, wrapping my scarf tighter around my neck. The barren trees held no color, the skies no birdsong. Clouds cast a shroud over the entire city that rivaled any bleakness I'd ever seen in my hometown.

I had no home, no job, no friends.

Where would I go? I couldn't go back to Mrs. Watson's. Her daughter-in-law was returning and would need her bed. Besides, the woman had already been more than generous. The Weinbergers were no doubt steeped in trouble if they actually had to close the factory, and shouldn't need to deal with my problems, too—not that I wanted to ask any more from them.

That left Maxine. Was she back in the city yet?

I reached into my purse for my Bible and pulled Victor's telegram from between its pages.

PLEASE RETURN TO BLEAK LANDING TO
ARRANGE ESTATE MATTERS.

I didn't need to go crawling to Maxine! I had options. I'd just have to implement my plan a little sooner than I'd anticipated. When I tucked the telegram back into the spot from which I'd pulled it, I saw that it was in the first chapter of Joshua, and my eyes fell to these words in verse nine: "Be strong and of a good courage; be not afraid, neither be thou dismayed: for the Lord thy God is with thee whithersoever thou goest."

With me. What a joke. If there was one thing I'd learned, it was that I was on my own. I returned the Bible to my purse, picked up my suitcase, and headed off down the sidewalk at a full clip. First stop: the Dominion Bank. And second: Union Station.

Chapter 34

Bleak Landing. December 27, 1943

I could feel my heart thumping away in my chest as the train approached the platform. Bleak Landing had changed little. Run-down houses still dotted the sad landscape, with only the odd new building here or a fresh coat of paint there. Campaign signs indicated that both Victor Harrison and Bruce Nilsen were running for mayor. That figured. Two losers competing for bullying rights. I was glad I wouldn't be sticking around long enough to have to choose between two such pitiful candidates.

I tried to ignore my sweating palms and gave myself a silent pep talk. *No reason to feel nervous. It's not like anyone is going to be here to meet you. You're here on business, a refined and mature woman now. Don't forget that.* I reviewed all the skills I'd gained since the last time I set foot in this place: *You've graduated from high school. You can operate a sewing machine. You've learned to cook and fix a lady's hair and care for fine clothing. You can type, file, and take shorthand. You have your own bank account and can find your way around the city.*

Determined to maintain my dignity, I wore the better of the two Caroline Weinberger outfits I still owned: a top-quality navy wool suit and silk coral blouse with a fluffy bow tied at the neckline. With my hair swept up and my matching hat and gloves, I knew I looked nothing like the pathetic girl who'd left town with Mr. Nilsen a lifetime ago. Yet strangely, my surroundings had me feeling very much like her. The sensation left my stomach reeling. I was glad my old house was not within sight. I was not ready for the feelings it was sure to stir up.

When the train stopped, I retrieved my bag and donned my winter coat. Taking a deep breath, I held myself as tall as possible and stepped down onto the platform. There had always been only one hotel in town—the Sundvolden, located right across from the train station—and I was certain that was still the case. The hotel had apparently been named for some fancy hotel in Norway, which was quite a laugh given its reputation for seediness. But I headed over there now, eager to procure a room before the gray December sky turned dark.

I paid two dollars for one night's stay and was given a key to a small room on the second floor that held a narrow bed, a table with two chairs, and a corner sink. The sight of two cheaply framed pictures on the wall made me grin. I was certain they'd been torn from an old calendar. One was a reproduction of Van Gogh's *The Starry Night*. I couldn't name the other but remembered enough from my visit to the Winnipeg Art Gallery to recognize it as a Monet—Maxine's favorite artist.

I left my suitcase in the hotel room, locked the door, and headed out onto the street. The land titles office had always been part of the Bleak Landing post office. I hurried so I would get there before they closed.

A middle-aged man with a balding head looked up when I pushed open the post office door. He immediately straightened and gave me an appreciative smile.

"Yes, miss. How can I help you?"

"Hello. My name is Bridget O'Sullivan." I nearly choked on the *O* but knew I had better use it if I wanted to claim family property. "My father died recently and I'm here to inquire about his estate."

The man stared at me a moment. "You're Paddy O'Sullivan's girl?"
I nodded.

"Well, I'll be. I'm new in town. Harley Robertson's the name. I heard tell the man had a daughter, but some say—" He cut himself off. "Well, it doesn't matter what some say, does it? I can look up the piece of property for you; that's easy enough. We'll require legal documentation in order to transfer the title. Do you have the deed?"

I'd been worried about this. "No, sir."

"All right." Mr. Robertson looked at me over the top of his glasses. "Well, a copy of your father's will and some government-issued identification should do it."

"Will?" I seriously doubted my father had ever made a will. And as for identification, the only piece I'd ever owned in my life was a card that identified me as an employee of Weinberger Textiles. Last time I saw it, it was hanging from its lanyard on a hook inside my closet door, and it had no doubt burned to ashes.

I slowly shook my head. "I . . . I don't know if my father ever made a will. Can you give me an example of a proper identification paper?"

"Birth certificate?"

I shook my head. "I was born in Ireland. But I grew up here. There will be plenty of people who can vouch for my identity."

"Absolutely. There's a law office just two doors down. If I were you, I'd get some legal advice. Then come back here with two witnesses who can verify that you are who you say you are, and we should be able to get this cleared up."

Law office? Bleak Landing has its own lawyer? Maybe things had changed more than I thought.

"They should be open for another twenty minutes or so." The man held out his hand to shake mine. "Welcome back to Bleak Landing, Miss O'Sullivan. It will be lovely to have someone of your . . . refinement living among us."

"Oh, I don't plan to stay." The words flew out before I could think. That admission might not help my cause. "But thank you. I appreciate your assistance, and I'll return in the morning." I shook Mr. Robertson's hand and walked in the direction he'd indicated. Sure enough, a new-looking sign graced the glass of a large window. I was wondering how much legal advice would cost when the words on the sign stopped me in my tracks.

NILSEN LAW OFFICE
BRUCE NILSEN, BARRISTER & SOLICITOR

When I closed my eyes to take a deep breath, I pictured Bruce's grinning face the night Maxine challenged him at the restaurant. His father had worn a similar expression as he pocketed my mother's neck-lace. And I could still hear the playground taunts of "Carrots" and "Woodpecker" ringing in my ears.

I can't do this, I thought. But just as I turned on my heel to head back to the hotel, I heard the door of the law office open with the tinkle of a little bell. And I heard a familiar voice.

"Can I help you, miss?"

In that instant, Maxine's words replayed in my head: *I wouldn't have had to say anything if you'd stood up for yourself and just talked to the guy! Who knows when or if you'll ever get another chance?*

I took a deep breath and slowly turned around. There stood Bruce, holding the door open. A look of shock and then recognition registered on his face.

"It's *you*," he said.

I swallowed. "Yes, Bruce. It's me—Bridget." I was so relieved he remembered me. I figured the act in the restaurant had just been a cover to impress his friends.

"No. It's *you*, the impostor from the restaurant. And still playing at the same game, I see. When did you recover your voice? I thought you didn't talk. How did you track me down?" He let the door close behind him.

"Bruce, it's me. Can we go inside? I have business." A light snow had begun to fall.

Bruce looked at me as if trying to decide. Abruptly he opened the door again, and indicated with one hand that I should go through. He followed me inside and the bell tinkled once more as it fell closed behind us. One desk, a filing cabinet, and two chairs for clients filled up the room. There was no secretary, no reception area. Not even a vestibule to buffer the cold winter wind.

Bruce stepped behind his desk. "Have a seat."

I did. "As you probably know," I began, my hands shaking, "my father died recently, and I've returned to see about his estate. Unfortunately, I don't believe he ever made a will, and I don't have the deed to his property. However, the gentleman at the land titles office suggested I could claim my father's land based on the fact that you and most of this town know me."

"So that's it." He sat back in his seat.

"Excuse me?"

"I wondered what on earth you were up to that night at the Fort Garry—what someone could possibly stand to gain by coming up with such an elaborate story. But now I know. You're after property that isn't rightfully yours."

"But I—"

"And furthermore, it never rightfully belonged to Patrick O'Sullivan in the first place. He won it by cheating in a card game. If you were his daughter, you'd know that."

I wanted to strangle him.

"I don't know how you managed to scrounge up so much information, miss, but I should think the fact that you did makes you a suspect in the disappearance of Bridget O'Sullivan. If I were you, I wouldn't come near this town."

What was he suggesting? I'm sure my mouth hung open, but once again I was at a loss for words.

"In fact, unless you want to be charged with fraud, you should get on the next train to Winnipeg and never come back. Who are you, really? You could do a lot better job of impersonating Bridget O'Sullivan if you had actually known her. But since she's probably been dead for five years, I'm guessing you never actually met. How'd you get information about her father's death or his land?"

"Bruce!" I finally managed to sputter. "Stop it! You know who I am."

"Then prove it."

I thought for a minute. "Ralph Neves!" How could he forget the jockey he'd portrayed back in our Grade Eight social studies class when we had to act out a current-events story?

"I beg your pardon?"

"You were Ralph Neves, I played the news reporter, and Victor Harrison was your horse! You must remember. Miss Johansen gave us an A!"

Bruce stared at me. "Anyone could have told you that story. Take my advice, Miss . . . Whoever-You-Are. Leave town before you get tangled up in something much bigger than you could imagine, with no lawyer to represent you."

He walked to the door and held it open, and there was nothing I could do but go.

Chapter 35

I sat on my narrow hotel bed, determined not to cry. It was a new day. Someone in this town was sure to recognize me. I thought immediately of Mrs. Harrison. She was such a kind woman, she would probably help whether she could tell who I was or not. But if Victor was running for mayor, he was obviously back to stay. How could I solicit his mother's assistance and avoid him at the same time? I rinsed out my silk blouse from the day before and hung it to dry while I pondered who else would be sure to know me. *Miss Johansen.* Was she still the teacher? I continued to weigh my options as I dressed in the second of my two outfits, a fitted emerald-green dress with black collar, cuffs, and belt.

When I inquired at the hotel desk I was told that Miss Johansen did, indeed, still teach at Bleak Landing School. Smiling confidently, I headed in that direction before I remembered that school would still be closed for the Christmas holiday and I wasn't sure where the teacher lived. Before I'd walked a block, though, I saw a familiar figure approaching: Mrs. Harrison! She hadn't changed a bit, and I could feel hope rising in my heart at the sight. Next to her walked a tall, well-built man whom I assumed to be her husband. With a jolt, I realized the man was much too young and too striking to be Mr. Harrison. Which could mean only one thing.

Saints preserve us!

I could suddenly see why Maxine had found Victor so attractive that day at Union Station.

Mrs. Harrison was talking animatedly. Victor appeared to be listening intently, nodding his head and keeping his gaze on the path in front of him. He had a limp to his gait that hadn't been there before, and suddenly I knew why he was home from the war.

As they stopped at the general store, he looked up in my direction. At first his gaze glanced right off me as he turned to follow his mother into the store. When he stopped to look back again, I could see a glimmer of recognition in his eyes, even from that distance.

I put up one hand to give a small wave. Victor Harrison might be a scoundrel, but I needed someone—anyone—to vouch for me. He turned and said something to his mother, and the two of them let the door close without entering the store. Mrs. Harrison looked up at her son and back at me. They started to head toward me, and I tried my hardest to smile.

"Hello, Mrs. Harrison," I said. With a swift glance up at her son, I added, "Victor." The glance was enough to confirm Maxine's assessment, although "dreamy" might have been a colossal understatement on her part.

"Bridget?" Mrs. Harrison studied my face, my hair—gazing at me with such intensity I could only stare at her throat, where a string of pink beads peeked out from beneath her coat.

"Yes, ma'am."

"Oh! It *is* you! Oh my dear, look at you!" She raised her hands as if she wanted to place them on my shoulders but lowered them again. "You're back! You're . . . you're *beautiful!*"

I could feel heat rising to my face.

"Bridget, I have a million questions! I got your letter, but I honestly thought we'd never see you again. What brings you back now?"

Victor had not said a word.

"I'm glad you know who I am." As briefly as I could, I explained that I'd decided to try to claim my father's property but that I held no deed or proof of identity. I told them about the fire and about my job coming to a sudden end. "I've already been to see Bruce Nilsen, but he insists I'm an impostor. So I'm soliciting help from anyone who can vouch for me."

"Well, of course we will!" Mrs. Harrison gushed. "We'll do whatever we can to help you get what's rightfully yours. Won't we, Vic?"

I looked up to find Victor staring at me. Would he side with his old pal Bruce? I knew he had recognized me, and now so had his mother. His jaw was set. When I glanced down at his hands, both fists were clenched.

Finally he spoke. "I don't know what Bruce is trying to prove, but we'll get to the bottom of this. Follow me." He turned on his heel and marched down the street so quickly that his mother and I had to run to keep up.

He swung open the door to Bruce's office. Bruce looked up from his desk in surprise, taking in the three of us.

Victor charged straight for the desk and leaned on it with both fists, his face about twelve inches from Bruce's. "Bridget O'Sullivan is back in town to settle her father's estate. What's this about you not granting her that right?"

Bruce sat back and scowled. "This impostor managed to fool you, Victor? Are you nuts? You knew that girl better than I did. This is *not* her." He looked at me. "I'm surprised you haven't hightailed it out of here yet, missy."

"The man at the land titles office said I needed two people to vouch for me," I said. "I've found them."

With a sneer, Bruce mimicked the pitch of my voice. "'*The man at the land titles office*' doesn't know what he's talking about. And even if he did, two people from the same family don't count."

Victor looked back at me with a scowl. Was he beginning to doubt my identity, too? He turned back to Bruce.

"Listen, Mister Fancy-Pants Lawyer," he said. "I don't know what you could possibly have to gain by not doing your job here, but sooner or later the truth will come out and it will not go well for you."

"On the contrary, Big Mouth. Sooner or later the truth will come out and it *will* go well for me!"

Victor's hands balled up again, and his mother stepped in when she saw Bruce's do the same. "Boys. Please. This reminds me of when you two used to scuffle in the barnyard over who could run the fastest. Now, Victor, if Bruce truly doesn't recognize Bridget—and that's understandable; just look at the gorgeous grown lady she's become—we'll simply have to find someone who does. It won't be that hard. Come along."

She took me by the arm and we headed back outside. I wasn't certain whether Victor was following, but after the bell tinkled, I heard his footsteps behind me.

"That rat," Victor said. What's he up to?"

"It doesn't matter." Mrs. Harrison still held on to my arm. "Now, Bridget, you must come home with us and stay as long as you need to. We'll get this all sorted out. You can share a room with Nancy, now that Peggy's married and gone. Where are your things?"

I didn't know whether to feel relief or angst. Given my rapidly depleting savings, I didn't dare spend one more night in the hotel. But accepting charity from the likes of Victor Harrison—even if he *was* inexplicably defending me from Bruce and not the other way around, and no matter how gorgeous he'd become—meant swallowing some awfully distasteful pride. Unfortunately, I was in no position to argue.

In no time, we'd gathered my few belongings from the hotel and were on our way to the Harrison farm in their pickup truck. This meant driving past my childhood home, and I steeled myself as we approached.

"Would you like to stop, Bridget?" Mrs. Harrison looked at me kindly.

I stole a glance at the shanty I'd called home from age seven to fifteen. It seemed even smaller now. Someone had taken the time to board up the windows, but the roof was missing nearly all its shingles. The screen door through which I'd overheard my father bargain for my virginity now hung at an angle by its bottom hinge. Even through a dusting of snow, I could see that Pa's garden was nothing but tangled weeds. I swallowed hard and shook my head slowly. "Perhaps I'll walk over later."

"Of course, dear. Whenever you're ready." We rode in silence a moment. "Your father's grave has a nice little cross on it. Our church saw to it."

When I looked at her in shock, she quickly added, "We have a fund for such things."

I was still pondering how Pa would have reacted to the idea of the Protestants buying him a grave marker when we pulled into the Harrisons' farmyard. It was just as I remembered, right down to the mongrel dog on the front porch—except now, instead of running to greet us, he lay with his chin on his paws, tail thumping on the floorboards.

Victor and I both reached for my suitcase at the same time.

"I've got it." He grabbed it and headed for the house. "Hey there, Bingo. Too lazy to get up and say hello, you old thing?"

The dog noticed me and limped over with an inquiring expression. I held out a hand to pet his nose and felt strangely warmed by his acceptance.

"Do you remember Bridget, Bingo?" Mrs. Harrison ran a hand over the dog's back. "I'll bet he does. Dogs have better memories than a lot of people."

We walked into the Harrison kitchen, and the rest of the family greeted me in surprise. I'd have known Victor's father anywhere. But the sight of his siblings made me realize why it might be difficult for people to recognize *me*—they had all grown up! If I'd stumbled across them in some other context, I wouldn't have known them. Nancy, Anna, and Bobby all said hello shyly.

Lunch was on the table, and Nancy set an extra place for me. I'd skipped breakfast, and the Norwegian *lapskaus*, a stew served with a lovely bread they called *fjellbrød*, was about the most delicious thing I'd ever tasted. Over lunch, I told my story again.

"Miss Johansen will vouch for you, Bridget," Mr. Harrison said. "Victor, why don't you drive Bridget over there after lunch and have a chat with your old teacher?"

Bobby piped up. "Miss Johansen's visiting her parents for Christmas, Pa. She prob'ly won't be back until Sunday evening."

My heart sank. Sunday seemed a lifetime away.

"Oh, surely we can find someone else who isn't in our family." Mrs. Harrison passed me a plate of cookies. "Of course, you're welcome to stay as long as you like, Bridget. But I'm sure you're eager to settle your business. Now, who can you think of who knew you well and might still be around? What about some of your old classmates?"

"There's Rebecca Olsen." Anna looked at Victor with a sly grin. I wasn't sure what the grin was about. I only recalled that Rebecca had always had a thing for Victor but little use for me.

I thought hard. "Francine Lundarson and Margaret Mikkelsen?"

Victor shook his head. "Francine moved to Saskatchewan, and I think Margaret joined the service."

"Mr. and Mrs. McNally?" I suggested. "I noticed their house was gone, but are they still around? Not that I really saw them all that often. I don't think they liked Pa much."

"They're still in town." Victor took a bite of cookie.

A few more names were tossed around, but it became clear that the O'Sullivans had not been popular in Bleak Landing. My best bet was Miss Johansen.

After lunch, Victor asked if he could talk to me for a minute. We went and sat in the living room I'd always admired. It was even cozier and prettier than I remembered, with the Christmas tree still standing in the corner, but I felt uncomfortable about just the two of us being in there. I could see his sisters moving around in the kitchen through the open archway.

"Bridget," Victor began in a near whisper, taking a seat on the chair nearest to mine. "It's true that a lot of people around here think you're dead. I wondered, too, until I saw you that day at Union Station. Then you sent my mother that letter. I'm glad you're all right and I'm glad you're here. I was afraid I'd never get a chance to apologize."

I waited, wishing I could escape. It wasn't that my old bully didn't owe me an apology. I just wasn't sure I wanted one.

"I know I was horrible to you when we were kids, and I knew better. My parents didn't raise me like that. I'm really sorry." Victor sighed and turned his gaze toward the window and the snowy farmyard beyond it. "I wish I could go back and do it over, respect you more. I know you had things tough, and I . . . well, I could have been your champion. I could have influenced the other kids to treat you more kindly."

The man was full of himself; that part hadn't changed. Still, the apology did seem genuine. When he returned his gaze to me, his face held the same contrite expression I'd seen all too often on Pa's after he'd beaten me black and blue and then recovered from his drunken stupor. Victor wasn't the same boy he'd been, I could see that. He'd gone to war and returned wounded. Who knew what all he'd seen?

"Bridget, I can't tell you how many times I've asked God to forgive me for the way I treated you." He'd been focused on my hands, which I had folded on my lap. Now he looked me in the eyes and I glanced away, feeling an unfamiliar ache at the warmth I saw in his. "Maybe—maybe your coming back here is my opportunity to make things up to you. Will you accept my apology?"

I felt cornered. Here I was, staying in his family's home. Victor was clearly well respected in this town, and I needed him to vouch for me. How could I say no? I nodded my head in silence. But I refused to look for very long into his remorseful blue eyes.

Chapter 36

*V*ictor had no idea why God was leading him to speak on forgiveness this Sunday, but it was the first Sunday of the year. Perhaps folks needed to make things right with others before facing 1944.

As always, when God gave him a topic, he examined his own heart first. He'd already worked through the issue of the German bullet that left him with a limp. With no name or face to attach to the soldier who'd fired that gun, Victor had chosen to forgive the Nazi army in general for this particular injustice.

Were there others he needed to forgive, areas where he was holding a grudge? *Show me, Lord,* he'd prayed. Instantly, Bruce Nilsen came to mind.

Victor had spent the last several days accompanying Bridget to various homes and businesses around Bleak Landing, but it seemed Bruce was a step ahead of them. Rumors abounded that an impostor was in town, posing as Patrick O'Sullivan's daughter in an effort to claim his property. This town loved nothing better than latching on to a good scandal. So far, everyone had said the same thing: "I remember Bridget O'Sullivan, but I've never seen *you* before, miss."

Victor hoped today's mission—visiting her father's grave—would prove more valuable.

"Think, Bridget." He walked with her to the little cemetery. "Is there a story you could tell, a memory you share with someone from the community that only the two of you would know about?"

She only shook her head, and he didn't press the matter further. After leading her to her father's grave, he brushed the snow away from the headstone and stepped away to give her some privacy. She didn't sit down, didn't cry, didn't speak. She merely stood there and stared.

And though he tried not to, Victor stared, too. At *her*. Having her in his home had shown him that although Bridget had changed very much on the outside, she was still the same hurting girl with the hard edge. Possibly she was hurting even more now. He knew she was not the kind of woman he ought to pursue. She came with so many scars, had so much difficulty relating to others. Not to mention that she still harbored scorn for him and his childhood bullying. And who could blame her? Still, his breath caught in his throat and his heart rate quickened every time she looked at him. He wanted desperately to undo the hurts that had broken her and to see her embrace the love of the Heavenly Father he was learning to trust more and more.

Bridget turned from her father's grave as though ready to leave. Then she stopped short at another headstone, about five graves over from her father's. Victor joined her to see what she was looking at so intently. The marker said: **ALBERT ROPER. JANUARY 29, 1892–APRIL 15, 1937.**

Victor turned to look at Bridget's face. It had grown pale, and he saw her shudder. "Do you remember Mr. Roper, Bridget?"

She nodded slowly, then pointed to the dates on the stone. "He died on my fifteenth birthday."

Victor nodded. "How about that?" Still, Bridget kept staring silently at the stone. What had this man been to her?

"What happened to him?" she asked.

"Complications of diabetes, they said. I only remember that because of Ma going on about the importance of looking after our health, holding Mr. Roper up as a bad example. I didn't really know him."

She turned from the grave so abruptly and headed back toward the Harrison farm with such a determined stride that Victor was forced to scurry to catch up. No more was said about Bridget's father or Mr. Roper.

It was a mild day, and when they got home he saw his siblings waging a snowball fight in the yard. He quickly scooped up a handful of white stuff to form his own ammunition, knowing he'd be nailed as soon as he got within range.

"Bridget! Join us!" Anna called out. "Girls against boys!"

Convinced that Bridget would scoff at the idea, Victor was surprised when she ran toward his sisters with a giggle and began to form snowballs of her own. He joined Bobby behind a hay bale and the two of them pelted the girls, who used Bingo's doghouse as their barricade. Soon they were engaged in all-out war. Only instead of the screams of bombs or the rat-a-tat of guns, this war was accompanied by delightful squeals of laughter and the happy barking of a dog who wanted in on the fun.

By the time the battle ended, Victor was soaked to the skin. The girls collapsed into exhausted heaps and began to make snow angels. When they stood to admire their creations, he caught a glimpse of a very different Bridget. Her face was aglow with delight, her smile stretching wide and her eyes sparkling with merriment. The joy of inclusion, of belonging, was clearly written all over her. This was the Bridget who had been buried inside the sad waif he'd gone to school with, the one who was never invited to play.

She'd been in there all along.

He wasn't sure how long he stood there, enjoying the scene. But somehow the moment made him ache with longing, and he felt that if he kept watching her, something inside him would crack in half. He brushed the snow off his coat and pants and headed toward the front porch. Just as he was about to pull the door open, a hard snowball clobbered him squarely on the back of his head. His hand flew to his hair and he turned around, expecting Bobby to be the culprit.

But it was Bridget O'Sullivan who stood there, a triumphant and mischievous smile lighting up her face. He grinned back at her and stepped into the warmth of the house to finish preparing his Sunday sermon.

Chapter 37

I sat between Anna and Mrs. Harrison in the front pew. The congregation no longer met in the Bleak Landing schoolhouse but had constructed a pretty, new white building that reminded me very much of Maxine's church in Pinehaven. I'd managed to push thoughts of Maxine from my mind for the most part. Until now. The experience of living out a piece of my childhood fantasy—being part of the Harrison family—had made me remember I still had issues to sort out with Maxine. And now Victor had the audacity to preach about forgiveness.

"Before we can truly forgive," he said, "we have to understand what forgiveness is *not*. When you forgive someone, it doesn't mean that what they did to you is okay. It doesn't invalidate the pain they caused. It doesn't mean they were right. It's not pretending an offense never happened. It's not necessarily even something we do for the offender."

I wondered where Victor was heading with this. I'd sort of believed all those things about forgiveness, and now he was saying they weren't true. If it wasn't any of that, then what was it? And why had he chosen this topic to talk about, anyway? Did he suspect my acceptance of his apology wasn't completely genuine?

I was still reeling from the knowledge that Mr. Roper had died the very day I left Bleak Landing. What did it mean? Would I have been safe if I'd stayed, or would my father have traded me away to some other old lecher? And how on earth did God fit into this picture?

"Mostly, forgiveness is something we do for ourselves," Victor was saying. "When we choose to forgive, we take the power away from our offender. They no longer wield control over how we feel or how we act. We are free to act in love instead of being held captive by our grudges."

These were new thoughts to me, and I looked around the room to see how others were responding. While most remained stone-faced, I saw a few heads, including Mrs. Harrison's, nodding in agreement. I hardly knew where to begin the list of offenders in my life, but God himself was right up at the top, for taking away my mother. Then there was Pa . . . Bruce and Victor . . . Mr. Roper . . . Mr. Nilsen . . . some of the mean girls at Weinberger's . . . which brought me back to Maxine. And once I acknowledged my need to forgive Maxine, I knew I needed *her* forgiveness, too.

For every person who had hurt me along the way, I realized, there'd been good people who had helped me. Miss Johansen . . . Mrs. Harrison . . . Mr. Weinberger . . . his daughter Caroline . . . Mrs. Watson . . . and, once again, Maxine. And her family. Now the whole Harrison family was treating me as if I was one of their own, welcoming me into the loving warmth of their home and trying to help me win back what was mine.

Had it really only been a week since I'd asked God to show himself to me? It seemed a lifetime had passed since the night of the fire, but now my eyes were slowly opening to something I'd failed to see before. A whole string of people had been supportive and loyal, all my life. Had they been God's way of showing himself?

"When we refuse to forgive," Victor went on, "it's like drinking poison and expecting it to kill the person who offended us. Instead, it only kills *us*. God wants more for us. He wants us to forgive each other and be truly free."

Like a real pastor, Victor sprinkled his sermon with passages of scripture and stories from his life. But it was that image of drinking poison that captured my mind, and I hardly heard anything else after it. By the time Victor had wrapped up his talk, I was swiping at tears. I remained seated while the congregation sang the doxology and gradually dispersed. I was vaguely aware of Mrs. Harrison still seated beside me. She handed me a handkerchief and waited quietly while the church emptied. When only the two of us remained in the room, she spoke gently.

"Do you want to talk, Bridget?"

I wept in earnest then. I felt embarrassed, but Mrs. Harrison only wrapped her arms around me and pulled me toward her. She stroked my hair and murmured softly. "It's okay. It's okay to cry. You've had so much loss."

When my sobs finally settled down, I looked into her caring face. "Did you ever speak to my father?" My voice was barely above a whisper. "Did you tell him I was all right?"

She stared back at me, as though gauging what to say. She nodded. "I did."

"And . . . ?"

She sighed. "He was relieved. I'm sure he was."

I knew what her next answer would be, but I asked the question anyway. "What did he say?"

She paused. "Nothing. He didn't say anything, Bridget." She patted my hand. "But I am positive I saw tears welling in his eyes. I felt certain he was grateful I'd told him."

I stared down at my shoes.

After she'd allowed some time for that to sink in, she asked, "What is God saying to you, Bridget?"

I swallowed hard. "I don't want to drink poison, like Victor said. I have a lot of people to forgive, Mrs. Harrison. I don't know if I can do it."

"Do you want to?" she asked.

I nodded.

"Then that's a terrific start. God knows your heart. None of us can forgive everything on our own, but he makes all things possible. Ask him for help, Bridget. He longs to meet you where you are."

"B-but . . . he's one of the people I'm angry with," I sputtered.

"Then tell him that. He can handle it. In fact, that's his favorite kind of prayer, because it's honest." She was holding my hand now, stroking one thumb across the top of mine. "And anyway, he already knows."

For the first time in my life, I prayed a prayer that wasn't merely a challenge flung out to God but was instead a genuine plea for help and strength. Out loud and with Victor's mother as my witness, I declared to God that I wanted to forgive those who'd hurt me and to be truly grateful for those God had sent to help me. I was beginning to see that, in some cases, people fell into both categories.

I spent the rest of that Sunday in quiet contemplation as a new sort of peace settled over me, calming my spirit in a way I hadn't experienced before. As darkness fell, I stepped out onto the Harrisons' porch, where Bingo lay curled up on the swing. He raised his head to look at me and thumped his tail a couple of times before laying his chin on his paws again.

"Hello, boy." I gazed up at the clear sky. I hadn't seen stars like that since I left Bleak Landing, and hadn't ever appreciated them in quite the same way I did now. Could it be true that the same God who created the stars cared for me and all my trifling sorrows? I leaned against the porch railing, a blanket wrapped around my shoulders. I heard the door open behind me.

"Want some company?" Victor was at my side, and for the first time maybe ever, his presence didn't make me feel tense. "Besides that lazy old mutt, I mean." We stood there in comfortable silence awhile.

"Sure is beautiful," I murmured.

"Mm-hmm." He leaned against the post and turned so he was facing me. "Sure is."

"You just don't see stars like that in the city."

He wasn't looking at the sky. His eyes were on me, his lopsided grin exposing straight, white teeth. I could feel my heart thumping.

"I hope you stick around, Bridget. I'd like to get to know you better."

I couldn't help but smile back. "What would you like to know? My favorite color? Shoe size?"

He studied my face, that old, familiar boyhood grin that used to make me want to punch him now warming my heart. Now, instead of mockery, I saw something like admiration in his smile. Had it been there all along, and I just missed it?

"I can't think of anything I *wouldn't* like to know about you." He turned his eyes toward the sky again and studied the expanse of stars. "If you could do something big with your life—I mean if money was not an obstacle—what would you do?"

I'd never been asked that before, and had to pause to think about it. "I don't know. Maybe . . . find a way to help poor immigrant kids get a better start in a Canadian school?"

Victor turned around and raised himself up to sit on the railing. "That sounds like a worthwhile dream."

"Yeah, well . . . unfortunately, money definitely *is* an obstacle. And even if it wasn't . . . it's pretty hard to imagine myself doing anything remotely *big*. I've got no home, no job, no family. Few friends. I can't even prove my identity." I pulled the blanket tighter around my shoulders. "Just when I thought I was moving up in the world, everything got ripped away. I feel so lost."

"You can't be lost as long as God knows exactly where you are. And he does, Bridget. God knows *who* you are, too. He knows your name. Sometimes that's all that really matters."

I took a minute to try to absorb that and asked, "How about you? What would *you* do?"

He paused, chuckling. "Never would have thought it in a million years, but this pastoring thing is kind of growing on me. I sure love it when I can help someone understand how much God loves them."

I looked at him out of the corner of my eye. "What did your mother tell you?"

"My mother? What do you mean?"

"About my conversation with her after church today."

"Nothing. Why? Should she have?"

"No. Never mind." I turned to look him squarely in the eye. "Thanks for your message this morning." I looked down and fidgeted with the edge of the blanket. "I've got a ways to go, I'm afraid."

Victor took a deep breath and let it out slowly. "We all do, Bridget." He was gazing into my eyes so intently, I couldn't look away. Then, with the back of his fingers, he gently brushed the side of my face and ran his thumb along my jawline, tilting my face up and leaning toward me just a smidge. Was he going to kiss me? And why did I find myself moving closer, hoping he would?

Whatever was about to happen was interrupted by a giant fur ball that suddenly wedged itself between us, nearly knocking Victor right off the railing into a snowbank on the other side.

"Bingo!" Victor scolded. "You sure pick the worst times to need affection." He hopped down and crouched to rub the dog's back.

"He's just jealous," I said. And frankly, in that moment, I found myself a little jealous of Bingo.

That evening, I asked Mrs. Harrison for some writing paper and sat down at her kitchen table to compose a letter to Maxine.

Chapter 38

First thing Monday morning, Victor pushed open the door to Bruce Nilsen's office and found the man sitting at his desk.

Bruce looked up. "Good morning, Victor. Do you have an appointment?"

"Oh, knock it off, Bruce." Victor sat down without waiting for an invitation. "It's not like you've got clients lined up waiting to see you."

Bruce glanced at the door as if willing a customer to walk in. "What can I do for you?"

"You can quit playing this stupid game. I don't know what you think you have to gain by being so belligerent, but you know as well as I do that Bridget O'Sullivan is who she says she is, and she's entitled to her pa's place." He leaned forward, his forearms on Bruce's desk.

"I don't know any such thing. *You're* the one who's been duped, Harrison. Or has that pretty impostor got you so addlepated you can't remember the smelly, skinny little woodpecker who used to sit in front of us? No one can change that much, that quickly. She doesn't even sound like Bridget!" Bruce lit a cigarette and leaned back in his seat. "Did I tell you I saw her in the city?"

"Bridget?"

"No. This impostor. She came up to me at a restaurant, with some friend who did all the talking. And guess what?"

"What?"

"She didn't even have Bridget's name right. Said it was 'Sullivan.' That's how I knew for sure it wasn't her." Bruce blew out a big puff of smoke.

"Well, how did she know *you*?"

"Beats me. Actually, I think she worked in the university offices. So she'd have had access to my student files, my home address. That's why she looked vaguely familiar."

"So you admit it! She looked familiar!"

Bruce let out a frustrated sigh. "Quit twisting my words! *Nobody* in this town thinks that girl is Bridget O'Sullivan, Victor! Nobody except you and your gullible family . . . and even *they're* probably questioning your judgment behind your back."

"All right, then tell me something else," Victor challenged. "If she really *is* an impostor, wouldn't she be trying harder to look like the 'smelly, skinny little woodpecker that used to sit in front of us,' as you put it? So we'd all recognize her?"

"Sure. If she'd ever actually met Bridget. My guess is, she knows just enough to know there's unclaimed property here and that the real Bridget is missing—or dead—"

"Stop it." Victor stared at him. Did Bruce really believe his own rhetoric? It was amazing what people could accept if they tried hard enough. He knew that was true from going to war and seeing Nazi propaganda pamphlets. He'd had enough.

"How did you end up with Bridget's locket?" he blurted. "And don't you dare argue with me, Nilsen. I know it's hers. Your father had something to do with her disappearance from Bleak Landing, and if you try to deny it I'll expose him to the whole town."

"I already told you, that locket has been in my family—"

Victor jumped to his feet and leaned across the desk. "Sell it to me!"

Bruce stopped in midsentence. *"What?"*

"You heard me. Any idiot knows it's not your family heirloom. It's no use to you. You're so determined it's a thing of value—it must be money you want. So let me pay you for it. How much do you want?"

"What do *you* want with it?" Bruce sneered. "Gonna let that con artist have the necklace *and* the land?

"You're the con artist, Nilsen. Name your price for the locket."

Bruce studied Victor's face, exhaling a long stream of cigarette smoke. "You can't afford it."

"Try me." Even as he said the words, Victor wondered if Bruce would call his bluff and name an exorbitant price. All he really had to trade was the old McNally property or whatever cash he might be able to get if he sold it. The money he'd saved to build his house was already spent on materials.

"All right. I'll name my price." Bruce tapped his cigarette in the ashtray. "I want you to drop out of the election."

Victor froze. Slowly, he sank to his chair. "Are you serious? I pull out and you'll give me the necklace?"

Bruce nodded. *"And* you keep this between us. Can I trust you to stay quiet?"

Victor looked out the window. Some kids hurried by on their way to school, lunch boxes swinging. He turned back to Bruce. "I've kept quiet about your sister, haven't I?"

Bruce went pale. His voice got very quiet. "You have."

"Anything else?"

"No."

Victor looked him straight in the eyes for a full ten seconds before speaking. When he did, one word said it all: "Deal."

Chapter 39

I waited until I saw children on the playground before approaching Bleak Landing School. Two newer-looking outhouses stood like a pair of soldiers behind the schoolhouse. Unlike the privy of my childhood, these outhouses were made without doors. Instead, each had a sort of fenced-maze entrance that provided privacy while remaining accessible. Little else had changed. Boys were building a snow fort on one side; girls forming snowmen on the other. They stopped their recess activity to watch me, and I heard muted whispers that did not raise my confidence.

When I stepped inside, I was instantly transported back in time by the familiar smell of the classroom—a combination of chalk dust, ink, and wet mittens.

Miss Johansen sat working at her desk and looked up at the sound of the door closing. My heart pounded.

"Good morning, Miss Johansen." I walked up to her desk with as much poise as I could muster. An expression I couldn't identify immediately covered the teacher's face. Mistrust? Recognition? I couldn't tell. "It's me. Bridget."

She merely looked at me, so I spoke again. "Bridget O'Sullivan? I know I've been away awhile. I'm really glad you're still here."

"I was told to expect you," she said.

"You were?"

She nodded. "Yes, I was told someone claiming to be Bridget O'Sullivan was in town and that she'd likely be asking me to vouch for her identity. Is that why you've come?"

"Does that mean you will?" I smiled. "Oh, I knew if anyone in this town remembered me it would be you, Miss Johansen."

The door opened, and Victor made his way through the rows of desks to stand beside me. "Good morning, Miss Johansen," he said.

"Good morning, Victor."

"Has Bridget had a chance to tell you her story?" he asked.

"I didn't need to," I said. "News travels fast around here."

Victor looked at me and back at the teacher. "Bruce has been to see you? That weasel." He removed his cap and thumped it against his leg in frustration. "I suppose he warned you not to believe her."

"It doesn't matter what anyone told me or didn't tell me." She looked back at me. "I remember Bridget O'Sullivan very well."

"Oh, thank you, Miss Johansen!" I wanted to hug her. "I can't tell you how relieved—"

"That's why I'm still unconvinced that *you* are *her*."

I couldn't believe what I was hearing. "B-but, Miss Johansen—"

"I remember all my students. And if you'll excuse me, I have twenty-four of them who need my attention now." She picked up a handbell and headed for the door to call the children in from recess.

"Wait. Miss Johansen," Victor said. "There must be some way Bridget can prove who she is. Surely you can think of something she could tell you that would convince you."

She stopped and looked at us, thinking. Had Victor managed to cast doubt on what Bruce had already convinced her of?

"All right," she said. "I loaned Bridget a book one day. Can you tell me which book it was?"

I stammered. "You—you loaned me many books, Miss Johansen."

"I mean I visited the O'Sullivans' home. After Bridget got in trouble at school. But instead of speaking with her father, I pretended to be simply loaning her a book. And I know exactly which book it was. Do you?"

I remembered the incident. I recalled the relief I'd felt. I recalled Victor's visit later that evening. Most of all, I recalled the beating my father gave me after he verified that I'd been in trouble. But for the life of me, I could not remember the book.

"Bridget?" Victor sounded hopeful. "Can you remember?"

I felt panic rising inside as I tried to think. "Um. *Pride and Prejudice*?" I didn't know if taking a wild guess would do more harm than good, but it was out there now.

Miss Johansen slowly shook her head. "That's what I thought." She moved toward the door again. "If you were Bridget, you'd have also remembered that your father didn't allow you to keep my book that day."

Victor dashed forward and took hold of her arm. "Miss Johansen, wait! That was a long time ago, and Bridget read *all* your books. Why, I bet she could tell you how many you had on your shelf!"

"Seventy-one!" I blurted. Why couldn't she have asked me that in the first place?

Miss Johansen looked at me. "I have no idea how many books I had on my shelf back then, nor how many I have now. More than that, certainly. You're wasting your time. And mine, and the time of my students."

"Please, Miss Johansen," Victor persisted. "There must be something else. Something that only you and Bridget would know."

The teacher shook her head and pulled her arm out of Victor's grasp, turning toward the door. Abruptly, she stopped and turned back. "There is one thing I can think of."

"Yes?" Victor sounded so hopeful, I was immediately frantic that it would be another question I couldn't answer. At this point, I was more worried about disappointing him than I was about losing out on my inheritance. If this continued, even the Harrisons wouldn't believe I was me.

Miss Johansen kept her eyes on Victor. "The town hall meeting and election is tomorrow night. Obviously, you'll be there." She turned to me. "Make sure *you're* there, too."

Then she marched to the front steps of the school and rang her bell as if her life depended on it.

Chapter 40

*A*fter we left the school, Victor and I walked in silence to the general store, where we found his mother selecting apples for her shopping basket.

"Got a couple more errands," Victor said without further explanation. "I'll catch up with you at home."

I wandered to the display of yarn and admired the selection while I waited for Mrs. Harrison to finish. On the way to the counter with her groceries, she found me studying a pattern for a beautiful scarf.

"I was always too embarrassed to admit I never learned to knit or crochet," she said. "In my day, not having such a basic skill was like—well, like not knowing how to read!"

And that's how it began. Once she found out I knew how to use a crochet hook, nothing would do but adding four hooks and a very large skein of red yarn to her purchases. Now she, Nancy, Anna, and I sat in the Harrisons' living room while I tried to pass along the skill Maxine's mother had shared with me.

"If you don't mind my asking, Bridget, who taught you?" Mrs. Harrison was catching on quickly, her chain already a foot long.

I told her about Maxine, how we met at the garment factory and how our friendship bloomed. How her family welcomed me as one of their own. "Much like yours has," I said softly.

"You must miss her."

I nodded but didn't mention our falling out. I'd mailed my letter to Maxine just that morning, addressed to the hair salon where she worked in case she'd moved. Of course, for all I knew, she no longer worked there, either.

"Will you go back to Winnipeg once your land claim is sorted out?" Nancy asked.

I wasn't sure how to answer. "I suppose if the factory reopens and I can have my job back." It was hard to imagine any kind of future for myself right now. I wondered how I'd even survive until tomorrow's town hall meeting. I told myself there was no point wondering what question Miss Johansen was going to ask to test me. Either I'd know the answer or I wouldn't. Still, the whole thing made me nervous.

"I hope you stay," Nancy said. Her sister nodded with a shy grin.

"I do, too," their mother agreed. "We need someone like you to class this place up, Bridget. Catch us up on the latest fashions and hairstyles."

"Will you put my hair in victory rolls, like yours?" Nancy asked.

"Sure!" I said. Before I knew it, Victor's sisters had set up shop in the middle of the living room and I was curling and pinning both girls' hair. "I'm not as good at it as Maxine. She's a trained hairdresser."

"You should invite her to come visit," Mrs. Harrison said as she worked on her stitches.

Never in a million years would I have thought I'd ever want Maxine to see Bleak Landing, but now the idea didn't seem so outrageous.

None of us had heard Victor enter the house. "Ask *who* to come visit?" His voice rang out from the kitchen, making my heart do that funny fluttery thing I'd noticed before. He leaned on the doorway to the living room, arms folded and held tilted at a cockeyed angle. "We takin' in more strays?"

I might have felt offended if it weren't for the ear-to-ear smile that lit up his face.

"Victor!" his mother scolded.

"It's all right, Mrs. Harrison," I said. "I *am* a stray."

"We were talking about Bridget's friend Maxine." Nancy fluffed her victory curls around her face with one hand while gazing into the hand-held mirror she clutched with the other. "She's an honest-to-goodness hairdresser!"

"The girl from the train station?" Victor said.

"The same." I smiled, remembering how smitten Maxine had been at the sight of Victor in his uniform. It occurred to me that they'd make a good pair, but something inside me objected to the thought.

"You free to go for a walk, Bridget?" Victor asked.

"Uh . . ." I looked around. "We're kind of in the middle of a project here—"

"It's fine, Bridget. Go ahead. The girls have enough victory curls to win the war, and I've got the hang of this stitch." Mrs. Harrison's crocheted chain was now longer than Victor was tall.

⌇

"I wondered if you might be ready to see your old place," Victor said as we headed out into the fresh air. "If you are, I'm willing to go with you. If not, that's fine, too."

I hesitated. We'd driven past my old home several times now, and that was getting easier. But was I ready for a close-up look?

"I need to check on something at my own property," Victor said. "If, when we get there, you don't want to go on to yours, we don't have to."

"Okay." I loved the way he said *yours*. He really did believe I was me, and somehow his believing in me made it easier to forgive him for all the pain he'd caused.

An overcast sky and absence of wind made for much more comfortable temperatures than January normally brought, but we still had to walk at a fast clip to stay warm. Hundreds of small birds twittered from among the bare branches of poplar trees and brought life to an otherwise barren landscape. Small snowdrifts made intricate patterns on the gravel road.

"Nervous about the meeting tomorrow?" Victor kicked a stone to the ditch.

"Yes."

"It'll be fine," he said. "I've been praying about it."

I had been, too. But somehow, I couldn't shake the notion that Victor's prayers carried more weight than mine. Knowing that he prayed for me filled me with an unfamiliar sense of well-being. It was almost as if my security didn't actually hinge on whether or not I could persuade Bleak Landing of my identity.

"You know what's funny?" I said.

Victor turned so he was walking backward, facing me. "No, what?"

"When I left Bleak Landing, I wanted nothing more than to become someone else—anyone but Bridget O'Sullivan. I never dreamed I'd be back here trying to convince people that that's exactly who I am."

"That's not the only funny thing." Victor spun around so that he was walking beside me again. He scooped up some snow to form a ball, tossed it in the air, and caught it. "*I* never dreamed Bridget O'Sullivan would turn out to be the prettiest girl in Bleak Landing. I'd have been a lot nicer to her if I'd known."

I intercepted his snowball, catching it myself. I ran ahead, turned around, and flung it at him. I missed by a mile, but the distraction gave me a chance to hide what I felt sure was a blush, and to recover from it.

We'd reached the old McNally property, now Victor's. I found it funny how country property always seemed to retain the name of its former owners. Victor's new digs would probably not be referred to as "the old Harrison place" until Victor was long gone. He showed me around, telling me about his hopes and dreams for his house and garden. A large stack of lumber waited under a heavy tarpaulin that he peeled back. He asked me to count the pieces while he jotted down the numbers on a little notepad.

I did so, distracted by the property next door.

"Ready to go have a look?" he asked softly.

I nodded.

"Shall I wait here?"

I nodded again. "I think I need to do this alone." My home had been the shame of my existence as a kid. How much worse would it be now?

With a deep breath, I strode over to the shanty and tried the door—half hoping that whoever had boarded up the windows had also nailed the door shut. To my surprise, it surrendered easily. The door swung open about a foot, until the bottom scraped on the floor where it had buckled. I squeezed through the opening and waited for my eyes to adjust to the darkness. Once I was in, I heaved the door all the way open to let in more light.

I surveyed the room. Our rickety kitchen table and two chairs—one overturned, the other with only three legs now—remained in their usual place. The rest was a shamble of broken bits of linoleum, scattered rags, random splinters of wood, and rat droppings. The old sofa that had served as my bed still sagged against the opposite wall, the remains of a blanket drooping to the floor. A curtain rod hung from the window by one end only, the curtain shredded and faded to a colorless heap where it met the floor. The ceiling had been falling in chunks. The walls were pocked with fist-size holes. And everything—*everything*—was filthy. How could Pa have been living here as recently as three months ago?

I could not bring myself to move from my spot, to go look into my father's bedroom. Mrs. Harrison had told me that after he died, she and two friends had come to the house and packed up his clothing for the missionary barrel. I joked that the missionaries probably didn't want them, but deep down I knew the joke wasn't funny. As I stood there now, I almost expected Pa to step through that bedroom door, to see me and start in about where I'd been and how he was going to teach me a lesson. I could picture him in his undershirt and trousers, suspenders hanging loose around his hips. He'd go for the willow switch he kept in the corner. I looked over there now, but the spot where it had always stood was empty.

I closed my eyes, willing the memories to fade. Instead, they only became keener. I could hear Pa's slurred speech, smell the bitter scents of whiskey and sweat. I thought I heard the crack of the willow switch and opened my eyes with a startled gasp, turning in the direction of the sound.

Victor stood in the doorway.

"You all right?"

That's when I realized tears were running down my face. I tried as hard as I could to make them stop, but they kept coming, accompanied by ugly gulps. In two strides, Victor was at my side. He wrapped his arms around me and pulled me close. "It's okay," he said. "It's okay. He can't hurt you anymore."

And there it was. I'd never told anyone, but Victor knew the truth. Maybe he'd seen my bruises when we were kids, or maybe he could just read my heart now. But however he knew, he *knew*. I sobbed against his chest. I had not been inside this house for nearly seven years. I'd never seen it in such horrible condition. But for the first time in my life, I felt safe inside its walls.

Chapter 41

$\mathcal{V}$ictor sat between his father and Bridget as the community hall filled with people. Most, he knew, had come for the free coffee he could smell percolating in the kitchen. There were sure to be sandwiches, pickles, and possibly even cake later if the women had pooled their sugar ration cards.

Mr. Lundarson pounded a gavel on the podium at the front and called the meeting to order. "Please rise for the singing of 'God Save the King.'"

In an off-key baritone, he led the group through the anthem. The last note dissolved into the sound of chairs scraping as everyone sat down, and he pounded his gavel again.

"As you know, tonight we get to hear from our mayoral candidates and will have a chance to ask them whatever questions we might have before we vote. However, we do have a few other items of business to cover, as well as a last-minute item Miss Johansen asked me to add to the agenda. And before we get to *that*, we'll hear news from the front. Who has a letter to share?"

One by one, three mothers and one wife rose to read letters, or excerpts from them, from their soldiers abroad. Victor listened, knowing from experience that the men worked hard to keep their words positive and hopeful. He could easily imagine what horrors they had left out. His time overseas seemed like a different lifetime now, and he sent up a prayer of gratitude that he was home. And then another for the men who were not.

"Thank you, ladies." Mr. Lundarson said. "Did we miss anyone?" He looked around the room. "If not, let's carry on with our business. First up: the drainage on Fattigdom Road."

Victor's knee bobbed up and down anxiously as his neighbors addressed an issue of a culvert in need of replacement and a corner that needed a stop sign because poor old Mrs. Jorgenson's cat had nearly been run over. He couldn't believe how passionate some people could get over petty issues. How long was this going to take? He looked around for Miss Johansen but couldn't spot her.

"And next on our agenda . . ." Mr. Lundarson looked down at his notes. "The issue of the Patrick O'Sullivan property on the edge of town. I don't think there's anyone here who isn't already aware that we have a visitor in our midst who is claiming legal rights to that property. I'd like to call her up now, along with Miss Elizabeth Johansen, Mr. Victor Harrison, and Mr. Bruce Nilsen. Look at this, folks. A teacher, a pastor, a lawyer. Bleak Landing's finest, right here." There was a halfhearted smattering of applause.

Victor supported Bridget's elbow as she rose, and followed her to the front. Bruce stood on the other side of the podium. There was no sign of Miss Johansen, and Mr. Lundarson called for her again.

"Well, no matter. We can proceed." He turned to Bridget. "Young lady, tell us your story."

Victor felt proud of Bridget. She stood tall and appeared confident, even though he knew she was probably shaking on the inside. Did she have any idea how lovely she was, how easily she outshone the women in Bleak Landing? Her navy suit perfectly complemented her red hair and fair complexion. He could understand how people didn't recognize her as the waif she'd been.

"My name is Bridget Mary O'Sullivan. My father, Patrick, and I came to Bleak Landing from Ireland when I was seven years old. We lost my mother, Mary, and my brother, Tommy, on the voyage. As you know, my father passed away, and I am here to claim his property. I do not believe he wrote any will, nor do I hold the deed. My only identification was recently destroyed by a house fire. Whatever birth record I may have had was left behind in Ireland. I am counting on the recognition of the people of Bleak Landing in order to redeem what is mine."

Bridget stepped back and Victor moved to the podium.

"My family has kept in touch with Bridget since she left town." He knew he was stretching the truth on that, but kept on going. "I was the one who sent the telegram to her at the home of her employer in Winnipeg, informing her of her father's passing. The fact that she received the telegram at all should be evidence enough that she *is* Bridget."

At this, he nodded toward her, and Bridget held up the telegram. He continued.

"And Ma and I both recognized her right off. There's really no reason not to believe her, unless you have an appetite for a cruel scandal."

"Now, Victor," Mr. Lundarson said. "No need for that."

Someone shouted from the back of the room. "Why did it take her so long to get here?"

"Ask her if she knows Patrick's middle name!" someone else yelled.

"How would that prove anything? Do *you* know Patrick's middle name?" a third mocked.

"Folks, settle down." Mr. Lundarson's voice rose above the others. "I'm giving the floor to Bruce Nilsen."

Bruce stepped forward and cleared his throat. As if he were standing in a court of law, he puffed out his chest and paced across the front of the room, one hand across his back.

"Miss . . . Sullivan, is it?" he stopped and looked at Bridget.

"O'Sullivan," she said quietly.

"Ah, yes. *O'*Sullivan. But there seems to be some confusion about that *O,* doesn't there?"

"My acquaintances in the city know me as Bridget Sullivan. I dropped the *O* when I arrived in Winnipeg. It was simply easier."

"Just like the *real* Bridget dropped her poor, lonely father?" Bruce asked. He turned to the crowd. "We can solve this very quickly, Mr. Lundarson. I'd like a show of hands—who in this room remembers Bridget O'Sullivan?"

Nearly everyone in the room lifted a hand, and Victor knew that those who did not were newcomers to the community.

"You may lower your hands," Bruce continued. "And of those who remember her, how many of you are confident that this is the same person?"

Six hands went up, including Victor's.

Bruce grinned. "I'd just like to point out that every person who raised a hand carries the last name of Harrison." His tone was dripping with satisfaction. "I would also like to point out that Victor Harrison here owns the property next to the O'Sullivan property. I think it's fairly obvious that this woman is in cahoots with the family and whatever plans they might have concerning the land. It would be a very convenient expansion, wouldn't it?"

"That's ridiculous," Victor said, but no one heard him over the hum that Bruce's accusation generated in the room.

Just then, heads turned toward another disturbance at the door.

"Ah, here she is." Mr. Lundarson pounded his gavel again. "Miss Johansen! Come on up."

The teacher was puffing, her face red and her hair mussed. "I'm sorry I'm late," she said, removing her coat and hat and handing them to a woman in the front row. "It took me longer than I expected to find what I was looking for." She took her place at the front, beside Mr. Lundarson.

"Miss Johansen," Bruce began again, "you taught Bridget O'Sullivan at your school, is that correct?"

Victor rolled his eyes. "Everybody knows that—"

"Can you tell us how many years Bridget O'Sullivan was your student?"

"Eight years."

"So you probably know her better than anyone. Yet even *you* don't recognize this young woman, is that correct?"

Victor wanted to shout "*Objection!*" like he'd seen in the movies. "Just let her tell her own story, Bruce," he said instead.

"I . . . can't say with one hundred percent certainty," the teacher fumbled. "But . . . no. I . . . I don't really think this is Bridget. She's just . . . she's just not the same person. But I have something that will help us." She pulled a folded sheet of paper from her pocket. "This is a poem Bridget wrote in class one day when she was in Grade Seven. She wrote it at her desk, handed it straight to me, and I've had it filed away all these years."

"And you're completely confident no one else has ever seen it?" Bruce asked.

"Absolutely."

Victor spoke up. "Wait a minute. You can't expect her to recite something she wrote so many years ago and never laid eyes on again. Who could do that?"

"He has a point," Mr. Lundarson said.

"I agree," Miss Johansen said. "But I know Bridget. If this *is* her, she'll be able to tell us what the poem is about. I know she will." She handed the piece of paper to Mr. Lundarson.

He scanned the page. "I really don't see how this—"

Another shout from the back interrupted him. "That's not going to prove anything!"

The room began to buzz again, and Victor didn't even notice until she began to speak that Bridget had stepped up to the podium.

Chapter 42

As I approached the platform, I could almost see my mother's face. I remembered the happy day we boarded the ship for Canada, the hope that shone in her eyes. Hope that was reflected in the smile on Pa's face, and Tommy's, too. We were a family heading off on an exciting adventure together, leaving our sad past behind us.

But the sadness had only begun.

Now it felt as though I was laying my heart bare before the very people who were rejecting me—who had rejected me throughout my childhood, too. This also felt like my last hope. I took courage from the smile on Mrs. Harrison's face, closed my eyes to the faces of the others, and offered up my poem as if I were a prisoner stripped naked before her accusers.

"*Once*," I said. "By Bridget O'Sullivan." As a hush fell over the room, I recited slowly, with my eyes closed.

I had a mother, once.
With smiles and laughter and lullabies
She stroked my hair and wiped my eyes.
I had a mother, once.

I had a brother, once.
All giggles and sunshine and kisses sweet
I rolled him a ball and tickled his feet.
I had a brother, once.

I had a father, once.
Before the deep sadness, the waves of the sea
Robbed him of all that he had—save for me.
I had a father, once.

I had a voice, once.
Like a lark, I could sing, I could laugh, I was free
To express all my words, all my love, ferociously
I had a voice.
Once.

Not even the squawk of an infant broke the heavy silence in the room. I looked at Victor's mother again and saw tears streaming down her face. Even his father appeared a little choked up. I couldn't bring myself to make eye contact with their son. I stepped away from the podium.

The crowd was looking at Mr. Lundarson, who still held the poem in his hand.

"That's it exactly," he said softly. "Word for word."

The community hall erupted into about forty simultaneous conversations. Mr. Lundarson kept pounding his gavel, to no effect. I took a deep breath and exhaled. The poem had come back to me verbatim because I'd carried it in my head long before I ever put it on paper in Miss Johansen's class all those years ago. Exactly when the phrasing began to form, I couldn't say. But when it had come time to complete Miss Johansen's assignment, all I'd had to do was write. I remembered how good it felt to finally see the words in black and white and to share them with someone, even if it was only one person. That night, and for many nights afterward, the phrases had replayed in my head as I fell asleep. They were almost like the mantra for my life.

Whatever the outcome, I'd expressed my poem aloud and survived. I could catch the next train to Winnipeg and find some other way to move on if I had to.

Finally, I looked into Victor's face. He was gazing at me with such intensity, I had to look away. What was it I saw in those eyes? I couldn't name it, but whatever it was, it made me feel something I'd never felt before. Something that made the thought of leaving him unbearable.

The room settled down, and Mr. Lundarson spoke again.

"Thank you, young lady, for that very eloquent recitation. Miss Johansen, are you satisfied that this woman before us is the author of this poem?" He held the sheet of paper high.

Miss Johansen was staring at me, and from the expression on her face, I thought she might burst into tears. "Yes, I am," she said. "I'm sorry I doubted you, Bridget."

"Wait a minute," Bruce broke in with an exasperated huff. "She could have discovered this poem any number of ways—"

"Oh give it up, Nilsen!" a heckler hollered.

"Put it to another vote!" someone shouted.

Mr. Lundarson pounded his gavel once again. "All right. You've all heard the evidence. If you believe this woman is Bridget O'Sullivan, please raise your hand."

Mr. Lundarson's hand shot up before he even finished the sentence. I wasn't sure if I was supposed to raise my own or not, so I left both hands at my sides and looked around the room. Hands went up everywhere. I scanned the room again. Only one small woman still held her hands down, and I recognized her as Bruce Nilsen's mother. I looked back at Bruce, who stubbornly refused to raise his hand and stood glaring back at his mother. Then slowly, and with a defiant expression, she, too, raised her tiny hand to shoulder level and held it there.

Mr. Lundarson pounded his gavel. "This might be the most wishy-washy crowd in the history of the world. But I think it's safe to say you may proceed with your quest to claim your property unchallenged, Miss O'Sullivan. Welcome back to Bleak Landing." He handed me the poem. "Now, let's move on to what you all came here for tonight: our mayoral debate and election!"

As I sank into my seat next to Mrs. Harrison, I realized I was trembling and my legs felt weak. She placed an arm around my shoulders and gave me a little squeeze. "Well done, Bridget," she said before leaning back in her seat to hear her son's campaign speech.

Mr. Lundarson continued. "Each candidate will have five minutes to speak. Then each will have another five minutes to answer questions. Afterward, everyone twenty-one years of age and older may line up in an orderly fashion and cast a ballot by placing an X next to the name of their preferred candidate." He gestured toward a makeshift voting booth in a front corner of the room, opposite the hall's kitchen. "Voting will end at precisely eight o'clock. Our scrutineers, Reverend Jorgenson and Mr. McNally, will tally the votes while we enjoy refreshments together, and then we'll announce our new mayor."

"Get on with it, Lundarson, I've got cows to milk!" called the heckler from the back of the room.

Mr. Lundarson shuffled some papers and cleared his throat. "First up, we'll hear from Mr. Bruce Nilsen."

Bruce approached the podium with the same confidence he had the first time. "Ladies and gentlemen. As you know, our world is at war. And our little town—safe though we may feel here—is not immune to the threats that face so many on this planet. We, too, could easily be overthrown by undesirables. When our forefathers founded this town, do you think they intended it to become a melting pot? Of course not. They'd be rolling over in their graves if they could see what's happening in communities surrounding ours."

I sensed some nervous shuffling in the crowd.

"I believe we need to stand firmly united to keep this town what our ancestors intended it to be. If people of lower cultural value are allowed to govern a culturally significant people, their inferiority will drag us all down to their level."

Did my ears deceive me? Was he paraphrasing Adolf Hitler? It sure sounded like it to me, and the reference wasn't lost on the Bleak Landing crowd.

"What exactly are you saying, Nilsen?" someone yelled.

"He's saying, let the low-life bums stay where they are!"

I had no idea who had shouted or whose side they were on. But it didn't matter, because Bruce ignored them both. "When this war ends—and we all hope it does soon—we'll be faced with an influx of people from all races, religions, and backgrounds—most of them looking for a handout. From us! They'll take our jobs. They'll claim our land. Can we afford this? I say *no*. We must take care of our own people first. It's what our great-grandparents fought for. It's what I stand for, too. That's why a vote for me is a vote for 'Peace, Prosperity, and Progress.' Thank you."

I'd seen the slogan on Bruce's campaign posters. Somehow he'd missed the point that those same great-grandparents he was citing had once been the "influx" to which he referred. A subdued smattering of polite applause followed, and then a chorus of low murmurs. I almost felt sorry for Bruce. I was certain he didn't stand a chance, and I doubted that Victor would need to say anything. The election was surely his.

"Thank you, Mr. Nilsen," Mr. Lundarson said as Bruce took his seat. "I'd now like to call Mr. Victor Harrison to the podium."

I wondered what Victor might promise the people of Bleak Landing if they elected him. Better roads? A new school? I'd heard him and his parents discussing ways to draw newcomers to the area once the war ended, particularly those who'd served their country and might be returning with seen and unseen wounds. He'd even talked about changing the name of the town to make it more inviting. All this was the direct opposite of Bruce's platform.

The room grew quiet, the people ready to hear what Victor had to say. But when he finally said it, I thought I'd heard wrong.

"Thank you, ladies and gentlemen. I'd like to take this opportunity to announce my withdrawal from the election. For personal reasons, I've decided not to run after all, and since he now has no opponents, I believe Mr. Nilsen here wins by acclamation. So, before I return to my seat, I'll say congratulations to him and may God bless his term of office."

Victor returned to the empty chair next to me and sat down. Nobody moved. I stared at Victor, then looked around to see everyone else doing the same thing. Had we heard correctly? When my gaze reached Bruce, I saw a slow smile of triumph cross his face. He was the only one besides Victor who did not appear shocked.

Mr. Lundarson returned to the podium, but he was clearly at a loss as to how to proceed. He fumbled through the papers in his hands. The room buzzed again. Finally, Mr. Lundarson pounded his gavel once more. "Ladies and gentlemen, this is a most unusual turn of events. However, according to our election bylaw, the deadline for any candidate to withdraw has passed. Ballots have been printed, and we still need to vote. I suppose the best I can do is ask you to respect Mr. Harrison's decision to withdraw and honor his wish. Are there any questions for the remaining candidate?"

"Let's just get on with it!" someone yelled, while heads nodded all around the room. Mr. Lundarson declared the debate period over and the voting open. I wondered what the point was now but sat quietly in my seat. Rules were rules.

Victor had disappointed me. In the last week, I'd come to think he'd turned into a man of real integrity and courage. Why on earth had he dropped out? If he wasn't taking this seriously, he never should have agreed to run in the first place. He was soon surrounded by people who were probably saying the same things I was thinking. I moved aside and stood by the wall.

Miss Johansen was the first in line to vote. When she was done, she came over to me.

"I'm so sorry, Bridget," she said. She searched my face, as though hunting for some glimpse of her former student. "I guess I . . . well, Bruce's warning carried a lot of weight, and . . . I suppose I've just never seen such a transformation in anyone before!"

"It's okay." It made me happy to know I'd changed that much. "I'm surprised you still had my poem."

We nibbled on sandwiches while she chatted about her hopes and dreams for the school. I told her how I'd completed high school, and she told me how sorry she was that I hadn't had a "normal" high school experience. She talked of the purpose she found in her work and how she hoped her board would soon be able to hire a second teacher or at least a helper for the students who needed extra assistance.

"Too many get discouraged and drop out, when all they need is a little more guidance. But if I give those students the time they need, the little ones suffer and don't learn their basics. It can be so frustrating."

At eight o'clock, the scrutineers carried the ballot box to the kitchen, where they sat in a corner tallying votes—to what end, I couldn't imagine. Bruce Nilsen would be the new mayor of Bleak Landing. Just one more reason for me to sell my property and get back to the city. That gave me an idea.

As if he could read my mind, Victor came over to me.

"Congratulations, Bridget! I knew people would come 'round."

I scooted over so he could stand next to me against the wall. "Thank you. I thought I'd be the one congratulating *you* tonight. Why did you withdraw?"

Victor smiled at me. He took a deep breath and grew more serious. "Like I said, it's personal. And I have my hands full, between the farming and the pastoring."

"Did your family know about this?" I knew they hadn't, and he shook his head. "They're not going to be very happy with you."

"I know." He gave me a sheepish grin. "They'll recover. So, what's the next step for *you*?"

This was my chance. "I'll be putting my property up for sale as soon as possible. You interested?"

Victor blinked about five times. "In *buying*?"

"Yeah." I stood as tall as I could, trying to sound like a person who understood business. "You could expand your own lot or maybe plow it up. There's enough there for a small crop of some kind."

He was staring at me. "I think merging our properties is a terrific idea, Bridget. But it will be years before I can afford—"

The pounding of Mr. Lundarson's gavel interrupted us again. "The votes have been tallied," he announced. "Mr. McNally, please tell us the results."

Mr. McNally stepped forward and consulted the card in his hand. In a loud and clear voice, he said, "One hundred and sixty-three votes for Victor Harrison. Two votes for Bruce Nilsen."

Chapter 43

$\mathcal{V}$ictor shook the last hand in a long line of well-wishers and looked around the community hall for Bruce. He expected him to be sulking in a corner somewhere, but he was nowhere to be seen.

Victor stepped outside and saw a light on in Bruce's law office half a block up the street. He walked over and went inside.

Bruce looked up from his desk and back down again, busying himself with some paperwork. "If you're here looking for my congratulations, you're wasting your time. And if you're just here to gloat, get out."

"Neither," Victor said. "I'm here to collect the necklace."

Bruce raised his eyes to Victor's without moving his head. "Pretty nervy for a guy who didn't hold up his end of the deal."

"I did." Victor raised both palms. "I withdrew."

"And then promptly voted for yourself—you and everybody else in this godforsaken place except for me and my own mother."

Victor didn't have the heart to tell Bruce he was the one who'd voted for him.

"C'mon, Bruce. You agreed that if I withdrew and didn't tell anyone why, you'd give me the locket. I did my part. Why are you so stubborn?"

Bruce sighed and looked Victor in the eye. "You threatened me."

What was he talking about? "Threatened you? How?"

"You brought up my sister. I suppose if you don't get your girl-friend's bauble, you'll tell everybody what happened to my sister."

Victor stared into Bruce's face. How had he taken that as a threat? The two of them had never discussed that awful day in the Nilsens' home, and Victor had wondered whether Bruce even remembered. They'd been so little. For the first time, Victor saw the pain in his old friend's face and realized he'd carried the guilt about his sister's condition all this time.

As gently as he could, he said, "Bruce, no one can say whether that fall caused your sister to be how she is. She could have been born that way."

"Exactly. And there's no point bringing it up now."

"Bruce, I wouldn't—"

"I had that necklace appraised, you know." Bruce tapped a pen on the surface of his desk. "It could bring enough to cover my sister's expenses for a long time."

"Then why haven't you sold it?"

"I figure if I can hang on to it until the war's over, maybe I can get even more."

Surprised that Bruce was divulging this much information, Victor continued. "But it's not yours, Bruce. You know it."

"Maybe it is, and maybe it isn't. Who's to say what Bridget traded it for?"

Victor felt anger rising in his chest again. *Lord, help me lay my feelings for Bridget aside for a moment.* "Bruce. Listen to me. It might do your heart a world of good to tell someone—besides me—what happened that day with your sister."

Bruce glared at him. "If you break my mother's heart, Victor, I swear I'll kill you."

Victor closed his eyes. Confidentiality dictated that he say nothing about the day he'd made a pastoral visit to Mrs. Nilsen, before Bruce ever returned to Bleak Landing. They'd sat sipping tea in her kitchen, and when Victor asked how he might pray for her, Mrs. Nilsen had begun to cry.

"You're a good man, Victor," she said. "I've never told this to anyone, but every Sunday I sit in church with this tremendous burden of guilt. No matter how many times I ask God to forgive me, it's still there."

Victor leaned in, encouraging her to continue.

"My little girl isn't right. Lars always said it was my fault, that God was judging me for past sins."

Victor sent up a swift and silent prayer for wisdom. "Oh, Mrs. Nilsen. That's simply not true. God loves you *and* your daughter very much."

"Lars once said it was too bad we didn't live in Germany. If we did, Mr. Hitler would have seen that our girl was put away and we'd have been spared the burden. He worked hard to keep her in that . . . that place," she sobbed. "And he refused to let me see her. Said it would hurt too much."

Victor allowed her to cry. When her sobbing subsided, he spoke with as much authority as he could. "Mrs. Nilsen, with all due respect, your husband was wrong. This was never your fault. You don't need to ask God's forgiveness for your daughter's situation, because there is nothing to forgive. You're a good mother."

He was never entirely sure if his words landed in her heart, but he thought he'd noticed a lighter countenance on Mrs. Nilsen's face the following Sunday at church. She shook his hand with a warm smile that seemed to return frequently in the weeks that followed.

Now Bruce sat before him, exposing what could well be the same false guilt—but in anger instead of remorse.

"Bruce," he began. "You were just a little kid. Yes, you should have told your parents what happened right away. *I* should have told. But I didn't. *We* didn't."

"So we're both to blame?" Bruce sneered. "You should be riddled with guilt, Preacher."

"I'd be willing to go with you to talk to your mother about this, Bruce. You might be surprised to find her relieved to hear the whole truth."

"Relieved? Are you kidding me? I swear, Victor, if you so much as breathe a word, I'll—"

"I know. You'll kill me."

Bruce only scowled at him.

"Hand over the necklace, Bruce."

"Is that an ultimatum?"

"No. I'm not going to tell your mother. It's not my story to tell. Do it for your own peace of mind. Do it because you need your old friend to know you still have a decent bone somewhere in your body."

Victor watched while Bruce let the words sink in. A lone tear escaped one eye, and Bruce quickly wiped it away with the back of his sleeve. He looked down at the floor with a sigh. With a sudden jerk, he yanked open a desk drawer, pulled out a wad of tissue paper, and tossed it across the desk. It skidded across the surface and nearly fell to the floor. Victor studied his friend's face, wondering whether he really could still call him *friend*.

Bruce refused to look up.

Victor carefully picked up the tissue and unfolded it. Inside—still completely intact, its green stone reflecting the overhead light—lay Bridget's locket.

He tucked it inside his coat. Bruce had not moved. "Thank you, Bruce. You won't regret this."

Bruce kept his eyes on his desk and dismissed his old friend with two words. "Get out."

Chapter 44

*T*was washing milk bottles at Mrs. Harrison's sink when Victor came in from the barn with the morning's milk. His sisters' task was to pour the fresh milk through the separator and fill the clean quart bottles with milk and the pints with cream. Victor would deliver the dairy products, along with eggs from the henhouse, from the back of his truck, where the winter air kept them cool.

"Need a ride into town?" he asked me.

I smiled up at him. "Yes, please. I can't believe the mayor himself is offering to drive me."

He ignored my teasing. "I imagine you're expected at the land titles office."

"Let's hope it all goes smoothly." I dried my hands and went to change out of the housedress Nancy had loaned me and fix my hair. By the time I put my coat on and headed outside, Victor was loading milk into his truck. It was a cold but sunny January morning, and the snow sparkled so brightly I had to squint. Victor was whistling as we climbed into the cab.

"You're happy today," I said.

"Why shouldn't I be?" He turned the steering wheel and we rolled onto the gravel road that led toward town. "I just defeated Bruce at his own game. The Nazis are sure to surrender any day now, and this awful war will be behind us at last. And if all that's not enough, I'm driving down the road with the most beautiful woman in Bleak Landing."

I tried to stifle a grin but couldn't do it. "Sure hope you're right about the war."

At the land titles office, Mr. Robertson was indeed expecting me. He didn't seem surprised to see Victor behind me, either.

"Well, congratulations to both of you! That was quite the performance last night. I can't remember when I've had a more entertaining evening, and I couldn't be happier with the results of both decisions."

"Thank you," I said. "How do we proceed from here?"

He gave me some papers to sign, and just like that, I was the new owner of the twelve acres my father had won in a card game all those years ago. I took the deed carefully from Mr. Robertson's hand and held it almost reverently. "How much is this property worth, Mr. Robertson? I'm looking for a buyer and will accept the first reasonable offer I get." Victor had made it clear it would be years before he could afford the place, and I didn't want to wait. Or rather, I *couldn't* wait. As much as I was enjoying my time at the Harrisons' place, and the Harrisons themselves, I couldn't just freeload forever. I had to survive, and that meant figuring out what to do next. Even if the thought of leaving them behind made me feel wretched.

"Can't say for sure, Bridget. Last piece of land sold around here went for twenty-five dollars an acre."

I immediately did the math. At that price, Pa's twelve acres would gain me three hundred dollars. Not a fortune, but nearly four months' worth of wages at the factory. Enough to keep me going until spring. Surely Weinberger's would be up and running again by then.

"But I'd hang on to it for a while if I was you," Mr. Robertson continued. "Once this war ends, land prices are sure to take a big jump—double for sure, maybe triple! I saw it happen last time."

"You don't need to rush, Bridget," Victor said. I looked at him. "I mean—it's none of my business, but I'm in no hurry to see Ma bawlin' her eyes out when you go."

I laughed. "Thanks, Mr. Robertson." I shook his hand.

As we turned to leave, Victor said to me, "She will, you know."

"You mean your ma?" We climbed into his truck.

"Yeah. She thinks you hung the moon."

I let out a snort. "Oh, she does not. She's just a very kind woman who'd do the same for anyone in my shoes."

"Nuh-uh. You don't know her like I do. She's been fond of you since you were a little kid." Without taking his eyes off the road, he added, "I guess I have been, too."

I pondered that for a moment, remembering the compassion I'd always experienced at Mrs. Harrison's hands. Though Victor was certainly beginning to win my affection, I couldn't say the fondness had been mutual when we were kids—or pretend that he hadn't had a lousy way of showing his. I responded the only way I could without lying or being unkind. "I've been fond of your mother, too."

Victor looked at me and grinned. "Guess I deserve that," he said.

I regretted my words immediately and opened my mouth to apologize. Then I quickly clamped it shut again. *Can't let that handsome face make a pushover out of me.*

We made the rounds of milk and egg deliveries, enjoying one another's company. At each stop, I stayed in the truck while Victor took care of the transaction. But on two of the five stops, customers recognized me and waved from their front doors, hollering, "Good morning, Bridget!" What a change from the week before!

"You're practically a celebrity now," Victor teased.

I had to admit I enjoyed just watching him climb in and out of the truck, his muscular arms hefting the crates and his handsome face smiling at his customers. A warm feeling came over me each time he took his place behind the wheel, as if I belonged at his side. I knew it was silly, but shaking it off was increasingly difficult. After we completed the deliveries, he surprised me by heading out of town toward Landeville.

"Where are we going?" I asked.

"The lumberyard where I got the supplies for my house. I had to reorder blueprints. They should be in now."

I sat back to enjoy the ride, trying not to think too hard about how to go about selling my land for top dollar. If I could make myself useful to the Harrisons, I supposed I could take advantage of their offer to stay longer. We chatted about what the economic forecast might be, and I felt honored when Victor told me about a couple of his experiences in the army, like trading the cigarettes from his rations for chocolate bars he had shared with some French children.

"How did it feel to come home wounded?" I dared to ask.

He remained quiet awhile. Finally, he spoke softly over the hum of the truck's engine. "Awful at first. I was in a lot of physical pain, and I was loaded down with guilt for surviving when so many others didn't."

"And now?"

"God has shown me that he spared me for a purpose. He's got work for me here; he wants me doing good—leaving this world a better place somehow." He pushed his cap back on his head. "And when I get frustrated with my limp, I remind myself that if I didn't have it, I'd probably forget what's important and go back to being the same arrogant reprobate I was before. In a way, the war saved me from myself."

"Well, I don't know whether or not you're a reprobate," I said. "But you *are* still a little arrogant." Though I teased him, the idea of returning to Winnipeg and not seeing him anymore was becoming less appealing every minute.

He grinned. "God's still workin' on me." He reached his hand across the seat and took mine. I didn't pull away. When he raised my hand to his lips and gently kissed it, it was all I could do to keep from grinning like a fool.

At the lumberyard, Victor ran inside and I sat contemplating what it would be like to be with him for always. I tried to tell myself it made no sense, but deep down, I had to admit that it was what I wanted more than anything.

My thoughts were interrupted when he quickly returned with some long rolls of paper. "Got 'em," he said, tossing them behind his seat. "Now, can I buy the lovely Miss O'Sullivan a cup of coffee?"

"I thought you'd never ask!"

At the cafe, we sat across from each other with steaming cups of coffee and apple fritters. Victor unrolled his blueprints on the table, eager to see them. As he pointed out the rooms of his house and explained what would go where, the joy on his face reminded me of Maxine when she opened her Christmas presents.

"How do you even know how to build a house?" I asked. The process boggled my mind.

"I helped Uncle Bud build two of them before I joined the army. He's a really good carpenter. He's going to help me out on mine. Pa will, too, of course."

"Is Bud your pa's brother or your ma's?" I'd seen the man in their home and around the yard a few times, but with his brown skin and black hair, he didn't fit the family mold. I'd assumed he was a hired hand from the Indian reserve down the road.

Victor thought about it a second. "Neither."

"Well then—how is he your uncle?" As someone with no relatives, I might not have much understanding of family relationships, but at least I knew what uncles were.

Victor shrugged. "Uncle Bud's just a close friend of my parents. We've called him Uncle Bud for as long as I can remember." He continued to describe his plans for the house as if having an uncle who wasn't really an uncle was the most ordinary thing in the world.

"See this right here?" He tapped his finger on one square on his blueprint. "This is the bathroom." He reached inside his coat pocket

Terrie Todd

and pulled out two full-color pages he'd torn from a magazine. He unfolded them and showed me photographs of the fanciest bathrooms I'd ever seen. "Which one's your favorite?"

I looked at the pictures and laughed. Marble tiles, glittery vanity tables with dressing-room lights, plush drapery, brass fixtures, and deep claw-foot bathtubs were all displayed in a colorful array.

"Are you serious? These are fancier than Caroline Weinberger's en suite in her family's swanky mansion!"

"Good! Which do you like best?"

I shrugged and randomly pointed at the one with more shades of green than pink. A huge grin covered Victor's face as he tucked the pages back into his pocket and rolled up the blueprints. What a strange man.

On the ride back to Bleak Landing, Victor asked me questions about my years in Winnipeg, and I found it easy to tell him all the things I'd learned—the things I was proud of and the things I wasn't so proud of, like abandoning Maxine.

"I won't blame her if she never forgives me," I said. "Except—she's not the unforgiving type. She might already have my letter. I hope to receive one back by the end of the week. If I'm still here, that is."

Victor grew quiet. We drove back through Bleak Landing, and at the end of town he stopped at his property and turned off the truck. He got out, came around to my side, and opened the door. He took my right hand. "C'mere. There's something I want to show you."

I stepped down onto the snow and followed him. Victor didn't let go of my hand, and I didn't pull away. In fact, I squeezed his hand tightly, wishing I'd never have to let go. When he squeezed back, I felt a surge of joy. The handsome Victor Harrison—war hero, devoted Christian, community leader—cared for *me*! How could it be true?

He led me over to the area where construction would soon begin on his. He stopped and seemed to be calculating something in his head for a moment. He moved a few more feet.

290

"Right . . . here." He stopped abruptly, turned, and placed both hands on my shoulders. "Stand right here."

I stood there, feeling more than a little silly. Then this strange man did something even stranger. He knelt at my feet.

"What on earth are you doing?" I asked.

"Bridget Mary O'Sullivan." He took both my hands in his. "Many years ago, I locked you in an outhouse just to impress my pals. I knew I was doing wrong and I've hated myself for it—especially now that I've gotten to know you." I felt his fingers trembling and clutched his hands more tightly, though I knew mine were shaking as well. "You have little reason to trust me. But I love you, Bridget. I want you to be my wife. And I promise, if you'll agree, this spot on which you stand will be your own private luxurious bathroom with every modern convenience ever invented. Because you deserve it. And I owe it to you. Will you marry me?"

My knees felt rubbery. I looked around, half expecting Bruce Nilsen to jump out from behind an oak tree to join his buddy in a rowdy laugh at my expense. My eyes began to sting. If this was only a cruel prank, my heart would never mend, because Victor Harrison had tunneled his way through its crusty shell and would stay inside it forever.

I could barely whisper. "Are you serious?"

"You bet I am," he said. "But is it all right if I stand while you think it over? The snow under my knee is melting through my trousers."

I laughed and pulled him to his feet. A few snowflakes had begun to fall.

"Listen, Bridget. This must feel awfully soon. I know it seems as though we don't know each other well. But in reality, we do. And I know you've hated me, for good reason." Victor looked down at his shoes, then lifted his blue eyes to mine again. In them, I saw utter sincerity and a love I desperately wanted to believe in. "But honestly? I've admired you for a long time, since before you ever left. I know we have a lot of things to work out. But I want to spend the rest of my life loving you, Bridget. I want to make Bleak Landing a better place, and I need you to help me do that. I don't want to let you get away."

Stay *here*? My head was spinning.

"And there's one more thing," Victor continued. "If you say yes, it might be a while before I can get you a proper engagement ring. But whether you say yes or no, I've got something to give you that's rightfully yours."

He reached deep inside his coat and pulled out a green velvet jewelry case. My heart pounded. Slowly, Victor opened the lid.

Inside, resting regally on the soft fabric, was my mother's locket.

Chapter 45

Surely I'll wake up any moment.

That was the only thought crossing my mind as I stood there in the exact spot of Victor's future bathroom with snowflakes twirling around me. But where would I find myself when I awoke? Back in Nancy's bedroom at the Harrison farm? In my sad little third-floor room in Winnipeg? In the apartment with Maxine? Just how much of all this was a dream, I wasn't sure, but one thing was certain: I could not possibly be staring at my mother's locket, having just received a marriage proposal from Victor Harrison.

The really strange part was, I didn't want to wake up. I desperately wanted it *all* to be true, and not just the part about the necklace.

"Bridget?"

I didn't want to take my eyes off the locket in case it disappeared.

"Are you all right?"

Slowly, I raised my eyes to Victor's face. He was smiling. He was *real.*

"It's snowing," I said stupidly.

He smiled wider. "You're right; it is. I should get you home. I'd love to put this locket on you first, though. May I?"

I nodded. Victor took the locket out and handed the box to me. "The box is Ma's," he said. "She doesn't know I borrowed it." With fumbling fingers, he opened the locket to reveal the faded likeness of my great-grandmother inside. "The locket *is* yours—am I right?"

"Yes," I whispered.

He closed it, stepped behind me, and fastened the locket around my neck. My hand immediately went to it, fingering the old familiar intricate etchings surrounding the emerald shamrock. I could still see it on my mother's slender neck. Victor moved back around and admired it.

"You look like royalty," he said. It reminded me of Maxine calling me 'Princess Bridget' and telling me I was a daughter of the King.

"Victor, however did you get this? *When* did you get this? Where—?" I wasn't sure which question to ask first. Instead of answering, he wrapped one arm around me tightly. The snow was falling in earnest now.

"C'mon, I'll explain on the way home." He walked me to the truck and opened the door for me. But in the time it took him to walk around to the driver's side and start the engine, it came to me. I knew. *I knew.*

"The election," I said. "You made a bargain with Bruce, didn't you? He had my necklace all along."

Victor turned to me with a grin. "I've been so busy planning how I could propose to the prettiest creature in Bleak Landing that I plumb forgot she was the cleverest, too. I should have remembered."

My eyes began to sting. "Victor! I can't believe you bargained with Bruce! Did you know people would elect you anyway?"

"Never crossed my mind."

I didn't know whether to believe him or not, but my eyes were too filled with tears to see the expression on his face. Why would he agree to such a deal—for *me*?

"I—I don't know what to say."

"No need to say anything. You've got back what is rightfully yours. That's all." He put the truck in gear and turned onto the road toward home. I sat in stunned silence, my hand fingering the locket.

Victor's family must have been anticipating our arrival, because when we pulled into their yard, they all tumbled out onto the porch, smiling and waving at us to hurry. Anna and Bobby jumped up and down like a pair of jackrabbits. What was going on? I looked over at Victor, but he appeared as puzzled as I felt.

"Do they know about any of this?" I asked, indicating the necklace. He shrugged. "I never said a word."

As soon as we climbed out of the truck Anna was by my side, tugging on my arm. "C'mon, Bridget! Come see!"

"Hurry, Bridget!" Bobby hollered before his mother succeeded in shushing him.

All of them were grinning like idiots, and they ushered me across the porch so urgently, you'd have thought I was bringing them a lifetime supply of chocolate cake.

"What's going on?" Victor asked.

"You'll see," his pa answered, smiling as much as the rest of the family.

I stepped into the kitchen and, for the third time in a single day, felt sure I must be dreaming. There, in front of the table with her hands clasped together, stood Maxine.

"Hello, Bridge."

Somehow I managed to sputter a weak "Max?" before I was caught up in her embrace.

"Oh, Bridge, I've missed you so much," she said, holding me tight.

I was too stunned to respond with words, but I hugged her back. The room swirled with people and color and noise. Someone removed my coat. Someone else guided me into a chair. Over the next half hour, the full story was sorted out. Maxine had received my letter and dropped everything to catch the first train she could. At the platform in Bleak Landing, someone directed her to the general store, where she explained that she was looking for me. The Harrisons' neighbor, Mr. Berg, happened to be in the store and offered her a ride. She'd been waiting for an hour, and, by all indications, had already made herself part of the family in typical Maxine fashion.

After a noisy lunch together, Mrs. Harrison settled Max and me in front of the living-room fire with cups of tea. "You girls need to catch up," she said firmly. I truly did feel like royalty when she put her daughters to work in the kitchen and shooed the menfolk out to the barn. Victor gave me an intense stare over his shoulder. I winked, and he half grinned as he disappeared out the door.

"Thank you for your letter, Bridge," Maxine began. "You have no idea how many letters I started to write to you. I didn't know where you'd gone, but I figured I could find you at Weinberger's. Once, I was *this close* to dropping a letter in the mailbox." She pinched together her thumb and pointer finger and held them up. "Somehow, though, every time I tried . . . it seemed . . . I just knew that the Lord was guiding me to give you more time. More space. That my leaving you alone was a necessary part of your journey somehow. I second-guessed myself so many times."

I nodded slowly. "You heard him right, Max." I felt awed by the reality that God cared enough about me to guide my friend in this way. "I was being so stubborn, and my stubbornness made me become desperate enough to finally come back here. It needed to happen."

I filled her in on the land claim, the town hall meeting, the poem, the election results . . . which brought me up to the present. I reached for the locket, but it had worked its way under my collar where no one could see it. I pulled it out.

"Look, Max."

She gasped. "That's *it*? That's the one?"

I nodded and told her the whole story, including Victor's proposal in "the bathroom." By the time I got to that bit, Maxine was bouncing up and down like a kangaroo and I thought she'd break the springs on Mr. Harrison's favorite armchair.

"Oh my gosh, Bridge! How romantic!" She grasped both my hands in hers. "Of course you said *yes?*"

I blinked back at her. *Had* I said yes? I thought I had, but I couldn't remember. The locket had stolen my attention, and I couldn't remember having given Victor a response.

"Oh for land's sake, Bridget. Tell me you gave the poor man an answer!" Maxine was on her feet.

"I . . . I guess I forgot."

"Forgot! Do you have any idea how insane you sound right now?" She pulled me up. "You want to marry him, right?"

Somewhere just below the surface, my twelve-year-old self was throwing a pigheaded tantrum at the very idea. But in my heart of hearts, I knew without a doubt that I yearned for nothing more than to become Victor Harrison's wife. I nodded, and that was all the confirmation Maxine needed. She led me through the kitchen, found my coat on a hook, and held it up. While I pulled it on, she opened the door and literally shoved me outside.

"Go! Go give him your answer right this minute, and don't come back until you've done it."

Oh, how I'd missed that girl bossing me around! I ran toward the barn, but before I reached it, I saw Victor looking down from the open loft above.

"What's going on?" he called.

"I didn't give you an answer!" I hollered back. "Can you come down?"

"That depends! What's your answer?"

I stopped where I was, praying he hadn't already changed his mind. "Yes! My answer is *yes!*"

Victor grinned. "Just so we're clear," he yelled, "what was the question again?"

I began to stammer. "Well—um—you—but—"

"Oh! You mean the one where I asked you to marry me?"

"Uh-huh."

Victor leaned on his pitchfork. "So that's a *yes*, then?"

I nodded. "Uh-huh."

"And I can build you a house? With the fanciest bathroom you ever saw?"

"Uh-huh."

"Get up here, girl."

I ran inside the barn and climbed the ladder to the hayloft, where he waited with a ridiculously huge smile. Without stopping to brush the strands of hay from my coat, I rushed straight into his open arms and the tightest, most welcoming hug I'd ever received. Eventually, he untangled himself and placed both hands on my shoulders.

"You sure about this, Bridget?"

I nodded.

"It's not just about the necklace?"

I shook my head.

"Kind of at a loss for words, aren't ya?"

I swallowed and gazed into his blue eyes. "I love you, Victor Harrison. Necklace or no necklace, I want to be your wife." I wrapped my arms around his neck and our lips met, softly. Victor ran one hand over my hair, brushing loose a stray piece of straw. Then he kissed me again, more intensely, and it felt as though some kind of delightfully hot blizzard was swirling around inside me.

"C'mon," he said. "Let's go tell everybody we're getting married."

When we walked back into the house hand in hand, Maxine was quivering with excitement like the Chihuahua we once saw at a pet store. She had managed to round up the whole family and they stood waiting, a stupid grin on every face.

"Bridget and I have an announcement," Victor began. But he didn't get to finish. A cheer went up, his sisters danced around me, his mother hugged me, his father patted him on the back, and Maxine beamed as if she'd just single-handedly negotiated an end to the war.

In a way, I suppose she had.

She wrapped her arms around me tightly. "Congratulations, Bridge. I can't wait to see you as a bride. You'll let me do your hair for the wedding . . ." She paused, biting her bottom lip. "Right?"

I hugged her back.

"Yes, Max. I'll let you—I *need* you—to do my hair for the wedding."

I felt a cold blast of air. Victor had opened the door and was heading back outside.

"Victor, where are you going?" his mother asked.

"Come on, Pa," he said. "Hurry up. We've got a house to build."

Epilogue

Hope, Manitoba. December 1, 1945

Dear Max,

Your letter just came and I'm thrilled that you're coming for Christmas! I hope your parents understand, but, as you said, with your brothers both home safe and sound, and after the reunion you all enjoyed at Thanksgiving, they can adjust to the idea of spending one Christmas without you.

No, I hadn't heard that Weinberger Textiles had been sold. Although that surprises me, it wasn't a shock to learn that Carlton died in a POW camp. I feel so sad for the family, but at least they know for sure now. I've already written them a letter and will plan to visit them in the spring.

I can't wait to show you the house! Were the walls up when you came for the wedding? I can't remember. Anyway, we moved in in August—just before a very bountiful harvest!—and have kept working on the finishing touches. We probably could have moved in sooner, but Victor insisted we wait until my "luxury bathroom" was complete, down to the last detail. Silly goose. But I have to confess, I do feel like royalty when I'm sunk to my chin in that deep claw-foot tub filled with hot water and bubbles.

As you know, Pa's old house was torn down last summer. Victor plowed the entire property into a field of rich, black earth, and we hope to plant it all to potatoes come spring. I am looking forward to seeing a gorgeous green crop as I stand at my kitchen sink. What an improvement!

I sure hope you noticed the return address, because it's official! My handsome husband has succeeded in his mission to have the name of our town changed—it just passed final reading in a town hall meeting last night. A few holdouts insisted we keep the name Bleak Landing, citing historic purposes—they felt we needed to honor the founder, whose last name was Bleak (or something close to it). But guess what? After a little more digging, Victor learned that the man's first name was Håp—Norwegian for "Hope." So he was able to persuade them we could have it both ways. The unveiling of the signs at both ends of town is set for New Year's Day: "Welcome to Hope!"

And a hopeful place it's turning out to be. Too bad for Bruce Nilsen that he didn't hang around to see it. With the opening of the gypsum mine set for *spring, we've got new people flocking this way. In fact, do you remember Michael, Vic's army buddy who stood up with you at our wedding? He got an office position with the mining company and has moved here! Michael asked about you the other day, and when I told him you might be coming for Christmas, I'm pretty sure I saw a twinkle in his eye. If I were you, I'd pack that turquoise dress that brings out the color in your eyes so well.*

So the mine is attracting veterans, and some of them are bringing war brides with them! One of them, Marie-Adorlee, is from France, and she has a little girl named Claire. Guess what? I am helping them both with English on Monday evenings. Not only that, but Miss Johansen has succeeded in convincing the school board to pay me a small salary—I think I told you I've been volunteering at the school since September, assisting the students who need extra help with reading and spelling, especially the kids who don't speak English at home. I never knew I'd love teaching so much, and can't believe I'm now going to get paid to do it.

And I am officially a pastor's wife! The congregation voted to keep Victor on permanently and has managed a small stipend for him, as well as the cost of a course in New Testament Greek that he's really enjoying. Our church family also keeps us supplied with food—so much that I've been able to share with the families of my students who need a little help. Can't tell you how gratifying that feels.

You asked what I call Victor's parents. Even though they've made me feel completely part of the family, I haven't been able to wrap my mouth around "Ma" and "Pa." But I've been calling them "Mom" and "Dad" and it feels just right. They are now the proud grandparents of Peggy's new baby, Richard Junior. Peggy brought little Ricky for a visit last week, and it's the most precious thing to be somebody's aunt! "Auntie Bridget!" Me! Can I make a confession? I volunteered to watch him while his mommy took a little nap, and the rest of the family was out doing chores, and I sang him an old Irish lullaby I remember my ma singing to me. I thought my heart might burst right then and there.

Not that life is without challenges, but I feel so blessed, Max! I once told you I didn't need a father, and you told me I was a child of the King. Little by little, each day, God is showing me that that is true—that I was never truly an orphan. He brought people into my life to help me along my journey—not the least of which was my dear friend Maxine. And Jesus was there all along. Can't wait for you to get here to celebrate his birthday with us!

Love,
Bridget

P.S. Please bring your good scissors. My hair is in desperate need of a decent trim.

Acknowledgments

I want to give a huge thank-you to Erin Calligan Mooney, my acquisitions editor at Waterfall Press, for believing in this project when it was still embryonic. To my agent, Jessica Kirkland, the well-deserving winner of the 2016 American Christian Fiction Writers Agent of the Year award. To Shari MacDonald Strong and Christy Karras for an outstanding job in cleaning up my less-than-stellar sentences, helping me flesh out ideas, and exposing my (sometimes) alternative facts! Thanks also to my family, for their ongoing support and enthusiasm. To Fire Chief Phil Carpenter, for his expert advice about how house fires spread. To my nephew and pastor, Nathan Weselake, who might just find bits of his sermons sprinkled throughout these pages. To my fellow Thesaurus Wrecks who so kindly reviewed the first draft and gave their valuable input: Jim Hamlett and Clarice James. Most of all, my thanks are due to my redeemer, Jesus Christ, master storyteller and main character in the greatest story ever told.

About the Author

Photo ©2016 G. Loewen Photography

*T*errie Todd is an award-winning author who has published eight stories with Chicken Soup for the Soul and two stage plays with Eldridge Plays and Musicals, and she has written a weekly Faith and Humor column for six years. Terrie's first novel, *The Silver Suitcase*, and her second novel, *Maggie's War*, were both published by Waterfall Press.

Terrie works part-time as an administrative assistant at city hall. She lives with her husband, Jon, on the Canadian prairies, where they raised three children and now enjoy the shenanigans of four grandsons. You can catch up with her latest escapades at www.terrietodd.blogspot.com and www.facebook.com/terrie.todd.31.